Sita Brahmachari

Tender
Earth

MACMILLAN CHILDREN'S BOOKS

First published 2017 by Macmillan Children's Books
an imprint of Pan Macmillan
20 New Wharf Road, London N1 9RR
Associated companies throughout the world
www.panmacmillan.com

ISBN 978-1-5098-1250-9

1 3 5 7 9 8 6 4 2

A CIP catalogue record for this book is available from
the British Library.

Printed and bound by CPI Group (UK) Ltd, Croydon CR0 4YY

For Esha and all young people who must find
a way to grow from this tender earth.

In memory of Simon Gould.
With love and thanks for keeping the Protest Book
safe and handing it on to the next generation.

'Days are scrolls: Write on them what you want to be remembered.'

–Bachya ibn Pakuda

SOME BRANCHES OF MY FRIEND TREE

BUBBE ♥ STAN

HANNAH ♥ MAURICE   LEYLA ♥ NURI

STELLA

REBECCA   KEZIA   PARI

TOMEK   LAILA
         (ME!)

AND MY FAMILY TREE

GRANDAD KIT ♥ NANA JOSIE

NANA KATH ♥ GRANDAD BIMAL

SAM (DAD) ♥ UMA (MUM)

DINESH ♥ ANJALI-
CHAMELI

MIRA   KRISH   LAILA (ME!)   JANU   PRIYA

Dear Reader,

How do we find our voice? *Tender Earth* is the story of how one girl, her friends and her community come to find theirs.

Some of you may have heard of the Levenson family before, through my stories *Artichoke Hearts* and *Jasmine Skies*. I have been asked many times by readers to write another tale in what I suppose has now come to be a family of books. Stories have to come to the writer – they have to grow in you over time.

And at last this story came. In it the baby of my first novel, *Artichoke Hearts*, is now twelve years old and, as the youngest member of her family, it's now time to find her voice . . . and discover what she'll use it for.

With my own children, and when I meet readers at events, we often discuss how difficult it is to know how to respond and act to things that we witness in the news and experience every day in our own lives: words and actions that disturb, cause fear, make us angry, upset, anxious or disempowered. Sometimes it feels hard to decipher the difference between truths and lies.

Tender Earth is set on this earth that Laila and her family and friends are born into and are now tending. Their journeys, from birth to growing up, contain mysteries, dreams and hard realities, and the young people in my story have many questions that they're searching to find answers for.

I hope that stepping into the shoes of these characters, as they walk the same tender earth as you, helps *you* to work out what paths you will walk, what banners to hold up and what words you might choose to write on them.

Love,

Sita x

P.S. I have to thank our neighbour Billie for helping us with the creature (to be revealed in Chapter One) that really did turn up in our kitchen – sometimes, as they say, the truth really can be stranger than fiction!

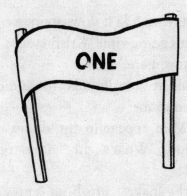

ONE

There's a snake in our kitchen.

'There's a snake down here!' I shout.

No one even answers.

It's slithering slowly across the floorboards, skirting the cooker.

'Funny!' Mira calls from her room.

'There. Is. A. Snake. In. The. Kitchen!' I shout again.

Krish jumps down the stairs, taking the steps in threes.

'What's "a snake in the kitchen" code for?' He laughs – and then freezes in the doorway.

'Mum! Dad! Mira!' he yells at the top of his voice. 'There's a snake in the kitchen!'

'That's what I said!' I shrug and watch it heading for the radiator.

Krish is busy videoing it on his iPhone.

'Jokes!' He laughs, and within seconds his Facebook page is pinging with likes and comments. Mum and

Dad haven't even made it downstairs yet.

'This thing's going viral!' Krish laughs.

'Some help you are!'

What would it actually take for someone in this family to listen to me?

Dad and Mira appear in the doorway. Dad's on his phone too. 'What's this video on Facebook about?'

I point to the snake . . . Its head is now snuggled up in the warmth of the radiator, so I bend down to get a closer look.

'Don't touch it, Lai Lai – it might be poisonous!' Mira warns. As if I was actually thinking of hugging it or something.

'What's going on?' Mum appears behind Mira.

I point to where the tail of the snake – I suppose snakes are *all* tail . . . anyway, the end bit of it, not its head – is sticking out. Mum's mouth falls open.

'Lai Lai, come away from it right now!' she orders, then turns to Dad. 'Sam! Please get that thing out of the kitchen!' She looks at him like *he's* responsible for putting it there.

'What do you want me to do, Uma? I'm not touching it till I know if it's safe!'

'I think *it's* more frightened of us, Dad.' I watch it coil up further behind the radiator.

'Good job I bagged it on video!' Krish loses interest and walks away.

'Where are you off to, Krish?' Mum asks. She's still hovering in the hallway, looking slightly green.

'Out of the reptile house!' Krish laughs, shaking his head.

The phone rings and I go to pick it up because it's obvious no one else is going to. It's Nana Kath.

'What's all this I'm seeing on Facebook about a snake in your kitchen? Is this one of Krish's practical jokes or something? He'd better not get up to any of that when he comes to stay with me!'

'No, Nana . . . it's real,' I tell her.

'I can see it's real,' she says, 'but how on earth did it get there?'

'Lai Lai, tell Mum I'll call her back.'

'Ask your dad if he's driving up on Saturday or Sunday with Mira and Krish.'

'Nana wants to know if you're going Saturday or—'

'Tell Nana we can't talk right now!' Mum's doing that gritting-her-teeth talking like it's *my* fault Nana won't get off the phone.

'She—'

'I heard,' Nana butts in. 'I suppose a snake in the kitchen *is* a bit alarming. Come and live up North with me and Krish, Laila! Hang on a minute . . . Hello, Betty, you've come at just at the right time – my Uma in London's got a snake in her kitchen! I know! Good idea, I'll ask them. Betty here says you should call the RSPCA.'

'Dad's trying to get through to them now,' I tell Nana.

'Good! Well, all I know is, never in all my life have I ever had a snake in my kitchen!'

I can hear Betty laughing in the background.

I wish Nana would give it a rest about moving to the country. She's got it in her head that it's 'a security risk' or something living here in the city. We all make a joke of it, but it actually makes me feel a bit nervous when she goes on and on about it.

'I think they have quite a few snakes in the countryside too, Nana,' I tell her.

'*Please* will someone get this snake out of the kitchen?' Mum sounds as high-pitched as our smoke alarm.

'I hope it's not a bad omen. Snake in the garden of . . .'

'Nana thinks it might be a bad omen,' I repeat.

'Just hang up!' Mum whispers. I don't know why she does this clenched-teeth whisper because you can hear her better than when she speaks normally.

'Please don't go, Laila. I'm not missing out on this!'

I leave the phone on the dresser so that Nana Kath and her friend can listen in.

'Can everyone just calm down? It's somebody's escaped pet. Probably harmless. I've read a few articles about this in the paper,' Dad informs us, contemplating the radiator. 'Someone will have left a cage door open.

4

Now, can everyone pipe down? I can't hear myself think.' He tucks his mobile between his chin and his ear. His face twists into a scowl as he's transferred straight to hold.

The call-waiting music finally ends and Dad explains the situation. There's a pause while he listens to what's being said, then . . .

'No, this is not a prank call . . . I agree it's a bit unusual, but there IS a snake in our kitchen. No, we don't know what kind. Yes, that's correct, that is our address . . . Contained? Well, it is at the moment . . . behind the radiator. Tomorrow!? You can't send anyone before then?' Dad's pacing up and down now. 'Nine o'clock first thing . . . OK . . . OK, if that really is the earliest you can come.'

He hangs up.

'You have *got* to be joking, Sam,' says Mum. 'What are we supposed to do till then?' She looks like she's about to blow.

'She suggested we should sit and watch it.' Dad shrugs.

'Helpful! And then what?'

'Look, I don't know, Uma!'

'Well, I've got packing to do,' Mira says, and heads for the hallway.

'I'll help you!' Mum follows, walking past the phone where Nana's still giving her friend Betty a running commentary.

5

'Didn't you hang up, Laila?'

'Nana wanted to stay connected . . .'

Mum listens in for a bit and sighs. I can hear Nana clearly from where I'm standing next to Mum. I think she's speaking loud for Betty's benefit.

'Is that you, Uma? I was just telling Betty about your snake . . . I've had to bring her a glass of water – she's nearly choked laughing! Says it's the best Saturday night she's had in ages!'

'Well, so glad we could provide the entertainment! I can't talk now – I'll call you in the morning.' Mum puts the phone down. 'Lai Lai, bedtime!'

As *if* I'm going to sleep after this!

So me and Dad sit on the sofa and watch that the snake doesn't go anywhere, though I have no idea what we're supposed to do if it decides to. Well, *I* watch the radiator and listen to Dad snoring till Krish crashes back in with a mate and jolts Dad awake.

'What! Has it moved? What's going on?'

'Here – it's behind the radiator,' Krish explains to his friend. 'Dad, this is my mate Ed – he knows stuff about snakes; he's doing a BTEC in reptiles.'

'Of course he is!' Dad laughs.

'No! Serious!' Ed says, looking a bit offended.

'I don't want you getting bitt–' Dad stands up and walks towards Ed, who has pulled on a pair of gloves that go right up his arm like the ones Dad uses for clearing brambles. Now Ed's carrying a plastic cage over to the radiator, ready to contain the snake.

'You just need to know how to handle them,' says Ed, lying on the floor on his back and squinting up behind the radiator. 'Aww, poor thing! It must be terrified.'

He starts to sort of tickle it slowly, as if he's a snake charmer, and he puts on a voice like he's talking to a toddler. 'Come on now, I won't hurt you . . . have you been out in the cold? You must be starving. Found a nice warm place behind there, though, haven't you? Not stupid, are you?'

Ed's shining a torch under the gap in the radiator and slowly, as if it really is listening to him, the snake starts to uncoil itself and twist around his long glove.

'Step back, Lai Lai!' Dad orders me.

'Nice markings. I think it's a corn snake.' Ed sounds quite excited. 'A young one by the look of it. Won't harm you at all . . . someone's pet come through the pipes probably.'

'Like Slytherin,' Krish jokes.

'Harry Potter's given snakes a bad name,' Ed says, without even a faint glimmer of humour. Like he's a defender of snakes or something!

'I think it's fair to say they had a bad reputation a little bit before that!' Dad says drily.

Ed ignores him and stands up slowly, holding the snake just behind its head. Now that it's all coiled up, it doesn't look as impressive as it did winding across the floor.

'Want a hold?' Ed asks me.

I stretch out my arm but Dad gets between us and holds open the cage.

'Leave it to me. I'll bung some signs up, see if anyone claims it,' Ed says as he leaves.

'Cheers, mate!' Krish laughs and shows Ed and the snake out, then punches the air, as if *he's* the hero of the day!

'What! *You* didn't do anything!' Mira says to Krish as she comes back downstairs in her PJs.

'I don't see any of *your* mates springing to the rescue, Mira.'

'Come on, you two!' Mum calls from upstairs. 'We've only got a few days left in each other's company. How about some brotherly and sisterly love?'

I call Kez. I think at least it'll be something funny to tell her, but of course she's already seen it. I didn't even know she was Krish's friend on Facebook. I don't think I'll bother getting an account when I am finally allowed one – it would be good to have some news that you could tell your best friend without them already knowing it.

I lie in my bedroom, drifting in and out of sleep. It feels weird lying on the mattress on the floor now that Dad's dismantled my high bed. It seems like such a long way between the floor and the ceiling, with so much empty space above me. Mira and Krish are still on their mobiles, chatting to their mates. This is how I go to sleep mostly, listening to one side of their conversations. It's relaxing, like being tuned into a radio where you know everyone who's speaking.

These are the last words I hear Krish say:

'I know, surreal, right? Only in our house!'

I'm staring up at the ceiling, smiling my way through a replay of the whole night. Maybe these sorts of things do only happen in our house, but I love this place exactly as it is. It's the house I was born in. I don't want anything about it ever to change. I don't want our noisy, random Saturday nights ever to stop happening. I don't want to be the only one left here with Mum and Dad. I want everything to stay the same.

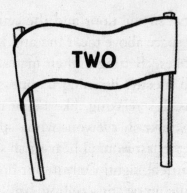

TWO

When you actually get the thing you've always wanted, how come it never feels like you imagined it would?

Me and Mira are lying top to tail on her bed. It's supposed to be my room when she moves out. Finally I'll have some space. It's at least three times as big as mine.

'How come all these photos are from when I was a baby?' I pick up a picture of Mira holding 'baby Lai Lai'.

'Awww, bless! You were only just born there! I had no idea that most people don't get to see their baby sister being born! I thought it was normal – you know what Mum and Dad are like.'

'Inappropriate!'

'Well, maybe it's not what people normally do, but . . .'

Mira stares at the photo.

'Are you crying?' I ask.

Mira nods. 'It's OK to cry, Lai Lai.'

'You sound just like Mum! Why does everyone want me to cry?'

'We don't . . . it's just that you *can* if you want to.' Mira looks all gooey as she goes through more ancient pictures of me.

'At least I know what it's all about! I think I might do a painting from this photo. You were sooooo cute!'

'Thanks! So I'm not any more?'

'Not AS cute! Look at those bush-baby eyes! Go on, Lai Lai, try your uniform on for me. I won't get to see you in it otherwise. Think of this as a dress rehearsal!'

I shake my head. 'I'll take a photo on my first day.'

'Oh come on, just one pic! You *are* getting your hands on my room after all!'

As she's practically pleading with me, I go over to the uniform laid out on her bed. I start with the skirt.

'What if I refused to wear it?'

Mira's half listening, texting at the same time.

'Hang on a minute, let me just answer this from Jidé.' She texts away and then sends. 'Sorry! Just go with it, Lai Lai. That's the whole point of uniform. You have to conform.'

'What if you don't agree with it?'

Mira looks up from her phone for a moment.

'No one believes in uniform!' She smiles at me but I don't smile back. 'It's rubbish, but just wear it, Lai Lai. I suppose I was lucky. They didn't bring uniform in till I was in Year Eight, but they're really strict about it now. No point fighting it.'

'What did you wear on your first day then?' I ask as I do up and undo the blazer to see what looks best. Neither!

Now Mira's flicking through a bundle of photos she's taken off her wall. She finds the picture of her first day at secondary school. She's standing in the garden wearing a floaty hippy top and a vintage-looking skirt, with leggings and Converse.

'You actually *chose* to wear a skirt?'

Mira pulls a *you'll-grow-out-of-it* big-sister face.

I check myself out in the mirror and yank the skirt up a bit because it's falling down over my non-existent hips.

'At least let Mum buy you a new skirt and blazer. She's desperate for you to have your own. Go on, Lai Lai. It swamps you. Makes you look even smaller.'

'Thanks!'

'You'll fill out.'

I turn sideways in the mirror. I am completely flat. I don't see much sign of it yet.

I look at the two of us in the mirror:

- My long, straight hair; Mira's new, short cropped hair that everyone says makes her look like that actress she's got a postcard of . . . Audrey Hepburn.
- My eyes still too big for my face, no make-up;

12

Mira's line of liquid liner she manages to paint on perfectly.
- My wide lips; Mira's full ones.
- My pointy chin; Mira's heart-shaped one.

Even though our features aren't the same, we definitely look like sisters. I like that we do. I blow out my cheeks to see what I'll look like more filled out.

'You're lucky – I don't think I even felt a cheek bone in my face till I was fifteen! What's with the puffer-fish face?' Mira holds her arms out to hug me but I pull away. 'Go on, Lai Lai – let Mum buy you a new uniform.'

'Has no one heard of recycling around here? What's the point of getting brand-new stuff all over again? I'm not going to like it any better.'

Mira grabs hold of my lapels.

'I tried to wear Krish's blazer once when I couldn't find mine, but Nana wouldn't let me. She said boy's blazers button up on the other side.'

'So what?'

'I know, but someone might notice.' Mira grabs hold of the material, pulling it in a bit at the waist and inspecting her work in the mirror. 'See? A girl's blazer would show off your waist a bit more.'

'That's just wrong! How can they gender a blazer? Anyway, I haven't got a waist.'

At least I've got Mira laughing now, which is a

relief – because if she starts getting all emotional again, I'm afraid that I will too.

Mira wraps both her arms around me.

'Why are you tearing up?'

'No reason! It's just that one day soon you will get a waist!'

'What are you going on about?'

'Ignore me! I just can't believe you're going to secondary school already . . .'

It's bad enough Mum and Dad moaning on about me growing up so fast. The truth is the recycling thing isn't the only reason I don't want Mum to buy me a new uniform. I actually like the idea of wearing bits and pieces of Mira and Krish's old school clothes. It makes me feel less nervous, like I won't have to work out who I'm going to be, like they'll be right there with me as they've always been till now.

'Don't go all silent on me, Lai Lai.'

'Can you *not* do that?'

'What?'

'I don't want anyone calling me Lai Lai from now on. Tell your friends that too.'

'But we've always called you Lai Lai.'

'You've always treated me like a baby.'

'OK, OK . . . Laila. Point taken!' Mira half laughs, half sighs. 'It feels a bit strange though.'

'Haven't you heard? There's this radical new idea to call people by their actual names!'

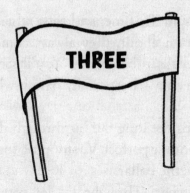

THREE

'Now, let's see if I can remember how to do up a tie.'

Mira's rubbish at it. Every time she slides the knot up towards my neck, I feel a bit panicky.

'It doesn't matter; I'll work it out.'

I pull away from Mira, but she keeps hold of the end and bangs on the wall. 'Krish! Can you come help Lai Lai with her tie?'

How hard can it be for my sister to call me by my name?

I want to scream!

Krish strolls in, headphones dangling around his neck; the tinny sound of his 'ambient' track leaking out.

He takes the tie back over my head and practises on himself. 'How d'you want it – fat or skinny?'

'How would *I* know?'

'You'd better hedge your bets for the first week then!'

I actually have no idea what he's talking about, which isn't that unusual because Mira and Krish say

15

stuff like this all the time, and then when I ask them what they're on about, they always come back with something totally rubbish like 'You'll see!' or 'You'll find out one day' – I especially hate it when they say that!

Krish loops the long tail bit through the knot and slides it up into a perfect V, stopping just where the button meets the collar.

'Slick or what? Thought I'd let you see what a regulation standard tie looks like, so you'll know not to do one again. The choice is strictly fat or skinny . . . Or not at all!'

Mira widens her eyes at Krish like she's warning him not to carry on.

'I didn't know you had a choice?'

'You don't, Lai Lai! Do as I say, not as I did!' Krish laughs. 'Forgetting or losing your tie is not an option; neither is refusing to wear one. Take it from me – you don't want to waste your life in detention over a tie.'

Krish does his robot walk back towards the door even though it hasn't got a laugh out of me since I was in Year Five. When is anyone going to wake up and see that I'm actually nearly twelve years old? Krish raises his – supposed to be Dalek – arms jerkily into position, ready to aim and fire.

'I am a u-ni-form – I will ex-term-in-ate you!'

'Not helpful, Krish!' Mira cuffs him on the arm. 'Get out of here!'

'By the way, don't call me Lai Lai any more!' I yell after Krish.

He pokes his head back around the door.

'What am I supposed to call you then?'

'Laila.'

'But I've *never* called you Laila!' Krish complains.

'And that's your logical reason for calling me by a baby name forever, is it?'

Krish scowls. 'I forgot, Your Honour. What about Kez? Is *she* going to call you Laila?'

I haven't thought about Kez. Mira and Krish are exchanging *that* look again. When I was little they used to spell out words that they didn't want me to understand. Then, when I got to the age when it was obvious I could spell whatever they were trying to hide from me, the knowing looks kicked in. They might as well get a loudspeaker and shout at the top of their voices: 'What's up with Lai Lai?'

Still, I suppose I *should* thank them for the spelling thing. It turned me into the best speller in primary school!

I will actually let Kez keep calling me 'Lai Lai' because she'd never shame me up by calling me that in front of anyone else, like Mira and Krish do. Anyway, it's always been Lai Lai and Kez. It wouldn't feel right for her to call me anything else.

'Make an exception for your brother. I don't think

I *can* call you Laila. It feels like I'm talking to someone else.'

'Maybe I *am* someone else!' I say, checking myself out in the long mirror.

'Deep!' Krish shrugs and plugs himself back into his music.

Me and Mira sit on her bed for a bit without talking, just looking around the bare walls. I chew on the inside of my mouth. This is so strange.

'So,' she says at last, 'I've left you a few books I used to love at your age.'

I walk over to Mira's shelves and pick up one of them. It's a novel with a girl's face on the cover. She's wearing bright red lipstick and has slightly fangy teeth. Kez has a whole shelf full of these she read in Year Six. Calls it her vampire moment. She used to go on and on about how they didn't really have anything to do with being *bitten* on the neck. I never got it. I drop it back down on the shelf.

'Vampires! Don't think so!'

'I was really into them for a while. But there's all sorts. I've taken the ones I can't live without. If you don't want them you can always give them away. Kez might want them . . .'

'She's probably read most of these,' I say, scanning the other titles.

It feels like Mira's only talking about the books because she's stuck for something to say. Now she takes her phone out of her pocket.

'Here, let's take a selfie! Krish, get back in here a minute,' Mira calls through the wall. 'I want a last picture of the three of us in my old room!' Mira widens her eyes at me like she still thinks it's outrageous for me to move in, though my bedroom's practically a box compared to this and she won't even be here. I *think* she's only joking, but I wish she'd stop going on about me taking her room, because I actually do feel bad about it – kind of guilty.

Krish comes in and squishes on to Mira's bed.

'Jump up, Lai Lai; you've got to sit next to me. Get us in the right order!

We jostle for places higher and lower so we can all fit in.

'Everyone say "Lai Lai"!' Krish grins this really stupid wide grin.

I elbow him in the side and stick my tongue out.

'That's a saver. Ping it to me,' Krish says, laughing at the photo.

When I'm on my own again, I stand for a long time and look at the person in the mirror. The truth is I've never really thought about me being on my own before. Maybe it feels worse than it would because of Kez. I just wish Krish and Mira weren't leaving at the same time. Mira going to college is bad enough, but Krish heading off too! He could have waited at least till I start secondary school. How am I going to get to sleep at night without listening to those two chatting on about nothing and everything on their mobiles? This stuff – this messing-around-in-our-rooms thing – is what we've always done. It's who we are together. It's who I am.

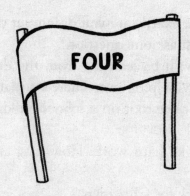

FOUR

Every time the doorbell rings it makes me jump.

What was the point of finally fixing it just as Mira and Krish are moving out?

Thinking about it . . . who's going to ring the bell or clank that letter box for me?

'That'll be Jidé,' Mira says, trying to make out that she's not that fussed.

Then the letter box clanks. Only one person still clanks!

'Or . . . Millie!'

Mira laughs as she run downstairs.

I creep out to the landing sofa – since the beginning of the summer holidays I've been sitting here a lot. In fact I'm here so much that Mum calls it my 'perch'.

Mum's beaten Mira to the door and now she's chatting away to Jidé and Millie.

'Quite a journey you're going on now, Jidé. Where are you actually staying?'

'In a volunteers' camp they've set up for us.'

'And what exactly are you doing out there?' Mum can never just ask one question.

'I think we'll be learning from the doctors there and generally helping out. There's a plan to build a well, and put the roof on a school building . . . that sort of thing!'

'Sounds like hard work. How long are you away for?'

'I'll be back for Christmas.'

'Well good for you, Jidé. Take care of yourself, won't you. And you, Millie . . .' Mum starts.

Now Mira's waving at Jidé and Millie while she tries to edge past Mum.

'Still enjoying the writing . . . ? In your second year already . . .'

'Can I get by, Mum?'

'Well, I'll leave you to your goodbyes. I was just on my way upstairs with this lot.' Mum scoops up a pile of washing she's parked on the side, walks up the stairs and finds me on my perch.

'Everybody's on the move, Laila.' She sighs, easing herself down beside me, and starts to fold the washing. 'Give me a hand, will you?'

Everybody except me, I think as I hunt through to find a matching sock of mine.

'Glad I got this upholstered,' Mum says, smoothing her hands over the sofa cover. 'We'll have to look after it now. Such a pretty little sofa . . . worth restoring.

They did a good job, I think. I like this faded gold paint. Your Nana Josie would have approved. Rattan's hard to get hold of these days.' Mum touches the flaky painted sides. 'It's a dying skill this lattice-work. I can still picture where it was in your Nana Josie's flat . . .'

I look around the walls at Nana Josie's paintings of Krish and Mira as toddlers, sitting on this sofa's faded cushions. There are no paintings of me on it, even though in reality I'm probably the one who's spent the longest sitting here. I've decided I think this is actually my favourite place in our house. I love to tuck my legs up and disappear into the jewel-coloured velvety sofa cushions. The little ruby-red one with the zip in the back is the most comfortable. Sometimes I can be snuggled up on here and people walk straight past and don't even notice me. Even though I've taken up Mum's name for it, it's actually not just somewhere for me to 'perch'. It's getting to be more like my nest. Apparently Nana Josie was about the same size as I am now. I fit here.

There's just one tiny painting of me on the landing. In fact it's the only painting Nana Josie ever did of me. I'm in Mum's arms when I was a baby. Mum says it's special because it's the last painting Nana Josie did before she died. Most of the people in the landing photos and paintings I don't remember, not like Mira and Krish do . . . some of them, like Grandad Kit, died before I was even born.

The photos on the staircase I love the most are of Mira and Krish holding me in their arms, as if they're afraid that they'll drop me. I really like the way the pictures of everyone are all mixed up together . . . There's one of Mum and Dad when they were young and actually quite good-looking. Mum looks just like Mira – or I suppose Mira looks just like Mum! If you look carefully you can sort of see all of us in these faces, especially me in Nana Josie. I feel like I belong to all the people on this staircase, and they belong to each other, but only a few of them belong to me . . .

Mum's finished folding the washing pile. I give up trying to find pairs and lay three single odd socks on top.

'One of the great mysteries of life!' Mum shakes her head. 'Where do they go?'

She leans back on the sofa and wraps an arm around my shoulders. She smiles up at her favourite photograph of her dad, Grandad Bimal, the one where he's clapping and laughing his head off. He looks so friendly. I wish I could remember him properly.

'Sometimes when I pass that photo I imagine I can hear his laugh,' I tell Mum.

'Me too!' Mum manages to splutter out before the tears start rolling down her face.

I wish I'd kept my mouth shut.

So, while Mira is downstairs saying her goodbyes to

Jidé and Millie, I'm here with Mum crying into her washing. This feels so sad. I wish I could ask Kez over right now. I wouldn't mind going into my old room and closing the door on all of this. I wonder if me and Kez will stay friends the way Mira, Millie and Jidé have stuck together.

Krish comes tearing out of his room wearing jeans and no T-shirt. Showing off his six-pack again. He leans over the balcony.

'All right, Millie! Fresh hair!'

'The bottle called it Pink Punk!'

'Looks good!'

'What are you up to?' Millie calls up to Krish.

'Doing this apprenticeship thing in an outward-bounds centre up North – staying with Nana Kath.'

'You'll need to get dressed then . . .' Millie says.

Krish looks down at himself as if he's *only just realized* that he's not wearing a T-shirt.

'Yes, can you get dressed, Krish,' Mum says. 'Poor Millie doesn't want to see your bare chest!'

'I don't think she minds!' Krish jokes, not loud enough for Millie to hear.

'You *so* fancy her!' I whisper.

'Shut up!' Krish goes to cuff me.

'Catch up with you later, Jidé!' Millie calls, and then they all start their goodbye hugs. That lot take forever.

Krish slumps down in the middle of Mum and me,

flinging an arm around Mum on one side and me on the other and making the washing pile topple on to the carpet.

'We've just folded that!' Mum groans.

'Don't worry, Mum! We'll be gone soon and it'll be dead peaceful and tidy with only Lai Lai—'

'*Laila*,' I correct.

Krish starts tickling me.

'Get off, Krish!' I squirm on the edge of the sofa. 'Would you mind not talking about me as if I'm not here?'

'OK, Lai Lai!'

'How many times have I got to tell you not to call me—'

'Did you hear something, Mum? An invisible force field?'

'Oh, shut up, Krish!' I belt him on the arm.

'Ow! I thought you were a pacifist!'

'I am, except when it comes to you!'

'You won't need to spy on us all from up here any more, Flappy Ears! Anyway, what are you complaining about? You're getting the best room in the house.' Krish jumps up, grabs me and attempts to turn me upside down.

'Get *off*!' I squeal, kicking my legs out.

'Oh, don't start that again, you two! The last thing I need now is someone getting hurt,' Mum pleads as she carries on up the stairs to her room.

26

'What do you mean, you *two*? *He* started it!'

'Say mercy!' Krish laughs. I swear he still thinks I'm in infants.

'Mercy.' I bash Krish on his shoulders so hard that his skin turns pink.

I'm upside down when I spot Mira and Jidé crushed against the side wall in the hall. For a second I think maybe it's just a long goodbye hug because Jidé's going to Rwanda where he was actually born, and I suppose that is a big deal so maybe that's why the long good— But no . . . not the way they're pressed together . . . tongues and everything! Gross!

'Put me down!' I pinch Krish even harder.

'Foul!' Krish laughs.

'You're foul!' I shout.

Mira and Jidé peel themselves away from the wall and appear at the bottom of the stairs, making out nothing's happened. Mira's hair looks all scuffed up though . . . what she calls 'distressed'. It's how I feel.

'All right, Jidé; thought you'd gone with Millie!' Krish waves down.

'Just off now. Say hello to Nana Kath for me,' Jidé calls up, but his voice sounds all dried out. It hardly carries up the stairs.

When they've said their goodbyes Krish goes off to his room. Mira's followed Jidé outside and they stand on the steps and talk.

After about half an hour Mira comes running up

the stairs and heads straight for her room.

She's crying. Proper puffy-eyed crying.

'Are you OK, Mira?' I ask as she runs past me. She turns to me, shakes her head as if to say *don't ask* and closes her bedroom door. But I can hear her sobs.

I knock gently on her door.

'Not now, Laila,' she manages to splutter out.

So I go back to my perch and listen to her trying to catch her breath. I've never heard her cry like that before. I wish she would let me in. Even *I* know those tears can't just be for a 'just good friends' kiss.

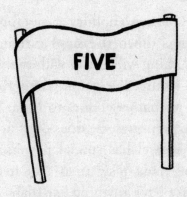

FIVE

'Mira – three things: Dad, straw and the camel's back! He'll flip . . . don't say I didn't warn you!' Krish laughs as he runs up the stairs.

I watch the whole leaving drama from the landing. Krish joking around, trying to lighten everyone's mood. Mum fretting over one last 'don't forget' item that Mira or Krish just *might* not survive without. And Dad giving his usual lecture: 'You'll have to leave some of this at home, Mira. This is a car not a Tardis! It'll never all fit in.'

It's always the same script. And then, in the end – miracle of miracles – everything *does* fit in. I think Dad likes to prove himself wrong with his excellent packing!

This scuffle, shuffle, huffing, moaning, forgetting stuff and going back for it is what I've always loved most about us going away together. This is how I remember the start of every one of our family holidays. Except this time it doesn't feel like the beginning of an adventure, or even a holiday . . . not for me, anyway.

Mira staggers down the steps carrying her easel. What special thing will I take with me when I leave home? I don't think I've got anything that means as much to me as that easel does to Mira. She told me once that the paintings she does on it are always her best. Like the easel has special powers, like there's something of Nana Josie in it that inspires her. I definitely don't have anything like that.

Mira rests the easel against the wall for a minute while she pauses on the stairs to get her breath back.

'Give it here then – but don't say I didn't warn you!' Krish takes the easel and carries it the rest of the way to the car.

'No way – that'll have to be for the next journey up!' Dad's definitely getting shoutier.

'But, Dad, I can't paint without it.'

Mira's standing on the pavement hugging the easel, as if she's about to go into battle and this is her only shield. Even *I* know there's no point in Dad arguing – that easel is the last thing in the world Mira's going to leave behind.

'I could wedge it, I suppose, but it's not exactly health and safety! Whoever's sitting in the front will need to get in and out from the driver's side.'

'We won't have to stop that often. Laila's not going to be with us puking all the way!'

Thanks, Mira!

'To be honest, this is an extra hassle I could do without,' Dad complains.

Mira's mouth is set in a pout.

'*I'll* sit in the front then,' Krish says, jumping in.

'Krish! Get out! *I'm* in the front!' Mira shouts.

I walk down the stairs and sit on the bottom step to get a better view. This doesn't feel right, watching Mira and Krish jostle for their place in the car. Until now I've always been the one right in the middle of all the family squabbles. You wouldn't think that this packing-the-car chaos and the same old argument over who gets the front seat would be something that anyone could miss, but I will!

After 'a quiet word' from Mum, Dad scowls at the car boot for a while as if he's struggling to work out a crossword puzzle. He sighs loud enough for everyone to hear him, opens the boot and, bag by bag, takes everything out again. He collapses the back seat and slides the easel right the way down the side of the car past Krish's shoulder.

'We'll probably get pulled over,' Dad complains. 'What if we have an emergency stop? Its legs will be straight through the front window.'

'I'll hold on to it,' Krish says.

'Dad, tell Krish he needs to get out!'

I can't believe that Mira's still going on about sitting in the front.

'I don't see why I should be crammed into the back

31

with all your junk,' Krish argues. 'You can sit in the front from Nana Kath's to Glasgow.'

Each time Dad forces something else into the boot, the easel shunts closer towards the front windscreen. Dad gives it a hard shove and finally slams the boot shut.

'Ow! That scraped my shoulder!'

'Well, you shouldn't have bogarted the front seat then!' Mira wades in.

'Oh, for goodness sake, you two, grow up!' Dad snaps.

There's someone coming down the street in a navy-blue business suit, wheeling a suitcase. Please don't let it be . . . It's Kez's mum, probably on her way to the airport. Why did she have to choose this moment to walk by?

'Is that Hannah?' Mum whispers, and disappears back inside the house.

Kez's mum inspects our bulging car like it's an exhibit in that museum of weird and curious things she took me and Kez to once.

'Have a comfortable journey!' she says wryly.

'Thanks, Hannah! Fancy trading places?' Dad jokes.

'On this occasion, I think I'll decline!' Kez's mum flicks back our car's wing mirror. 'You'll definitely be needing your mirrors . . .' Then she spots me sitting on the steps. 'Oh, hello, Laila. We haven't seen you for ages. We were just saying the other day, when the coast's clear –' she nods towards our car – 'you should come on over.'

'Thanks.'

I've never witnessed a scene like this outside Kez's, but I suppose she doesn't have brothers and sisters to argue about everything, even though she wishes she did.

Kez's mum pauses by the tree to read the sign that Ed's posted up.

Corn Snake found
Call Ed: 0653351511

'No more reptiles turned up in your house then, Sam?' She laughs.

'None that I know of!' Dad shakes his head.

'That's a relief.'

Hannah peers into the car and taps on the window 'Good luck, you two!'

When she's gone Dad leans into the front seat and starts the engine. It's his signal for the countdown. Just at the last moment Mira jumps back out of the car. I move aside on the step because I think she must have forgotten something else in her room, but instead she grabs me under my arms and pulls me up into a hug. I make my legs heavy and hold on to the banister so she can't actually lift me off the ground. I know I'm light but I wish people would get out of the habit of whisking me up. I can feel the tears on Mira's cheek as she squeezes me so tightly that my sides hurt. Then she turns around, runs back down the front steps, hugs Mum again and gets back in the car. Krish winds the window down as far as the easel will let him and peeps his head out as if he's a prisoner or something. He sticks his hand through the window and mouths, 'Help!'

Mum's throat makes a strange sound somewhere between a laugh, a cry and a choke. She's leaning her back against the garden wall as if she needs it to hold her up.

'See you, Lai Lai – I'll be back to annoy you for a weekend before Christmas!' Krish shouts.

I stick my tongue out at him.

'See you in a couple of days. I'll call!' Dad has to shout over the noise of the engine. It sounds a bit cranky.

I walk past Mum and head back up the stairs to my landing perch, picturing Krish laying odds on how long it will take before Dad has to turn back for some last forgotten thing.

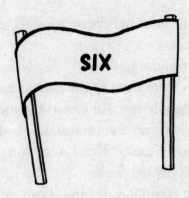

SIX

Mum stands for a while on the pavement, then turns towards the house, climbs the front steps and closes the door behind her.

I inch to the back of my perch, curling my feet up under me.

'You all right up there, Lai . . . la?' Mum's voice sounds weak. She coughs and tries again. 'You know what – I think I'll have a cup of tea,' she says, as if that's a revolutionary idea. Then she stops and looks up. 'Do you fancy one, Laila?'

Now *this is* a revolutionary idea! It's the first time she's got my actual name right without hesitating, and it's the first time anyone in this family has ever thought to ask me if *I* want a cup of tea.

'Yes, please, Mum!'

'Do you have milk and sugar?' she asks.

'Um . . . yes!' I call down. But I don't know. *Do I have milk and sugar?*

*

Mum's got it into her head to start cleaning the kitchen shelves.

'Why are you doing that?'

'I do clean from time to time, you know!' she tells me, but I've hardly ever seen anything move off those shelves. And from the amount of dust Mum's whipping up, it looks like a very long time since anyone's even dusted them.

I'm on the computer, flitting about on YouTube. I take a sip of tea. I'm not sure I like the taste it leaves on my tongue.

'How do you like it?' Mum asks.

'A bit sweet.'

'Sweet enough as you are?'

I pull a face at her that's the opposite of sweet.

'I think that's enough computer time now,' Mum says as she finishes clearing a shelf.

'I'm watching Priya's new music video. She's done the choreography on it. It's got loads of comments. Want to see?'

'What a talented family we've got!' Mum says, and comes over and reads the title over my shoulder: 'Holi-Spring!'

I press PLAY and we watch the dancers in their bright silk clothes padding out rhythms with their feet on a huge drum. It looks like they're outside Janu's House of Garlands refuge in Kolkata . . . Now one of the dancers breaks through the skin and there's this slow-motion fall to another drum and the dancers are suddenly on a New York street, moving to a dub-step beat. Then all the dancers start throwing powder in rainbow colours. Powder reds, blues, yellows and greens fly from the hands of the children in Kolkata on to the faces of the New York dancers. It's funny and beautiful. Then the two streets and all the dancers sort of merge together and they're doing a dance that's a sort of fusion of everything – just a mass of colours moving.

'Stunning! When I was growing up I used to have to imagine your Aunt Anjali dancing – I never actually got to see her perform till I went to India. She must be so proud of Priya and Janu . . . they're proper trailblazers in their different ways, aren't they?' Mum says.

Trail-blazers . . . what does that mean? That they're bright flames . . . brave, I suppose.

'Laila, I *really* think you've had enough screen time, don't you?'

I do a huge uncontrollable sneeze and say, 'I think *you've* had enough cleaning time, don't you?'

'Laila, why are you itching?' Mum takes hold of my hand, turns it over and inspects the crook of my arm.

'Probably all the dust you're making!'

It does look a bit red and raw.

'Your skin's really dry just there. We'll have to keep an eye on that. You haven't had it that badly since you were a baby!'

'It's nothing,' I mumble, and go to Skype Kez.

'How could we let it get this dusty?' Mum tuts. 'I'm not having you getting eczema again. This house is going to look worse before it looks better, but I think it's time we had a proper spring clean.'

'It's autumn!'

'Autumn clean then!'

Now Mum decides that one shelf at a time won't do, so she's taking everything off and making a pile in the middle of the room.

I press Kez's photo ID on Skype, listen to the dialling sound for a few seconds and then her face appears. I lean in to get a closer look.

Me: Have you dyed your hair?

Kez: Yep! Like it?

Me: Yeah, looks good on you.

Kez: Have Krish and Mira gone then?

Me: Yes.

Kez: You OK?

Me: It feels weird here! I saw your mum. She said to come and see you. You free?

Kez: Sorry, Laila, I've got Saturday School.

Me: How long for?

Kez: Pretty much all day.

Me: I thought it was just in the morning?

Kez: There's loads of preparation to do for my bat

mitzvah. They're putting on extra classes at shul for us now.

Me: Tomorrow then?

Kez: We've got family over.

Me: After the first day at school?

Kez: Mum thinks Sundays will be the easiest for us to meet up – till after my bat mitzvah anyway. She's worried I'm going to get too tired with Saturday school, physio and everything.

Me: Are you tired?

Kez: A bit. Got a few more tremors than normal. Nerves don't help.

Me: About school?

Kez: Yeah! It'll be all right though; once I find my way around . . . get to know where the lifts are and everything.

Me: We can go around together, if you want?

Kez: You don't know where you're going either. Anyway, we might not be in the same tutor group.

Me: Yeah, we are. Seven Dials. Didn't you get the letter? I like the name . . . Like in Covent Garden. All the tutor-group names are based on things to do with seven, apparently. Krish told me the tutors choose the names, so you can kind of see how interesting they are before you meet them . . . or not!

*

39

I watch Kez's face. She tips her head forward so her bright red curls fall across her face and I can't read her expression.

Kez: It doesn't always happen, getting in the same tutor group.

Me: Yeah, but we will definitely be together, won't we? That transition woman said she thought—

Kez: She said friends can't always be together.

Me: But we will.

Kez: I'm in Seven Oaks . . . apparently.

Me: You can't be – they must have made a mistake.

Kez: I don't think so, Lai Lai! It's not that bad. We'll see each other all the time—

I start to cough uncontrollably. I'm trying my hardest to stop so I take a glug of tea, but that makes it worse and now I'm spluttering all over the screen. I wish I could get a hold of myself. Mum brings me some water and eventually the coughing stops.

Me: I'm only choking because Mum's gone on a cleaning frenzy. There's dust everywhere! Sorry, Kez, I've got to go!

Kez: Lai Lai . . .

Me: See you Monday!

I break the connection.

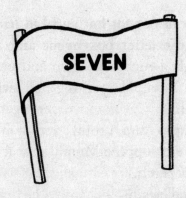

SEVEN

I stare at Kez's text for a while as the dust floats through the air around me.

> Are you pissed off with me about something, Lai Lai?

> No, should I be?

> You shouldn't, but I feel like you are x

I am.

There are too many things floating around that no one's talking about . . . Not just dust either. Why isn't Kez kicking up a stink about us not being in the same tutor group? If anyone can fight for something they really want, Kez can . . . unless . . .

I start to cough again, and scratch at my arm. Mum's abandoned the shelf mess on the floor in the middle of the room. It looks like a junk heap.

'Mum!' I call out for her and I'm halfway up the stairs when the letter box opens and an envelope slides through. I run back down and pick it up. It's addressed to Mira. The writing's all swirly, kind of old-fashioned.

I'll take it up to Mira, I think, and then I remember she's not here. I suppose Mum'll post it on to her. I drop it on my perch.

'Mum!' I call again.

'In here!'

I find her in Krish's room, picking up clothes he's left strewn around and hanging them back in his wardrobe. She pushes the door further open so I can see even less of her face. I think she's trying to hide her tears from me.

'Mira and Krish *are* coming back you know, Mum.'

'I know I'm being over the top!' Mum says from behind the wardrobe door, where she stays sorting clothes for much longer than she needs to. Eventually she blows her nose and comes to sit next to me on Krish's bed. She wraps her arms around my shoulders too tightly. Her eyes look pink and sore. She picks up my arm and turns it over. 'Laila, you've got to stop scratching this or you'll make it bleed.'

'I'll stop scratching if you stop cleaning and crying!' I say.

At least this makes her laugh.

42

'Deal! I don't know what's got into me really.'

'I'll help you put the things back on the shelves if you want.'

'That's sweet of you. You know me; I'll feel better after a good cry – but I wish I'd never started on those shelves downstairs.'

I scan Krish's bedroom. At least Mum hasn't tidied everything up . . . yet. Krish's things are all still here. His Tottenham posters, his festival programmes, Grandad Kit's beret with medals . . . and that funny painting that Nana Josie did of Grandad Kit eating fish and chips where the fish on the plate is actually eating the chips! All waiting for Krish to come bowling back in. Even though it looks stupidly tidy in here, it doesn't feel so final, him going away – he's only gone to stay at Nana Kath's after all.

'I'm going to get changed,' I tell Mum, and walk through to Mira's room, where all my clothes are now stacked up in her wardrobe. Mira's bedroom feels different. I can't get my head around this being *my* room. I scan the patchwork of empty frames where Mira's photos, pictures and posters used to be. It's so empty in here.

'How about we decorate! You can choose the colour – within reason!' Mum's remembering the time Krish wanted to paint the whole room black with light-up stars on the ceiling. 'What do you fancy?'

Her voice is all high and broken, like she's forcing herself to talk. 'Any ideas?'

I shrug. 'When will Dad be back?'

'Monday afternoon. He'll be here by the time you get home from school.' Mum sighs. 'It's quite a drive to Glasgow and he's got to drop Krish off in the Lake District with Nana first. That's a long drive, and then I suppose it'll take a bit of time to settle Mira in. He's booked into a hotel for tonight, then he'll break the journey and see Mum and Krish on the way back.'

'Didn't you want to go too? See where Mira's living?' I ask. 'I could have stayed over with Kez.'

Though I wonder. Last summer there were only two weeks when we didn't see each other. This summer we've only seen each other for two days. She's always got something else on. So, thinking about it, I don't know if it actually would have been possible for me to stay with her . . . Seems like every time I ask, she's busy.

'I can't miss your first day of secondary! No, I'll visit Mira soon; find out how she's settling in. Anyway, I don't think they could have squeezed me in that car! And you know what Mira and I are like – maybe best not to get too emotional!' Mum smiles.

I nod a bit too enthusiastically, which makes Mum laugh.

'Why don't you ask Kez to come over and help

you plan out your new room?'

'How many times do I have to tell you, she's not coming over any more?'

Mum looks a bit taken aback.

'Sorry, Laila. Yes! I forgot. Dad told me it was a bit awkward when she was over the last time.'

'Just a bit!'

'When did you last see her? Have you been over–'

The home line rings. There are only a few people who call on it now that Dad's had this code put on to stop the marketing calls. Mum says we only really keep it for Nana Kath, because she never thinks it's a proper call unless it's on the landline.

'Sorry, Laila. I'd better get that,' Mum says as she runs down the stairs.

I sit on my perch and listen to Mum chatting away to Mira – I can't believe she's calling her from the car – she isn't even at college yet! Afterwards she speaks to Krish, and it's hard to describe how I feel, like nothing's left here for me.

I'm sitting on something, so I shift over. I'd forgotten about the letter. I read the envelope. The writing's sort of shaky, as if the person was finding it difficult to keep their hand steady.

On the back is written something that makes me think that whoever this is from hasn't met up with anyone in our family for a long time.

If the addressee no longer lives here, please return to:
Simon Makepeace
The Caring Community
22 Railway Road
Finsbury Park
London, N4

I'm about to call down and tell Mum about the letter when she comes running upstairs, grabs the little wooden stool on the landing and heads into Mira's room. I follow her through.

'I thought this was supposed to be my room now. What are you doing? Mira said I could have those books.'

Mum's standing on the stool, reaching for something pushed to the back. She takes down two books with Mira's drawings all over them.

'What are they?' I ask.

Mum sort of hides them under her arm like she doesn't want me to see.

'Oh, they're Mira's diaries. She forgot them. She wants me to store them up in the loft.'

I hold out my hand for Mum to pass them to me because it looks like she's struggling to keep her balance, but she won't hand them over.

'You haven't read them, have you?' Mum asks, looking at me strangely.

'No! Have you?'

'Of course not,' Mum says.

'You're not even tempted?' I say as she heads for the door, but she doesn't answer me.

Mum is right above me in the loft storage cupboard putting Mira's diaries away. I wonder what's in them that she so desperately doesn't want me or anyone else to know about. I pick up the letter for Mira and turn it over. I don't know why I feel annoyed with Mira for not wanting me to read her diaries . . . after all that is the point of diaries, to keep things to yourself. But it's like no one in this house thinks I'm capable of understanding anything.

'You all right there?' Mum says as she comes back down to the landing. 'What's that?'she asks, looking at the letter.

I place it by my side so she can't see.

'Nothing! Just a letter Kez sent me when she was at her summer camp. It's private!' I can't resist saying.

'Has something happened between you two, Laila, because if it has you can always talk to me . . . ?'

'No! Everything's fine!'

'OK!' Mum says, like she doesn't believe me but she's decided she's not going to push any harder for now. 'Do you fancy giving me a hand with the shelf-mess?'

'Yeah! I'll come down in minute,' I say.

When Mum's gone I slip the envelope inside the little velvet cushion cover, zip it up and hide it behind some larger cushions. No one's going to look in here.

As I walk down the stairs I knock into the frame of an old black-and-white photo of Nana Josie when she was young. She's on the South Bank by the river, selling her paintings. Now I stop to look, I can see that it's true: I really do look like her.

EIGHT

'Why keep all this stuff anyway? I should get a giant bin bag and chuck it all out! I mean, look at all these bits of old pottery . . . a lid for something . . . and there's half a beach worth of holey stones here. We can keep a few, but honestly . . . !' Mum picks up a big white pebble and looks through the hole at me.

'Don't throw those out, Mum – they're from the competition Mira and me had this summer.'

Mum smiles and puts the pile back on the shelf. 'Well, perhaps we can return a few next time we go!'

Now Mum's holding up a drawing I did in Year Six that I thought was useless, nothing like Mira could have done. I know Mum only keeps it because she's trying to make me feel good about my art.

'You can chuck that!'

Mum sighs and shakes her head.

'I should have made a scrapbook for your art . . . like I did for Mira and Krish. Maybe now I'll get around to it. I've been meaning to mend this old picture frame for about five years. I suppose that says it all!' Mum shrugs and drops the broken frame into a bin bag.

I pick up a dusty box with a crack through the lid. I'm about to hand it to Mum when I wipe a finger over the top and it comes up shiny. It's painted in what looks like varnish and has a delicate painting of a bonsai tree on the lid.

'It's all chipped at the edges. We've got to be brutal. Bin it!' Mum says.

'I like this. Can I keep it?'

'It's broken, Laila!' Mum sighs. 'We're not getting very far with clearing things, are we?'

Seems like I'm annoying her, so I throw the box in the bag – but as I do, I hear something rattle. I lift the box back out and open it.

Inside is a black silk drawstring purse. I loosen the strings and see a silver-grey bauble the size of a giant marble, with patterns of stars, moons and suns cut into it, like a tiny little universe. At the top is a hook with a cream-coloured ring, threaded through with a faded blue ribbon.

Mum leans in to get a closer look.

'Oh, thank goodness we didn't throw that away!' She inspects it more closely. 'I'd given up on ever seeing this again. It was your Nana Josie's rattle when she was a baby. We hunted and hunted for this after she died because she wanted you to have it. Has it still got its chime?' I rattle it and it rings. 'That's what I remember . . . such a sweet soothing sound.'

'But I thought Nana Josie didn't give me anything.'

'You were just a baby when she died, Laila. You were her last painting.'

'I know all that. But you mean she actually *gave* me something, just for me?'

'Yes, she did. She adored you, Laila. It made that time bearable, having a baby around.'

Mum's inspecting a few other little boxes more closely now.

'So Mira had the easel and the charm thing that she lost, Krish got Grandad Kit's war medals and one of Nana's paintings, and *I* got a baby's rattle that's been lost for nearly eleven years?'

'Perhaps it doesn't seem like much.'

'Yes, it does seem like much. It seems like a lot actually. Only no one bothered to tell me about it. Maybe you want to throw me away too!'

My eyes are stinging with tears of anger, but I clench my teeth together so they don't fall and I run up the stairs to the landing with the box. I go into Mira's room and place it on one of her bookshelves, open the box, tip the chime out of the drawstring purse and take it back to my perch. I feel like I want to keep it close while I read . . .

I find the ruby-red velvet cushion, take out the letter that's addressed to Mira and open it.

Dear Mira,

You may not remember me . . . but we met once in the hospice. I was a great friend of your Nana Josie's and I know the two of you were very close. I seem to remember Josie used to call you her 'fellow artist'!

Anyway, the point of writing to you is that I would like you to come and collect the Protest Book Josie made me the guardian of. Of course if you'd prefer I could send it, but it's heavy and the post isn't what it used to be.

Josie gave me firm instructions that one day, when I had done with it, I should pass it on to you. I was thinking of addressing this to your parents, but then it occurred to me that you must be an adult by now, and with the world as it is, I'm thinking now's the time to hand it over.

I hope your family still live at the address Josie left me - if not, I suppose I'll have to do some research and see if I can trace you online. Hopefully I won't have to! I thought I'd try by letter first.

*I do like a letter. Myself and your Nana
Josie have written quite a few and got a
few replies too, but you can read those in
the Protest Book.*

*I hope to meet you again soon to hand
over a very special book - it contains so
many of the things Josie and I stood up
for . . . about fifty years of campaigning,
letter writing and protesting all in all. No
wonder it's heavy!*

Yours,

Simon Makepeace

I should tell Mum about this. I know I shouldn't have
opened it, but I've heard Mum and Dad talk about
the protests Nana Josie went on. Sometimes when we
sit and watch the news together and there's a march
like the one to make refugee people welcome, Mum
or Dad say, 'Josie would have been there with her
banners.' I asked Dad why we don't do that, and he
said he'd been on his fair share – but I've never been
on one with him.

I had no idea there was an actual book with the
things Nana Josie felt so strongly about written down
in it. At least Mira and Krish remember her. It doesn't
seem fair that Mira gets to go and meet Simon and

have the book too. I put the letter back in the envelope and tuck it inside the cushion cover. What if I went to pick it up for Mira, just to have a read and give it to her when she comes home?

I rattle the chime and it makes a sound like a sweet clear voice that carries on singing in my ears for ages until it gets interrupted by the home phone ringing.

It's Dad. I can hear Mum talking to him.

'Is Krish OK? I know she's going to spoil him rotten. You drive carefully up to Glasgow; make sure you're not too tired. Laila's been in a bit of a state. I'm leaving her to cool off for a bit. I know, emotions running high! It's odd, isn't it . . . of all the things, she decided to open that little box. No, no, I won't, don't worry. I'm going to go through everything with a fine-tooth comb from now on.'

Mum comes upstairs and sits down gently next to me, like I'm bruised or something and she's afraid to put any pressure on me in case I hurt more.

'Funny how you love this little landing sofa so much. When I see you sitting up here I always wish your Nana Josie had lived long enough to get to know you.' Mum looks up at the paintings of Mira and Krish sitting on this very same sofa.

'She waited for you to arrive, you know. She loved you to bits.'

'But she didn't *know* me!' I pick up the little rattle and make it ring again.

'I'm so glad it hasn't lost its chime. I know we've been a bit taken up with Mira and Krish leaving and you starting secondary school too –' Mum cuddles me – 'but you *do* know how much we all love you, Laila, don't you?'

'You don't have to say it, Mum. I *know*.'

'All right then. I've made the bed up for you in your new room. Why don't you go and start getting moved in?'

'I will in a bit.'

I always thought the night before secondary would be me and Kez together, and in a way it is . . . with me going over that vile day at the beginning of the summer holidays when everything seemed to change between us. I don't know why I keep raking over every detail. It's not going to make a difference going back over it. No one else except me and Kez seem to understand how awful it was. I let the chime roll around my hand. Maybe if Nana Josie was alive and she'd got to see me and Kez growing up, like Bubbe has, I could have talked to her about that day. I've been over it so many times I've actually got a name for it. It feels like a lot longer than two months ago . . .

The Day of the Unfriendship Bench

'By the tree,' I text Dad.

He comes straight out, opens both sides of our

stupidly narrow doors and joins us on the pavement.

We start walking up the steps while Dad folds Kez's chair and carries it up after us.

'This is neat. Much easier to fold than the old one,' Dad says as he stacks it down the side of the house.

'My motorized one's coming in the summer,' Kez says, pausing halfway up and holding tight on to me until my arm trembles too. 'I didn't realize I was so tired. I'll never make it up to your room. Let's just stay in the kitchen today, Lai Lai.'

She's not making a fuss, but she's in pain – I can tell. I can always tell.

We're just sitting at the table listening to a bit of music when a text pops up on Kez's phone.

'It's Bubbe. I forgot I've got physio today. I've got to go anyway. Nature calls!'

'Sorry, Kez. I wish we didn't have so many stairs. Are you OK?'

'Not great. They're adjusting my medicines again.'

'Dad! Kez has to go!' I call upstairs.

'You've just got here!' Dad shouts down. 'I'm sorry, I'll have to call you right back.' He looks a bit stressed as he runs down the stairs and opens up both sides of the front door again so we can walk out together. He's got Kez's wheelchair carried down, opened and ready for her before we've even made it to the door. 'Come on then, girls!'

56

Kez and I are on the top step when Dad runs up and scoops her off her feet like he used to do with both of us when we were little.

I hear Jidé's voice as he comes around the corner. He's on the phone to Mira. When are they not!

'Yeah! Right outside; I'll be up in a minute!'

'Need any help?' Jidé asks.

Kez blushes and holds her face away from Dad's chest, but then he wobbles and nearly loses his balance.

Jidé runs up the steps and holds Kez's back to steady them both.

'Thanks. I just lost my footing for a minute,' Dad says.

'Hi, Kez, how's it going?' Jidé asks, touching Kez on the shoulder. She flinches away from him as he climbs the steps. 'Hi, Lai Lai!'

I move aside to let him through.

Kez closes her eyes like she wants everyone to disappear.

Dad's still out of breath as he lowers her into her seat. He wipes the sweat off his forehead as if the weather's the reason he's so puffed out.

'There you go, Kez.'

'Thank you!' she whispers. Her head's bowed.

'It's nothing.' Dad puffs. 'Really is a nice bit of new kit this! So much lighter than the old one.'

I wish he would stop going on about the chair,

like it's a new car or something.

'At least *the chair's* lighter,' Kez says.

'I didn't mean . . .'

I glare at Dad.

As soon as he's out of earshot, Kez's smile fades. We don't talk as I follow her into the park to the nearest bench on the main path that leads to school.

'Can we just talk here for a moment?' Kez asks.

I sit down on the bench and she looks straight into my eyes and comes out with it. 'That's the last time that's happening. I'm *never* being carried up and down your steps again.'

'I'll tell Dad he should ask you if you want help . . . being carried.'

'I *never* want to be carried,' Kez snaps.

'Sorry, Kez!'

'It's not your fault, but I mind, Lai Lai. I really mind now. Maybe if I was built like you I could put up with it for a bit longer, but it feels wrong, especially in front of Jidé too. I felt like an oversized kid.'

'Jidé wouldn't think anything—'

'You don't get it! I don't care what anyone else thinks. *I'm* the one who had to be carried by your dad. Maybe after they've tried this tendon-lengthening thing I'll be able to get up your steps myself . . .'

'But when are they doing that?'

'Not sure. But in any case it might not make *that* much difference. We'll just have to switch things up.

You can come over to mine any time.' Kez wriggles around a bit in her chair. 'I really need a pee! Now I *do* have to go! Don't worry about walking me back.'

I watch Kez till she's on the pavement. I tell myself if she looks back and waves it'll be all right.

But she doesn't.

'We'll just have to switch things up.' Kez's voice echoes through me. It started that day – the feeling that everything was going to change. I ring Nana Josie's chime till it starts to sing through my mind and calm me down like a lullaby.

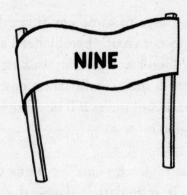

NINE

I wake up on my perch with my hand still clasping Nana Josie's chime. Someone's put a duvet over me. I must have fallen asleep so early. I tuck the chime inside the cushion cover, and as I do I feel the letter from Simon Makepeace.

'I didn't want to disturb you. You must have been exhausted. At least you've had a good night's sleep.' Mum yawns her way downstairs. 'I can't believe you actually slept on that!'

'I did!'

'It can't be that comfortable; there's no room to stretch out.'

'I curl up anyway.'

Mum sits down next to me and tests the springiness of the seats. There is none.

'It's got horsehair stuffing. The upholsterer asked me if I wanted it restuffed – maybe I should have . . .'

It's like Mum's been hit by a thunderbolt. She suddenly grabs hold of my arm, where my eczema is definitely getting worse. It's started itching on the other arm now, and a bit in the crease behind my knees. The thing about the scratching is that most of the time I don't even realize I'm doing it.

'It could be the sofa you're allergic to! Make this the first and last time you spend the night here, OK?'

'I can't be allergic to it. I've been sitting here for years.'

'That's true . . . but you've never slept on it before. Maybe your skin will settle down again when you get used to your new school. I'll get some cream for you later. Are you worrying about starting secondary? Do you want me to walk in with you, just on the first day?'

'Yes, OK, a bit, no! Which question do you want me to answer?'

'Sorry!' Mum laughs. 'I would like to walk you in though . . .'

As if *that* would help! I might as well take along a loudspeaker announcing to everyone how nervous I am: 'Baby of the family arrives at school, walked in by her mummy!'

'I'll be fine, Mum!' I say, shrugging off the duvet and going through to Mira's room to get dressed.

I inspect the rings under my eyes in the mirror, then put on the school uniform laid out ready on the chair. Mira was right. I should at least have got a blazer of my own. I'm lost somewhere inside this one. I pull the skirt up where it's sliding over my hips. Nothing fits except the tie.

'Mum, I've decided I do want to have my own uniform.'

Mum gives my oversized blazer and me a sideways glance, but carries on cooking.

Five, four, three, two . . . right on cue, the smoke alarm goes off. I grab a tea towel and waft.

I used to think the alarm going off all the time was funny when Krish and Mira were around, but now when the shrieking noise starts I'm the only one here left to waft the smoke away and it makes my head ache.

'You know, Laila, it's not very helpful to wait until the first day of school to finally agree to having a new uniform!'

'I thought you wanted me to have one that fits.'

Mum attempts to unstick the pancake from the bottom of the pan with a spatula.

'OK, we'll go at the weekend.' She sighs.

I sit at the table and eat my way through the extra-crispy pancake.

Mum places a mug of tea in front of me.

'Milk, no sugar, there you go! I won't have time to make pancakes every day, but as I'm starting late this morning, you're in luck. I'm going to have to get more organized from now on though! Maybe I'll leave cereal out at night so you can help yourself . . .'

'Thanks, Mum.' I take a sip of tea. I think I'm getting to like the taste.

After breakfast Mum insists on taking a photo of me in the front room.

'A new uniform would have been better, but the first day of secondary school is the first day of secondary school – history in the making!'

'I think it's happened to quite a lot of people before. Do you *have* to, Mum?' I groan.

She's holding up her iPhone and clicking away.

I force a smile.

If Mira had been here I would have asked her to do my hair in a French plait, and Krish would probably be trying to pick me up or make my tie more fat or skinny. They would be standing either side of me like cheerleaders, building me up.

'The first-day photo's a tradition!' Mum says. 'There you go . . . posted to Facebook.'

'Were you posting stuff when Mira and Krish started secondary?' I ask.

'No . . . but!'

She shows me the photo. Even after all that sleep I still look tired, and the blazer makes me look like I'm wearing a black box.

'Like it?' she asks.

'What difference does it make?'

'Oh, don't be grumpy, Laila.'
I groan at her status update.

My last baby off to secondary school!

Great. I'm right next to Krish's video post of the snake
in our kitchen. It's got tons of likes and comments. I
read over a few of them again.

Where ARE you? The Tropics?
Is that seriously in your house?
My ma says you have entered the cycle of
change! Janu X
Quiet night in with a Cobra!
Sorry, can't make it over for dinner tomorrow!
Have to file my nails!
You call the RSPCA? What did they say?
BTEC in Reptiles? Is that sssssssssssserious!
Just an ordinary Saturday night in the Levenson
household!

Remembering the madness of that day cheers me up.
'What's so funny?' Mum asks.
'Nothing! Just those comments about the snake!'
Mum shudders. 'Don't remind me! I'll say goodbye
before we open the door.'
She opens her arms and I let her hug me properly
until her phone pings us apart.

'Some messages for you!' She hands me her phone.

Mira: Good luck, sis! xxx
Nana Kath: You've put her in a boy's blazer!
Krish: Skinny crew then!
Hannah: How did it happen so fast? Share your
    pain!
Nana Kath: And why does she look so
    exhausted? What time did she go to bed?
Priya: Rock that look!
Anjali: Pretty girl!
Dad: Our beautiful baby Laila at secondary . . .
    Noooooooooooooooooo!

I pull the tie even tighter to try to stop myself from
welling up. What *is* the matter with me? It's up to
Mira and Mum to do the crying . . . not me. That's
how it's supposed to be.

I step out of the door and walk down the steps.

'Be careful how you cross the road, Laila; people
don't always stop at that crossing,' Mum says as I shoo
her back into the house. She laughs and closes the
door.

Jeff the postman is standing by the tree reading the
snake poster.

'No one claimed it yet then?' he asks.

'Don't think so,' I say, trying to get past him before
he starts up one of his 'chats'.

'Is that you off to secondary, Laila? It feels like five minutes since you were born! I remember . . .'

Oh, not again! I must have heard this the-day-you-were-born story a hundred times before.

'. . . I came to the door to deliver a parcel, and your mum answered with her own little parcel wrapped-up in her arms! You can't have been more than a few hours old.'

This weird little nervous laugh comes out of my mouth. 'Well, I've got to go!' I say as I squeeze around Jeff's trolley.

There are a few people I know a bit from my year group in primary walking the same way in as me. We don't exactly say hello, but they don't seem to mind when I walk along with them. Everyone looks smaller in their uniforms, especially compared to the older years. Some of them look like giants. I listen to the Year Sevens chatting together, asking about each other's summers, wondering what the tutors will be like, worrying about getting lost, feeling stupid in their uniforms . . . I *could* chip in, but I feel so on the outside. It's not their fault. I suppose I've never really made much of an effort to make friends with anyone except Kez.

Everyone gets pushed and jostled and there are so many students taking up the pavement that I feel a bit panicky. I look down the path to the Unfriendship

Bench. I tell myself that if I don't walk past it, then maybe everything will go back to how it's always been with me and Kez. I follow the pavement to the second entrance into the park. No one else is walking this way except a really old lady with an ancient dog that can hardly walk itself. I can't tell which of them is waiting for the other. She smiles at me and I smile back. I don't think I've ever felt this lonely.

I'm at the school gates now, looking down the path towards the bench. It doesn't feel any better looking at it from this side. I wait for a minute or so longer to see if Kez is coming.

'Waiting for a friend?' the lady at the gate asks.

I nod.

She taps her watch. 'Dearie! You have two minutes to get into school.'

I nod.

'You'd better go on in now. You don't want to be late on your first day!'

In primary I think some teachers used to think that I helped Kez. That she depended on me instead of the other way around – the way it actually is.

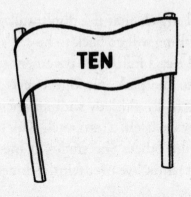

TEN

I check down the list of names in my tutor group. Kez is definitely not on it. After what they said in our transition meeting, I still don't understand why we're not together. Unless . . . I just can't get the idea out of my head that Kez has somehow made this happen.

You could ask for two people you especially wanted to be with, but the only person I really cared about being with was Kez, so I didn't write down any other names. The only other person I know is a boy called Carlos. He only came to our primary in Year Six and he didn't speak much English then. It's incredible how good he is now though. I think he's Spanish, but I'm not sure. I don't know him that well.

Our tutor's called Mrs Latif. She tells us that she teaches Philosophy and Ethics and a subject called Citizenship, which I've heard Krish talking about. It was his best subject and he was really gutted they didn't do it as an exam. Mrs Latif is explaining why she chose 'Seven Dials' as our tutor-group name:

'Always so many different pathways to explore from the same starting point, or roundabout to be precise! Anyone know where Seven Dials is?'

I've been thinking that at secondary I should speak up more than I used to in primary, especially when I know the answer.

'Well, it's in Covent Garden,' Mrs Latif answers as no one puts their hand up.

Mrs Latif is tall and has a long, slim face with high cheekbones, dark eyes with thick lashes, perfectly sculpted eyebrows and a tiny diamond nose stud. Her lips are painted plum colour and her silvery headscarf is decorated at the side with diamond jewels. She wears a plain black dress and heavy silver jewellery. Her nails are painted the same plum colour as her lips. I love her shoes . . . they're like brogues but silver. It doesn't seem fair really. If students have to wear a uniform, why don't teachers?

Mrs Latif says she's just started teaching here, and at her old school she taught Religious Education.

'So you will be my philosophy ambassadors here!' she says.

Above the whiteboard she has a sign mounted on bright blue card:

This school welcomes
believers of all religions and none

I read it over a few times. I think it's a good thing she's written it up there on the wall so everyone knows, because when I watch the news lots of the things in the world where people fight with each other seem to have something to do with what religion they do or don't belong to; what they believe or don't.

Mrs Latif takes her black marker pen and makes columns on the board under the headings:

| Name | Hobbies | Connected Lands | Languages |
| Beliefs | Religion | Favourite Subjects | |

I didn't think tutor time would be about stuff like this. Mrs Latif goes around the class taking the electronic register. She does it as fast as she can.

'Now. I thought we could start by getting to know a few things about each other! In a minute I'd like you to walk around the class with your notebooks, asking each other questions. I've put a few suggested headings up here to get you started –' she taps the board – 'but you can add whatever categories you like. We're just making a start at getting to know each other. Try to fill in as much as possible for as many people as possible in the time that we've got. In the next few weeks everyone will have met everyone else. Any questions?'

A girl sitting behind me puts her hand up.

'Is belief the same as religion?' she asks.

'This is exactly the sort of question I was hoping for . . . what's your name?'

'Pari.'

'Hi, Pari.' Mrs Latif thinks carefully before she answers. 'No, actually – I don't think they're the same. They're connected though. It's complicated, but that's the kind of thing we can debate in tutor time. You can also keep an eye out for any news that can feed into our discussions.'

'Excuse me? What does Connected Lands mean?' Carlos asks.

'Make a guess!'

'I'm from Spain, but my family live all over the world . . .'

'Where?' Mrs Latif asks

'Well, my uncle's from Cuba. I have relatives in Mexico, France and Spain, America and Canada.'

'You've got it! But, like I said, you don't have to stick to my categories; they're just to get you started. Come on then! See how many people you can meet and how much of the globe we can span in the next few minutes.'

The room gradually fills with noise.

The first person I meet is someone called Stella. She says she doesn't see why we should be talking about 'personal stuff' on our first day at school, and when I talk to her the only question she will answer is her name: Stella Hetherington.

'What's it got to do with her or anyone else what I believe in?' Stella asks.

I don't think Stella realizes that Mrs Latif is standing right behind us.

'The thing about secondary school, Stella, is that it can open the door to a whole other world you never knew anything about, *if* you're willing to step through.'

'Like we need any more doors open? I know where I'm from!' Stella mumbles under her breath.

Mrs Latif ignores her.

I tell Stella my name and move on because her lips are sealed and it's just getting embarrassing.

The next person I talk to is the girl called Pari who asked the question about belief. She shows me what she's written in her book under the categories.

Name: Pari Pashaei
Languages: English and Arabic
Hobbies: Athletics and Reading
Connected Lands: Iraq/UK
Beliefs: Fairness, Justice, Human Rights
Religion: Islam
Favourite Subjects: History

She peers at my book. 'Your religion bit looks a bit complicated!' She laughs, reading over my shoulder.

'It is kind of hard for me to fill in.' I shrug. 'Maybe I haven't done it right.'

Name: Laila Levenson
Languages: English
Hobbies: ??? Dance?
Connected Lands: India, Poland, UK, America
Religion: Hinduism, Christianity, Judaism All/
    None?
Favourite Subjects: ?? Not sure

'Do you believe in one of these religions then?' Pari asks.

I look at the sign above the whiteboard.

'I'd say none.'

'But you know about them, right?'

'Not really. Well, a bit . . . I mean some people in my family do.'

I wish I could sound a bit more convincing.

Pari looks at me like what I've just told her hasn't made anything any clearer. She points to my name, I think to move the conversation on.

'Your name sounds a bit like my mum's . . . she's Leyla.'

Mrs Latif holds her hand in the air and counts down her fingers from eleven to one. Everyone's staring at her by the time she's done. She does actually have eleven fingers!

She holds her left hand in the air for us to all have a proper look.

'Introducing my baby finger!' she says, wiggling her

little finger – and the baby offshoot wiggles too. 'Anyone else got an extra digit on their fingers or toes?'

No one puts their hand up.

'Well, there isn't another teacher in this school who'll do that countdown from eleven to one, so you've got one more count to be quiet . . . but don't test that extra digit! It's fiercer than it looks!' Mrs Latif jokes and everyone bursts out laughing – but she quickly does the countdown again and starts to look really mock-fierce as she gets to her sixth finger.

'Now let's just have a quick go round of what we've found out about each other in that short time.'

She writes the title: 'Seven Dials Harvest – Day One' on the board.

'How many languages have we got listed? Mr Keegan, our Head of Languages, will be interested in this. Only give me a new one if it hasn't been said before!' Mrs Latif starts going around the class and adding to the lists. People are from all different religions too:

Quaker, Islam, Christianity, Judaism, Sikhism, Catholicism, Jehovah's Witness, Hinduism . . . I can't believe how long each category goes on for – especially 'Connected Lands' and 'Languages'.

When we've pooled it all together, there are fifty-two different countries this class is connected to.

'How many countries are there in the world then?' a girl I just talked to asks.

I look down at my list. Her name's Milena, and her family's from Bulgaria.

'Debatable. One hundred and ninety-five or six?'

Milena whistles.

'But of course borders between countries do shift over time,' Mrs Latif answers, 'and not often peacefully.'

When she says this she puckers her lips like she's thinking of saying something else, and then she makes a popping sound with them as if to bring herself back to what she's doing.

Mrs Latif circles a language on the board called 'Lingala'. 'Who does this belong to?' She scans the class.

A girl I haven't met yet puts her hand up really shyly.

'Ah, Carmel!' Mrs Latif smiles encouragingly at the girl as she tells us that her parents are from Cameroon.

'Millions of people speak it,' she says, looking down at her desk.

I think she's a bit embarrassed. I know how she feels. I hate it when teachers spring questions on you that you weren't planning to answer.

'It sounds like a song . . . Lin-ga-La!' Mrs Latif almost sings the word and makes Carmel smile. And even though she does still look embarrassed, she seems kind of happy too.

Stella puts her hand up.

'I speak Italian and my grandpa on my mum's side speaks Cornish – does that count too?' she asks.

Mrs Latif adds 'Cornish' to the list of languages. 'I'd love to hear some Cornish. Do you speak it?'

Stella shakes her head.

'Could you ask your grandad to teach you some and then we can all learn a bit? And yes, Stella, it counts. It *all* counts.' Mrs Latif looks at her watch. 'Now hand your notes in and tomorrow I'll write up the lists in more detail. This is just the beginning of our map of Seven Dials . . . It's been useful to have this double lesson so we could make a good start, but it's still just a sketch at the moment and we'll be filling in more detail every day.'

'Do we have the same tutor *all* the way up the school?' Stella calls out, screwing up her nose.

'That's how it's organized in this school.' Mrs Latif smiles at Stella, who kicks against the back of the chair in front of her. 'I think it's a real opportunity for us all to grow up together!'

I'm sure Mrs Latif notices the look on Stella's face, but she focuses on the back of the classroom like she hasn't seen.

'Now, we'll gradually go over the rules over the next few weeks, but I should tell you all straight away that I've got one rule in this classroom that I will not tolerate being broken.'

She looks deadly serious for a moment, then her mouth springs into a dazzling smile. How does she make her lipstick stay on so perfectly? She takes her green marker and writes something on the board that I can't see until she's finished.

'No matter what else is happening outside of here, in the wider world, this is what I expect in *my* classroom . . .'

MUTUAL RESPECT.

She underlines the words three times. 'Everyone know what "mutual" means?' she asks, scanning the room for an answer and letting her gaze rest on Stella for the tiniest second.

A few people murmur the answer.

'Each other! That's right. Now, I'm going to send you on your way with my ethical question of the term . . . always a good one to get people going, I find! It seems that there's a lot of talk about "truth" at the moment. Apparently there's something called "post-truth" – a term that's officially in the dictionary – so I think we do need to look into it. When we say something's *post*-something, what do we mean?'

She writes examples on the board.

Post-Modern
Post-Natal
Post-Script
Post-Truth

'After,' Milena calls out.

'So what comes after truth?' Mrs Latif raises her eyebrows and shakes her head.

I'm not sure if she's actually asking us or whether she's just putting the question out there.

She turns back to the whiteboard. 'Who knows? But I always think a good way to examine something is to look at its opposite. The opposite of truth is . . .'

She doesn't turn around and a few people including Pari call out, 'Lie.'

Mrs Latif nods as she writes two questions on the whiteboard. 'This could be viewed as the same question, but it sometimes helps to play around with an idea. To turn it on its head.'

Is it *always* **wrong to lie?**
Is it *always* **right to tell the truth?**

'So, Seven Dials, that's tutor time over! No easy questions, no easy answers! Exercise your minds – that's the most important thing. Off you go now to your first lessons.'

Is it always *wrong to lie?*
Is it always *right to tell the truth?*

Maybe I should just call Mira and tell her that I opened her letter.

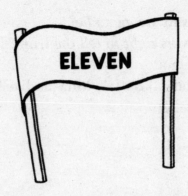

ELEVEN

I spend the whole of break-time looking for Kez but it's impossible to spot anyone with this many people wearing exactly the same clothes. The school is a maze of corridors. I wish they hadn't done away with that block Mira told me about – it sounded kind of cosy – only for Year Sevens, like a mini school on its own.

I don't actually see Kez till I'm standing in the lunch queue, lining up to have my thumb scanned. She's sitting at a table surrounded by people.

Now that I'm here, it does feel a bit like being in a factory. Finally it's my turn to lay my thumbprint on the reader. As soon as I do, my name comes up on the screen: 'Laila Levenson,' it tells me. 'You have £20 credit.' I walk along the canteen and choose a cheese sandwich, an apple juice and a piece of flapjack.

At the end of the line a dinner lady scans the packets on another screen. 'Hurry along. Next one!' she says after I've scanned my thumb on the reader again.

Altogether it costs £3.50. A light flashes up. 'You have £16.50 credit.'

I look around for a space somewhere near Kez, but the seats are all taken. I pause with my tray, trying to work out if she's seen me, but she's deep in conversation so I scan the room to see if there's anyone else I even vaguely recognize to sit with. I spot Pari from my tutor group.

She smiles at me with her eyes and shifts over. It's so loud in the dinner hall with all the echoey voices and the clatter of trays that it's hard to hear over the din.

'All right? Lilah?'

She pronounces it Lee La instead of Lye La . . . or Lie La.

'It's Laila,' I say.

'Oh, OK – it's just my mum's name is pronounced differently,' Pari explains. 'What do you think of Mrs Latif? She seems really on it, doesn't she?'

I nod. Though I'm not that sure what 'really on it' means. 'That was good that thing she got us doing to get to know each other. I've never done that before.'

'Me neither,' Pari says.

'Do you know anyone else in our class?' Pari has to almost shout over the din of the lunch hall. It's strange how the noise builds up in waves and then calms down again for no reason that you can work out.

'No!' I mouth and shake my head.

'Nor me! Want to sit next to each other in class?' she shouts back, pointing to how we are now – side by side.

I nod and smile and we give up trying to compete with the noise and get on with eating. Pari takes ages to finish her sandwich. Her empty packet's got a big red sticker over it saying the sell-by date.

'You should take that back. It was best before yesterday. Did it taste all right?'

I'm not sure she can hear me. I point to the label, but Pari shrugs.

'It's OK. It's not from here. They never go off on the actual day.'

She hasn't got anything else to eat so I split my flapjack and hand half to her.

'It's a bit weird this money-on-your-thumb system, isn't it?' I say.

'I'm not doing that. My mum doesn't like the fingerprint thing. That's why I'm going packed lunch.' Pari turns the packet over so I can't see the date any more.

I wish I hadn't made a thing of it now, so – as it seems a bit quieter in here, and I suppose I need to cover my embarrassment somehow – I find myself telling my 'Money on Your Thumb' story, even though I've always got really annoyed when Krish and Mira tell it about me.

'When I was little I used to hear my brother and

sister coming home and complaining about having no money on their thumbs. I kept trying to kiss their thumbs better and they could never understand what I was doing until one day I told them and then my brother scared me to death saying how at secondary school they insert a little chip under your skin, just like with a dog or a cat . . .'

Pari laughs.

Two older girls, maybe in Year Nine or Ten, turn and smile at us with a 'bless!' look. 'Did we ever look that tiny?' I hear one say to the other.

Pari slides a bit closer to me so we're shoulder to shoulder and lowers her voice.

'My mum gets worried about security cameras everywhere and stuff like that. She thinks they'll take your prints and then share them around with everyone. I told her they're not allowed to do that, but she doesn't trust them.'

I feel sort of excited. I've only been talking to Pari for a few minutes but there's already so much I want to ask her, to find out about her. Just for a bit I actually forget about Kez completely. On the way out of the hall I spot her again. The first thing I notice is that she's got make-up on, even though you're not allowed to wear it – black eyeliner and mascara. And as well as dying her hair – it's a mass of wine-red waves – she's pinned it up high in a beehive. She must have been practising new looks from that vlog she follows.

'Hi, Kez!' I call to her. She turns around and smiles her most confident 'I'm all right, please don't fuss over me' smile. She's in Super-Kez mode. Some people might see her new motor wheelchair first today, but with the way she carries herself about the place she's making sure it'll only ever happen once.

'This is Becks . . . Rebecca,' Kez tells me, introducing the girl beside her.

'Hi!'

'Laila's my best friend . . . from primary,' Kez tells her.

'Hi!' Rebecca smiles, and I try to smile back but something about the way Kez added 'from primary' makes me feel like I'm her 'used to be' best friend, though maybe I'm reading too much into it. Even if I am, I'm so happy Pari's at my side and I'm not standing here on my own.

'This is Pari – she's in my tutor group,' I say, and regret it straight away because Kez colours up like I'm trying to make a point. She's definitely feeling guilty about something.

'What's your tutor like?' Rebecca asks.

'Clever, funny, stylish, Muslim, beautiful!' Pari answers, holding up all the fingers on her left hand and wiggling the little one on her right hand. 'And she's got an extra finger!'

'Random!' Rebecca laughs. 'But lucky you . . . Ours

is –' she pulls a strict face, giving herself a double chin, and mimics a low, gruff voice – 'I expect one hundred per cent Attendance, Attention and Attainment. At the end of the day you're here to learn! There's nothing flighty and silly about an oak tree, is there? So you're Seven Oaks and I expect you to live up to your name!'

I bet Rebecca's really good at acting, the way she slips into that voice.

'He didn't quite put it like that!' Kez laughs. 'But yeah . . . that's him all right! Did you count how many times he said "at the end of the day"?!'

Kez purses her lips and puts her head on her chest to get a double chin.

'At the end of the day, Kezia, it's not a beauty pageant! Make-up is not allowed to be worn in school! If I see it again you'll be on concern! You're all aware of the system we have here, aren't you? You get a warning . . . and just to be clear, this is *your* warning, Kezia. If you don't heed it you'll be on concern, and if you don't pay attention to the concern . . . it's a detention.'

'He *did* say that! You were told!' Rebecca laughs.

Kez shrugs. 'I think he's all right in a solid sort of way.'

I bet Kez actually likes the fact that he's treating her the same as everyone else. She hates it when teachers treat her differently. She has her iPad on her knees and she's checking out her timetable.

'Can you believe this new app they've asked me to trial? 'Seems like I've got my own personal satnav!' They've loaded in my timetable. All I have to do is log in my room number – see!' Kez shows us the screen. She types in 'DT room twenty-four', and a map and instructions spring up.

There's a red arrow pulsing our 'present location', then another arrow pops up for DT twenty-four with a list of instructions:

- **Turn right**
- **Take lift 3 to floor 2**
- **Turn right**
- **DT is second on your left.**

'We better get going then, Vimana!'

'Who's Vimana?' Pari asks.

Kez taps the side of her power-chair. 'I thought I'd give my chariot a name!'

'Isn't that the name of the charity you're raising funds for at your bat mitzvah?' Rebecca asks.

Kez nods.

I've heard the name before, but I can't work out where.

'This app's smart. If they change classrooms, the teacher has to register a change of room and it redirects you. Good, isn't it? But the "golden pass to the lifts" is a bit OTT.' She says it like 'HOT', dropping the 'H' and adding a 'T'.

I laugh.

'What's "ott"?' Rebecca asks.

It's a bit pathetic how happy it makes me that she doesn't know what Kez means and I do.

Kez raises her hand towards her blazer pocket where the golden lift pass sticks out of the top.

'This is! OTT,' she says. 'Over The Top! When people go a bit overboard – as in making me a gold lift card like I especially need one.'

'I get that sometimes!' Pari says.

Kez pulls a bit of a 'that's unlikely' face.

'Not because of *me* . . .' Pari stops short like she forgot to be on her guard for a moment. 'I mean, it's different . . . but I still get what you mean.

Kez looks at Pari like she's trying to work her out.

'Oh, yeah! Well, it's a bit crap, isn't it?'

Pari nods.

Kez is acting really confident, but it doesn't fool me. I can see by the tension in her leg and arm how stressed she is.

She sees me seeing, and I get it. Kez doesn't need someone in secondary school who knows her like I do . . . who can tell when she's covering things up.

'See you later!' Kez waves over her shoulder as she heads off through the crowded hall.

No fuss. This is exactly what she wants, and I

wouldn't be her best friend – or at least her old best friend 'from primary' – if I didn't listen to her.

I catch sight of Kez and Rebecca before the lift doors close. She twiddles the bit of hair that's coming loose from a clip and smiles my way. I twiddle a strand of my hair too. Then she holds her golden lift pass up and pulls a face at it. The twiddle-hair thing is our code – mine and Kez's. It means . . . well, it *used* to mean: 'I know who you are and you know who I am, no matter what anyone else in the world thinks.'

I want to run over to Kez and take Rebecca's place. I want to say to Rebecca, 'You can go now. I'm the one who knows Kez best.' But that isn't what Kez wants. The lift doors close, and Rebecca and Kez are gone.

Pari looks from me to the lift and smoothes her headscarf.

'I like the colour of her hair,' Pari says. 'Is it dyed?'

I nod.

'It suits her.'

It's true. It does. But it feels too weird to be talking about the person who has been my best friend forever with a girl in my tutor group I hardly know anything about . . . yet. It's strange how it feels like I've known her for a lot longer than half a day. The only other person I've ever felt like that about is Kez when I met her on the first day of nursery.

*

What is Dad doing walking towards the school gates wearing that beret and holding his arms out as if he's going to try and lock me in a bear hug?

'Hi, Lai . . .'

I shoot him a warning look. I can't be Lai Lai here.

'Hi, Laila,' he corrects himself. 'You look so smart! I hardly recognized you.'

'That's because I'm identical to everyone else!'

'Not to me you're not!' Dad laughs and tries to kiss the top of my head, but I duck and he ends up kissing air.

'Do you have to wear that beret?'

'What's wrong with it? I bought it in Glasgow with Mira. She thought I looked OK,' Dad says, touching the top of his head. 'Anyway, it keeps my head warm!'

I shoot Dad a you-are-totally-embarrassing-me look.

'Oh yes . . . the memory is indeed merciful. I forgot about the total-rejection stage!'

'Dad!' I laugh and bash him on the arm. He grabs my hand, then links arms with me. I let him.

'So Krish and Mira are all settled in. Two down, one to go!' He starts going on about Mira's new flatmate with her purple hair, ripped jeans, red braces and more piercings than skin: 'Ah well, that's art school for you! Expression is all!' Dad flings his free arm about like a dancer, so I break my arm-link with him.

'Dad! Just walk normally!'

'You're not allowed to find me this cringe-worthy yet,' Dad jokes. 'I need you to give me till Year Eight at least.'

'Please, Dad!'

Eventually we put some space between us and the stream of uniforms, and I let him link arms with me again.

'How was it then? Your first day?' Dad asks, as we pass the Unfriendship Bench.

'Fine.'

'There'll be a fine for every time you say "fine"! Money-on-your-thumb operation go all right?' He does a thumbs-up sign.

'Yes, Dad!'

'And how did Kezia get on?'

'I only saw her at lunch. She seemed fi . . . OK,' I tell him.

'"OK" is banned too! I thought you and Kez were going to be in the same tutor group.'

'Me too, but we're not.' I shrug like it's no big deal.

Dad looks at me as if he's checking that I'm really all right about it.

We cross the road and walk past the tree outside our house.

'Ed says he'll keep the poster up until someone claims it,' Dad says, tapping the trunk.

'I was thinking, if no one *does*, maybe—'

'Not a chance, Laila! Mum's not keen – and to be

honest, I'm not either. You have to feed them chopped-up mice and things, you know!'

Gross! I hadn't thought of that. 'What will happen to it if . . .'

But Dad's not listening; he's staring at the deep crack that's running all the way along our front wall. The wall that stops our bit of front garden from falling on to the pavement looks like it's about to collapse.

'When did that split apart?' Dad asks. 'The last time I looked it wasn't much more than a hairline crack.'

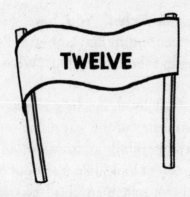

TWELVE

'Want a cup of tea, Dad?' I ask.

'Thanks, Laila.' He looks a bit surprised.

I come to the table with two mugs and take a sip of mine.

'When did you get a taste for tea?' Dad laughs.

'Since I did!'

'Everything all right with Mum? She should be back from work soon. Funny! Mum starting work at your old primary and you starting secondary at the same time!'

Dad sips his tea and looks at me as if he's waiting for me to say something.

'Hang your blazer up, Laila.' Dad picks up the plates and cups from breakfast that are still on the table, puts them in the sink and starts unloading the dishwasher. 'We'll need to help out a bit more around the place.'

'Mum's being weird . . . cleaning.'

'That *is* suspicious behaviour! She told me she'd

rearranged a few things.' Dad looks towards the shelves a bit doubtfully. If anything, now that she's shoved everything back on them all higgledy-piggledy, they look even messier than before.

'Did Mum tell you I found the chime Nana Josie gave me?' I ask, but I'm not sure he hears because he has this faraway look on his face. 'Dad?' I touch his arm. 'Do you want to see it?'

'Sorry, Laila, I was miles away.' Dad kisses me on the forehead like he used to before bed when I was tiny. 'I'd love to see that again. We hunted everywhere for that little rattle . . . I thought it was lost for good.'

'It nearly was,' I say, running upstairs. I unzip the cushion cover and feel around for the chime. It doesn't look like a rattle. No one would ever let a baby put this in their mouth. Whoever gave it to Nana Josie when she was a baby definitely meant for someone to ring it for her . . . it's a chime, not a rattle. I slide the letter about the Protest Book further into the cover and zip the cushion up again.

Dad walks up the stairs to find me. 'Let's see it then.'

I sit down on my perch and he sits next to me. He holds his hand out and, as I place the little chime in his palm, it rings. A smile spreads across Dad's face.

'Stars, moons and suns. Pretty!' Dad yawns and leans his head back on the cushions and I lay my head on his chest. 'I remember my mum asking us to give this to you,' Dad says with his eyes closed.

The way he says 'my mum' makes him seem like a little boy. I've hardly ever thought about how Dad was when he was young.

When Mum comes back I make her some tea too.

'How was work?' Dad asks.

'Tough,' Mum says, putting some files down on the table. They say 'Confidential' on the front. 'But once I'm back in the swing of it, it'll be easier – the more I get to know the children. Some of them have quite complex needs. Anyway, I promised myself I wouldn't bring it home.'

Dad looks at the pile of files on the other end of the table and raises his eyebrows.

Three is an odd number to sit around a long table that used to have at least five of us eating at it. Usually more with Mira and Krish's friends and sometimes Kez too. Dad's cooked way too much food.

'We'll never eat that much,' I tell him as he ladles some into my bowl.

'Yes . . . and I met one of Mira's flatmates. Seemed really friendly . . . Punky-grungy type.'

'That's not a thing!' I groan.

It's going to be so boring around here without any proper banter.

'Do we have to eat at the table every night?' I ask.

Mum nods. 'So, are you going to tell me about school?'

'I like my tutor. I've told Dad about her already – I can't be bothered to go over it again.'

Mum looks disappointed. 'Tell me one thing you learned,' she asks.

'I'm not at primary any more!' I sigh.

Mum pulls a begging face and holds one finger up.

I give in. 'Lingala is a language that millions of people speak in Africa.'

'Which countries in Africa? Never heard of it!' Dad says, looking it up on his phone. It's so brilliant how they ask me a question and then don't believe what I'm saying.

'You interested in Geography?' Mum asks.

'It was in tutor time. A girl called Carmel speaks it.'

'Here we go. It's spoken in Angola, Congo . . .'

'She's from Cameroon,' I say. 'Can we *not* talk about school now?'

'Fair enough. You must be tired. Oh! I've got you a remedy for your eczema and some cream.' Mum takes a little pot of cream and a little glass tube of her white sugary homeopathy pills out of her bag. She taps one into the lid and tips it on to my tongue. 'Take another in the morning. Let me have a look at your skin.'

'Stop fussing, Mum.' I hold out my arm and she smoothes the cream over it.

'This should soothe it at night especially.'

*

When I hear Mum and Dad switching their lights out later, I drag my duvet out to the landing. I feel inside the ruby-coloured cushion for the chime and I take out the letter from Nana Josie's friend and read it over and over again . . . What difference would it make to anyone if I went to pick up the Protest Book, instead of Mira?

Is it *always* **wrong to lie?**
Is it *always* **right to tell the truth?**

I could just say to Mira that the book arrived by post, and give it to her when she gets home. She probably wouldn't even be that bothered if I read it. She's got loads of things of Nana's after all. Maybe Mrs Latif's 'Connected Lands' category isn't just about countries in the world; maybe it means the lands of the past too. Everyone else in this family seems to have a connection to Nana Josie except me. I look at the address on the letter. It's not that far. Would it be *that* wrong of me to go and pick the book up myself?

'Is this sleeping-on-the-landing thing some kind of protest, Laila?' Dad asks, picking up Simon's letter to Mira. I must have fallen asleep reading it.

I snatch it off him before he can read anything.

'What's that you were reading?'

'Nothing,' I say – but why did he ask me that? How can sleeping on the landing be a protest? 'Protest about what?' I ask.

'I don't know, Laila, you tell us. Krish and Mira going away? Starting secondary school? Or is all this feeling so unsettled something to do with Kez?'

He waits for a minute for me to answer, and when I don't he sighs.

'Well, if you want to talk . . .'

'I don't,' I jump in, before he can say any more.

'You'd better get ready for school then.' He sighs and carries on down the stairs.

I tiptoe down the first three steps and sit on the stairs so I can hear Mum and Dad talking.

'She's curled up on that sofa like a frightened little kitten.'

Is that what Dad really thinks about me?

'She was reading a letter, but she wouldn't tell me about it.'

'Yes, there was something she was looking at from Kez the other day . . . I wish I knew what was going on between those two,' Mum chips in.

'Don't get involved, Uma – whatever it is, they've got to sort it out for themselves.'

Now I can't hear much . . . except for one word: 'puberty'. It's such a vile word. I suppose it serves me right for eavesdropping. I cringe, cringe and cringe some more at the thought of Mum and Dad talking about me like that. I hate this house without Mira and Krish in it.

After Dad's gone to work, Mum runs around getting her things together and keeps asking me the same questions over and over again: 'Have you eaten enough breakfast? Sure you've got everything?' She straightens my tie and puts my gym bag by the door even though I've told her we don't have PE today.

'Set off in twenty minutes!' she tells me as she runs out of the door.

I can't stand all the fussing around.

I'm actually glad she goes into her school before me now.

THIRTEEN

'So how's your first week been, Laila?' Mum asks, as she tidies up the landing sofa and plumps the cushions around me. Maybe that little velvet cushion isn't the best hiding place for the letter after all.

'Mum! Do we have to talk about school now?' I ask.

If I look over the whole week, I think I've seen Kez to talk to about eight times. Mostly I go around with Pari – and I like her, but it's not so easy to get to know someone from scratch. There are so many gaps in what you do or don't know about each other . . . and what you feel like you can ask. I like Mrs Latif's tutor time more than anything else – the way she asks questions that run through your mind whatever you're doing through the day. Probably the best lesson of the week was Citizenship. I think it's my favourite subject. I don't know why they don't have it in primary; it's like learning about everything together. It sort of helps you join things up. I suppose the other thing that's got me thinking is about starting up dance again. Mrs Latif asked if anyone was interested in an after-school dance club she's thinking of setting up next term, and me and Pari both registered for that. Even though I was too shy to go to ballet without Kez when she gave it up, I think maybe seeing Priya's videos has sparked me up again . . . and if Pari comes too . . . But if I told Mum *that*, I know she would get so over-the-top happy and go on about how talented I was at dance and how I should never have given up ballet. Those are the main things I would tell Mum if I was going to tell her anything, but I don't – and no matter how patiently she smiles at me, waiting for an answer, I won't. School feels long enough, and I don't want to have to go over everything again now I'm home. I think she's just as relieved as me when the phone rings . . .

It's not Mira, Krish or Nana Kath calling. I can tell by the way Mum answers the phone.

'What a lovely surprise!' Her voice is all high.

There's the usual polite asking after all the other aunties, uncles and cousins in India, then . . .

'Ah! Yes, Anjali, I spotted that on Facebook a while back . . . A final fundraising push – it's a massive target he's set himself.'

I'm good at deciphering the other half of a phone conversation. I think I would make quite a good codebreaker, like those women in Bletchley Park in the war. I think that was the last film Kez's gran – our bubbe – took the two of us to see. I can't remember when I started calling her my bubbe too, but I've always sort of thought of her as my other gran. Anyway, if I'm right, the Facebook thing will be about Janu raising money to open a new refuge in his village.

'Laila was watching one of Priya's videos the other day. She's doing so well in New York. A bit of a star, isn't she? Near Central Park! Swanky . . . I know – Mira was talking about going to stay.'

Mum's in deep listening mode now.

'Of course. It'll be our pleasure to have Janu stay here. That's generous of Hannah to offer to put him up but, no, he must stay here. We'd be offended if he didn't. There's no question. We've been waiting to repay your hospitality. Really? Has it taken that long? I know it's not easy to get a Visa these days, but he's only visiting for such a short time. Well, yes, I suppose . . .'

I jump up and lean over the banister so that I can hear Mum better.

'To be honest, Anjali, it'll cheer us all up. And it's perfect timing with Krish and Mira away . . . We've shrunk to just the three of us. It's so quiet around here! I know, Laila keeps reminding me they'll be back, but . . . Just let me know when you've booked the flights, OK? Email me the details . . .'

Up until now I think I've just about managed to work out everything that Aunt Anjali has been saying on the Kolkata end of the line, but for this next bit I have no idea.

'For Mira? Really? Sounds intriguing . . . is he? What's he called his charity? Barefoot Trust? Well, good luck to him!'

I sit on the top stair and watch Mum walk up and down the hallway as she chats on to Aunt Anjali. They always take ages to say goodbye even after it's obvious that they kind of have. You think they've finished and then they start talking about something new.

When Mum's finally hung up, I take the stairs three at a time. I lean on the banister hard and swing my body around the bottom. The post groans and shakes a bit.

'Don't *you* start doing that! That staircase is rickety enough as it is!' Mum says. 'Guess who's coming to stay?'

'Janu!' I laugh.

'Did you hear *everything*?'

'Pretty much!' I nod.

'Anyway, glad it's put a smile on your face.'

I go up to Mira's room, close the door, stretch out on her bed and text Kez. I think maybe Janu coming will change things between us. It could give us something that's about me and her again.

> You'll never guess who's coming to stay!

Are you keeping that snake?

> No!

Are you keeping that snake?

Well?

> Janu!

Oh yeah! Mum said he might come over. You know they're working together on his new refuge . . . the one in his village? I think she wants to show him round some of her community builds. Have you checked out his website? We're fundraising for his charity at my bat mitzvah.

> Yes . . . your friend Rebecca said.

I can't help that accusing tone that keeps creeping in between us.

I lie on the bed and look around the walls where Mira's photos used to be and I get to thinking this: the gaps between me and Pari are because of the things we *don't* know about each other, but with Kez and me it's like we know too much. I can't pretend I'm not upset that Rebecca knows things about Kez that I don't, especially when they're things that were always between just the two of us. Janu's work at the

103

refuge was something *I* shared with her, like she shares her grandma with me and doesn't mind that I call her my bubbe too. But I have no idea how to explain why I'm being so off and moody with her, and I don't think Kez knows either. The one thing it never was before with me and Kez was awkward . . . kind of sour. *I* wanted to be the person to break the news about Janu coming to stay. Why did she already have to know?

I wait to hear Mum and Dad go up to bed, then google 'Barefoot Trust Orphanage, India'. It doesn't take me long to find Janu's new website. There's a photo of him and a description of the refuge in Kolkata that me and Kez raised money for in primary school. There's another photo of him standing on a plot of land by a river where he plans to build a refuge that's going to be called 'Vimana'. I don't know why it annoys me so much that Rebecca knew that name before I did and that Kez has named her new chair after it and didn't think to mention it. I wish I could tell her how it makes me feel, but when I try to work out what I would say it just sounds petty. It's not like Janu belongs to me or anything. It's not like anyone belongs to anyone really. Maybe that's what Kez is trying to tell me. Have I been clinging on to her too hard?

These thoughts flick through my mind as I click on the different pages of Janu's website. It looks really slick, with quotes and photographs and video clips. I press the PLAY arrow and Janu's talking.

> 'Like my own mother, many disabled children born into poverty are abandoned, often left on the street at the mercy of others who would exploit them. I walk barefoot for a future for every one of them.'

Janu smiles with his eyes. You can't tell if he's sad or happy.

> 'Please join me on my barefoot journey.'

Then a computer-generated building plan flashes up.

> 'Vimana Refuge is to be designed and built in consultation with Hannah and Maurice Braverman of the award-winning Out of the Box community architects in London. 'Out of the Box' specialize in open-access buildings. Their services are generously offered free of charge.'

And nobody thought to tell me. I wonder if Kez actually came up with the name Vimana. And if she did, why should it matter? I really hate thinking like this, but I can't seem to stop . . . Why *should* she have to tell me everything? It's not up to me what she gets involved in . . . but I suppose it's what we're used to. Maybe she feels as uncomfortable about what's happening between us as I do. My head aches from trying to work things out. I just wish I could switch off my brain.

There's a gauge showing how much money Janu still needs to raise to get the refuge up and running for a year, and there's a holding page, like it's not been set up properly yet.

Why Barefoot?
Find out by signing up and following in my footsteps!
www.barefootblogger.com
The Barefoot Blogger plans to walk from the earth on which he will build his refuge, around London and New York and back to his village . . . collecting stories on his barefoot travels, and funds, as he goes.
Please click here to receive updates.

I click on the link and enter my email address, even though he's already got it. I suppose Kez must have done this already.

FOURTEEN

'I don't get why you have to go to his house to pick him up, Mum?'

'It's not that easy for some children, Laila – to make that transition between home and school,' Mum explains. 'Now, are you sure you've got everything organized? Sorry I've got to rush out. Dad'll be back from his conference soon and he's planning to go in late for a few days after so you're not on your own.'

'I'm fine, Mum – stop fussing!'

I go through to the kitchen and switch through the radio stations till I hear a song I like. I think Mira liked this one too. She used to sing those lines about a new dawn, a new day. I know the tune but I've never really listened to all the lyrics before. It does what the words say . . . makes you feel good. I turn it up really loud so I'll be able to hear it upstairs.

I sit on my perch and look at the photo of me and

Krish and Mira on her bed before they left. It makes me happy and sad at the same time. I can't wait for Janu to be here. It's far too quiet. I can actually hear bits of the house creaking. The staircase nearly talks to you when you walk up and down it, and the boiler downstairs makes a hissing, sighing noise. I can hear it from here. I think about calling Mira, but I suppose it's my guilty conscience that makes me press on Krish's number instead. *Please* answer.

Krish: How's it going, Lai Lai?
Me: Laila. Remember?
Krish: Oh yeah!
Me: All right. How's your work thing?
Krish: I'm loving it. I have to help all these city kids do abseiling, climbing and rowing and stuff.
Me: You're a city kid!
Krish: I know – that's why I get them. I think I could actually live here though. It's so chilled with the mountains and lakes. That's what I bike through every day! It's good for my lyrics.

I hear Nana say in the background, 'All very well, but he's eating me out of house and home!'

Me: Is Nana spoiling you?
Krish: What do you think? Good job I'm doing all this exercise! How's it going in the holding pen?

Me: It's good so far. I like it. We've got this great
   tutor. She teaches Citizenship.
Krish: That's a bit of luck.
Me: Janu's coming to stay!
Krish: Serious? Tell him to call me when he gets
   here. How long for?
Me: Not long. He's going off to see Priya in New
   York afterwards.
Krish: Tell him he can have my room if he wants. I'll
   see if they'll let me have a few days off, but I'm
   not sure. Someone's just left . . . I might even get
   their job if I play my cards right and then I can
   actually live at the centre. You moved into
   Mira's room yet?
Me: Not yet.
Krish: Get in there quick or Mira will have it back!

I can hear Nana Kath in the background telling Krish
it's time for breakfast and he needs to get off
the phone.

   Krish: Hang on a minute, Laila.

Krish tries to muffle his voice a bit . . . but I hear
anyway:
   'It's Laila. She's off to school in a minute. I think
she's on her own.'

Me: Hello! I'm OK on my own! That's not why I called.

Krish: All right, don't blow a gasket!

Me: I'm not. I wanted to tell you . . . I found a chime of Nana Josie's, a kind of baby's rattle.

Krish: Oh yeah! I chose that for you.

Me: What do you mean, *you* chose it?

Krish: When Nana Josie was ill in the hospice, she told me and Dad to go to her flat and choose something for you.

Me: Why didn't you tell me?

Krish: I think cos we lost it . . . You don't even remember being given it, right?

Me: That's not the point.

Krish: Anyway, good you found it. Ha! Funny if you think about it . . . you having a go at us all for treating you like a baby – then that rattle shows up!

Me: It's a chime!

Krish: Whatever!

I can hear Nana talking to Krish again. 'Is she all right there on her own, Krish? Where are Sam and Uma anyway? One of them should be in. Tell her she should be getting ready for school now. She'd better not be late. Has she had a good breakfast? Ask her if she's remembered a snack?'

I know where Mum gets the multiple-questions-never-waiting-for-an-answer thing from now.

> Krish: Hang on, Nana; I can't hear what she's
> saying.
> Me: Krish, do you remember one of Nana Josie's
> friends called Simon?
> Krish: The hippy painter guy? Yeah! He used to ride
> a bike everywhere. Not like the mountain bike
> they've given me. His had flowers and bells in the
> wheels. I remember that. Yeah, he was a legend.
> Me: I don't know about a bike – I just found a
> photo of him, that's all. Just wondered if you
> knew him?
> Krish: Simon was sound. I used to sit by Nana's
> pond with him sometimes and watch the
> tadpoles. I wonder if he's still around . . . Gotta
> go! Nana Kath's getting on my case.

I decide that it's safer to keep the letter from Simon with me in case Mum or Dad get tempted to have a nosey around or a tidy-up of the landing and find it. So I tuck it into a zip section at the back of my school bag.

I've still got a bit of time so I check my email to see if there are any messages. Maybe Mira's emailed. There's actually nothing from her, but there's already an update alert on Janu's blog, so I log in.

Priya's 'Holi Spring' video that I watched the other day has been loaded up on to this page too. At first I think it's a bit weird that it's on here. Then, after I've watched it a few times, I get why it's there. The faces of the children are so happy, just having fun chucking paint-powder at each other like any other kids. It's not like those appeals you get on TV that make you feel miserable . . . like how do I even start to help?

I love watching Priya dance. She makes you think that she could do anything. The way she smiles and draws you in, it's like she sweeps you up with her, so you start to believe that *you're* dancing too. She's spinning so fast in the video, it's like she could just take off and fly.

At the end there's a tiny bright yellow footprint that you can click on to donate.

When I watched this clip with Mum, I don't really think I understood what it meant . . . but now, seeing the children in Janu's House of Garland's refuge in Kolkata throwing paint at the people in the park in New York and them throwing bright-coloured powder paint back, all laughing and playing together . . . I feel as if I do understand.

I read the slogan that's at the head of the page again.

Barefoot Blogger

Because we all walk on the same earth

I catch the time in the corner of the screen. I can't believe it's already nine o'clock.

I grab my bag and run as fast as I can down the road. There's hardly anyone about. One boy wearing our uniform gets off a bus, but he doesn't look like he cares one way or the other if he's late or not. I'm sprinting towards the school gate but Miss O'Brady, who nearly always stands there, blocks the way and hands me a pass to take to reception.

'Now then, dearie, too late for the gate – what's your name?'

'Laila Levenson!'

'Oh, I didn't know there *was* another one! I knew your sister Mira a little and your brother a bit better!' She laughs. 'Now, what's wrong with me that I can't recall his name . . . ?'

'Krish,' I pant, desperately trying to catch my breath.

'Oh, yes, that's the one! Now calm yourself down now, Laila, sweetie. No need to get into such a state. I can see you've made an effort to make up for lost time.' She winks at me. 'I'll pass that on to your form tutor – who is it you're with?'

'Mrs Latif.'

'Oh, Mrs Latif – that lovely young woman. You'll have no problems there then . . .' She turns and takes hold of a boy's shoulder. 'Don't be trying to sneak past me with your cheeky grin, Connor.' Miss O'Brady gives the laid-back boy I saw near the bus a late pass too. 'Get along with you now, young man. Wherever is your sense of urgency?' She taps him on the back and 'Connor', who must be in Year Nine or Ten, rolls his eyes at me as if to say 'Good luck!' and walks slowly through the gates.

'Whatever is he like?' Miss O'Brady shakes her head. 'Right, you feeling more like yourself now, young Laila?'

I nod.

Connor turns around and waves at Miss O'Brady as he walks into school.

She laughs, waves back and shakes her head. 'The cheek of him! Just like your brother. Though I have to say, I always had a soft spot for your Krish, even if he *was* so often late! Will you tell him Miss O'Brady asked after him?' She shakes her finger at me suddenly, as if she's just remembered what her job is. 'Don't let me be seeing too much of you here at the late gate, Laila Levenson . . . get on your way now!'

*

'Sorry I'm late,' I tell the receptionist and hand her the late pass.

'Nameclassreason?' she fires, without looking up.

'Laila Levenson, Seven Dials, I forgot my keys and had to go back because my mum's not going to be in later.'

Is it *always* wrong to lie?
Is it *always* right to tell the truth?

'You're on concern,' the receptionist tells me, in a voice that sounds like a recorded message. 'There'll be a note home and next time it'll be a detention.' She presses so hard on the paper that the bit of hair escaping from her clip bobs up and down as she registers my name in the late record.

Pari's bagged a place for me next to her. She slides her backpack off the seat and I slip in beside her.

'Thought you weren't coming,' Pari whispers. She looks really pleased to see me.

FIFTEEN

'How about sunshine yellow for one wall? That'll brighten up the place a bit.'

Mum folds the colour chart so that I can only see a little oblong of yellow card.

I shake my head. 'That's Kez's favourite, not mine.'

'Well, let's put some posters up at least. These walls look so empty with all the gaps. How about we make a start on Sunday?'

'I'm seeing Kez on Sunday. It's the only day she can meet.'

The landline goes.

'Oh! That'll be Mira,' Mum says. 'She was out when I called earlier.'

I take up position on the landing.

'Do you think you'll be able to come back to see Janu? If it's the expense . . . I'll let you know when we've got his dates. Apparently he's really keen to see you. No, not yet. She's still sleeping on the landing – see if you can have a word. No! No more snakes in the kitchen or anywhere else! Don't think so . . . the sign's still up on the tree. I'll just see where she is . . . I can take a guess . . .'

'Laila, Mira wants to talk to you,' Mum calls up.

I pretend not to hear.

'Maybe she's in the bathroom. I'll get her to call you back later.'

I go through to Mira's room and take the lid off the little varnished box. I like the colour. It's sort of orangey-red and the bonsai tree is delicately painted in gold. It's such a shame there's a crack in it. I take out the little silk purse and place Nana Josie's chime inside to keep it safe. I feel a bit nervous about taking it out of the house for the first time. I would hate to lose it, like Mira lost that artichoke charm that Nana gave to her. I place the letter from Simon and the purse into the big front pocket of my dungarees. The charm sticks out a bit, but I pull on my hoodie and zip it up so you can't tell it's there.

'What time will you be back, Laila?'

Mum's finally letting me go out on my own sometimes, but this is always the last thing she asks before I walk out of the door. It kind of spoils the going out in the first place.

'I don't know! I'll be out all day probably. I need to catch up with Kez.'

I glimpse myself in the hallway mirror. I try twisting and piling my hair into a beehive like Kez's, but it's

117

too flat and shiny so it just flops down. I give up and let it trail down my back.

'Don't forget your coat. I think it's going to rain. You got your mobile on you?' Mum asks.

I feel for it in my hoodie pocket.

'Yes, it's here! See you later!'

I pick up my coat, but when Mum goes back through to the kitchen I dump it back in the hall. It's not even cold.

I suppose in a way Kez's parents have turned their flat into a sort of showcase for their work. Janu's going to love it. It'll give him so many ideas. Each of the walls is a screen that can be pulled back so the whole thing opens out into one massive box and then can be closed up again. I love the way the buildings they design can be small or huge, depending on how many boxes you have. I can see why they've won awards for coming up with the idea. But they say they would never have thought of it without Kez's input, so the awards should belong to her too because everything was done in consultation with her. I think that's true, because they've used her experience of what it's like not to be able to get around your own home easily to create it, like the invisible wall grips and easy-grip floors so she doesn't have to use her chair so often

Mum and Dad don't understand why it's such a big deal for me that Kez won't come to ours any more.

But why would she when she can be completely independent here? I suppose when our house was built, about a hundred years ago, they didn't think about access or stuff like that.

I remember when Kez moved back into her flat after it had all been redesigned. I gave her some parachute silk to hang from her ceiling to make her room look like a rainbow marquee. Kez's mum strung fairy lights along the edges of the coloured silk, and we used to lie on her bed staring up at the ceiling, talking for hours. In the summer Kez opened the window and the breeze would get under the parachute silk and it would billow and blow like sails, projecting its colours right across the wall. It made me feel like we were in our own little cocoon. I wanted it to be like that for us two in my new room too, but now it looks like that will never happen.

I ring Kez's doorbell and Bubbe answers.

'Ah, my Laila!' She smiles, and squeezes my shoulder. It feels strange now that I'm taller than her.

Kez walks slowly out into the hallway and opens her arms wide. I didn't expect this. We hug for ages, like we're long-lost friends, which I suppose we are in a way. This feels like the sort of hug Kez gave me after she came back from her summer camp though, as if she's been on this huge journey without me and she wants to make me feel better because I've missed out.

I have a word with myself.

Laila, don't make such a big deal about it. You can always come and see her here . . . and after her bat mitzvah's over she'll have more time for you. If she's not in pain, and things improve, maybe she'll come over to yours then and sit on your bed in your new room and you can plan it all out, maybe decorate it together, and things will be more or less back to how they were before.

'Have you heard this one? I love it.' Kez plays a song on her phone that I've never heard of. She holds a pretend microphone to her mouth and sings the whole thing. 'I'm thinking about doing this for the audition for that school concert. What do you think?'

'It sounds really strong. You'll definitely get in.'

I take the little silk purse out of my dungaree pocket, loosen the drawstrings and tip out the chime.

'I brought this to show you. You said you wanted to see it.'

'It's really sweet. I like the cut-outs! You should shine the silver up. I bet it would really sparkle.'

Kez half looks at the chime as she finds another track but then she checks out a photo that's just been sent through.

'I think I like it as it is, so you can see how old it is—'

'Hang on a minute, Laila!'

She angles the screen slightly away from me, but I've already seen a picture of her and a boy with dark curly hair.

'Who was that?' I ask

'Oh, that's Adam,' she says, and quickly flicks on to another photo that she doesn't mind showing me.

Now she's grinning at a photo of her and a whole group of people from her summer camp with their arms thrown around each other. I keep thinking she's going to tell me who all these people are, but it's like she's back there with them now. Their faces are splatted in mud and Kez is still wearing a riding cap. It looks like they've been on a trek . I'm just about to ask Kez about the horseriding and the people in the one when she scrolls on to the next photo.

I slip the chime back into the purse in my pocket and wait for Kez to remember that I'm in the room.

'Shall we do nails?' She points to a toilet bag by her bed. I take out a bottle of navy-blue nail varnish. 'Mine first!' She reaches forward and rests her hands on my lap.

'I don't know if I'll be any good at it!' I say, opening the lid. It smells really strong.

I start with her left hand, easing her fingers straight as I brush in one direction over the first nail.

'That's so much smoother than I could do,' Kez says, inspecting her nail and holding her hand out for me to continue.

'How's Pari?' Kez asks.

'All right.' I shrug.

'She seems really nice. I saw her the other day on

her way back from school. Said she has to take the bus to the station and the tube home. It sounds a long journey.'

'How about you – are you all right? Met some new people?' I try to make the question not sound loaded, but it does.

'Well, there's Becks . . . I know her from Saturday school – you know, at the synagogue – but I didn't think she was coming here. I thought she'd be going to Jewish school.'

Kez pulls her hand away from me so she can flex her fingers, then rests her hand back on my knee again. She seems really stressed. 'Honestly, Laila, I couldn't believe it when she sat next to me in tutor time on the first day. Her sister's in Year Eight so she's introducing me to a few people . . .'

She trails off when she sees the look on my face. We both sit there in silence for a moment, trying to find something to talk about. I can't get used to these empty pauses between us – like the ghost pictures on Mira's wall, it feels like this is turning into a ghost friendship.

'I know I've been giving it all the beehive and eyeliner . . .' Kez breaks the silence. Then she winces and waves her fingers in the air.

'Sorry, am I hurting you?' I ask.

'It's more of an ache!' She gives me this really sad look like she's not talking about doing nails at all, and then she slowly relaxes enough for me to take back her hand. 'I'm sorry we haven't got to see each other much. I can't believe how busy the week is with shul Friday evening and Saturday too. I'm behind with everything . . . homework included.'

'You hardly ever used to go to the synagogue,' I say.

Kez looks a bit exasperated with me, like I just don't understand.

'It's for my bat mitzvah, Lai Lai. I want to get it right. Anyway, except for Becks, everyone else is learning Hebrew at Jewish school so we're getting together later . . . Bubbe's going to help us. I didn't think I would get so into it, but you know how Bubbe makes everything into a story.'

I do know. But it feels like it should be me and Kez sitting together with Bubbe while she tells her stories . . . not Kez and Becks. I finish Kez's nails in silence. I wish I didn't feel so jealous all the time.

'Do you want me to do yours?' she asks, wafting her fingers around.

I shake my head.

'What time are you seeing Rebecca today then?' I ask.

Kez blushes. 'Not till later.'

'That's OK then!'

'But . . . Sorry, I forgot to say . . . I missed my physio this week too, so Dad reorganized it for today. He didn't know you were coming over and he only told

123

me this morning or I would have called you so I'm going to have to leave in about half an hour. If I'd known about that I wouldn't have organized for Becks to come over later. Really, Laila, you wouldn't believe how much there is to learn for shul. I've only just got to grips with translating my parsha . . .'

I have this knot in my throat that I can't seem to swallow.

'What's a parsha?' I ask quietly.

'It's like the portion of the Torah I've got to learn to talk about at my bat mitzvah. I'm only on the first Aliyah . . .'

I know the Torah's the Jewish holy book, so I suppose an Aliyah must be a verse or psalm or something like that. I don't want to ask though, because not knowing for sure makes me feel a bit dim.

'I was just really looking forward to hanging out today.'

Kez looks up at me through her tangle of hair and I can see she's upset too. Even though we've been carrying on as if everything's the same, nothing is.

For the first time ever, I don't know how we're going to find enough to say to fill even another half an hour. I definitely won't show her the letter about Nana Josie's Protest Book now. Or ask her if she thinks it would be safe for me to go and get it by myself.

'Why are you scratching your arm?'

'Got a bit of eczema, that's all.'

'I didn't know you had that.'

'Apparently I did when I was a baby . . . it's come back.'

'Hang on a minute. I've got cream for when I wear my arm brace and it rubs.' Kez opens her bedside table drawer and takes a out a tube. 'Try this.'

I pull my arm away from her.

'No! I'm fine.'

'Please, Lai Lai . . . let me!'

Kez gently dabs the cream over my arm. She looks up at me and whispers, 'Promise you won't get upset if I try and explain something. I've wanted to tell you the truth about this since I got back from camp. We've never lied to each other, have we?'

'You have now!' I pull my arm away.

'Please don't be in a mood with me, Lai Lai.'

Maybe this is one of those situations when telling the truth might not do any good at all. Because I'm pretty sure I know what she's going to say . . .

She takes a deep breath, then comes straight out with it, like she's been storing this up for ages. 'I *asked* to have nobody I knew from primary in my tutor group.'

'Nobody! Not even *Becks?*'

I say her name the way Kez does, like she's known her forever.

'Don't be like that, Lai Lai. She's not from

primary . . . and I didn't know she was coming to our school . . .'

I shrug like it doesn't make any difference to me one way or the other.

'. . . I thought it would be better for both of us to try and meet new people. Bubbe warned me I should explain to you before we started school – she said we should sit down together and talk about it. I wanted to, and I kept trying to find a way, but I . . . just couldn't.'

'I guessed anyway. I can tell when you're lying.' I keep my voice really flat and I won't look at her so I don't risk getting all emotional. 'Thanks for telling me about Vimana too!'

'Sorry, I should have . . .' Kez's voice trails away.

She looks like she's about to cry. A bit of me wants to hug her and tell her not to get stressed out over us because I don't even really know why all this has got to be such a big deal . . . except I can't tell her that because to tell the truth I don't think I've ever felt this angry with anyone before.

'Lai Lai, I want you to understand; at camp it was like finding this really big family. I never thought I could go somewhere where I didn't know anyone and then do all those activities. It was easier than I thought it ever could be and I met so many great people. I didn't feel so on my own!'

'But you've never been on your own! I've always

been around and I'm always thinking about you . . .'
I'm having to bite the inside of my mouth really hard
to stop myself from crying.

I look at Kez's bedside wall; at all the photos of me
and her when we were little. There's one of us standing
by our pegs with our matching drawstring bags. Kez
and Laila, always by each other's sides.

'How's your new room?' she asks, keeping her eyes
on the photo wall.

'I dunno; it doesn't feel like mine. Mum keeps on
at me to decorate.'

We're just surface-talking now. It doesn't mean
anything. I look up at the parachute silk and fairy
lights.

'My mum had this really good idea. Why don't you
take a video of your new room and we can all design
it together?' she suggests.

'What's the point? It's not like we can hang out in
there, is it? Even if you wanted to!'

'Please, Lai Lai.'

The hurt feeling just bursts out of me.

'You can call me Laila from now on.'

Kez winces.

'But . . .' She looks down at her nails.

'Nobody's calling me Lai Lai now. It sounds
babyish.'

'Am I nobody?' Kez whispers.

'No, but *I* am . . . Obviously or you wouldn't have

gone out of your way to ask for me not to be with you.'

Kez takes my hand. 'I know I should have told you . . .'

I won't look at her.

'Laila, please . . . OK, if this is how you want it . . .'

'Don't turn it on me. It's not about what *I* wanted.'

Kez looks up at the ceiling for ages, and when I don't say anything she fills the silence with: '. . . We're decorating too. The parachute's coming down. I'm just going to have it plain – all this feels a bit childish.'

'Yes, really childish.' I get up and walk out without turning back.

'Are you going, Laila? Everything all right with you girls?' Bubbe calls out to me as I pass the kitchen.

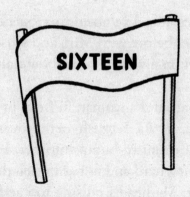

SIXTEEN

'Everything all right with you girls?'

Bubbe's voice echoes through my head as I run all the way to the station.

I arrive at the underground and my phone buzzes.

It's a text from Kez.

You OK?

I don't feel like answering, so I head straight in then change my mind. The last thing I need is Kez or Bubbe worrying about me and calling Mum or Dad. I step out on to the street and text back.

Fine. Sorry I was in a mood.
See you tomorrow at school.

I wait for a while to see if Kez messages me back, but then the screen goes blank. Why can't I ever remember to charge it? I touch my card on the reader and walk down the escalator. I've taken this journey into town so many times before with Mira and Krish and Mum and Dad, but on my own it somehow feels completely different.

I squeeze around a woman in front of me carrying a wide suitcase. As I brush her shoulder she tuts loudly, like I *meant* to bump into her. I can feel my heart thumping hard and fast as I reach the bottom of the escalator. My head's pulsing too and I feel a bit faint. I think I've been holding my breath. I open my mouth and take a huge gulp of grimy underground air, and the tug-of-war voices in my head crank into overdrive.

'You haven't got a clue where you're going. You should have looked up the address.'

'Just do it! You know where Finsbury Park is. Pari makes this journey on her own every day. When you get there you can always ask someone the way.'

The overhead electronic information board flashes that the train will be here in three minutes. I look down at the track where a couple of mice, the exact same colour as the grey of the rails, are chasing each other into the tunnel. They're cute and tiny. I could never feed one of those to a snake. I wonder how they survive down here without getting crushed.

There's a poster opposite where I'm standing. It says: 'I am a Refugee.' It has a picture of a doctor wearing a white coat talking to an old lady in a hospital bed. Underneath it says: 'Dr Ahmed Habib, from Afghanistan, NHS Consultant.' The photo reminds me a bit of the one we have of Grandad Bimal on our landing by Edinburgh Castle, when he was really young and had just passed his exams to be a doctor.

A crowd of boys in football hats and scarves appears on the platform. They must be about fifteen or sixteen years old. I think the team's Arsenal. If Krish was here he'd probably get into some banter with them. Every time one of them says something, the next one in the group ramps it up a bit louder. The boy with the scarf is listening to music on oversized headphones and he raps along, half dancing, half mucking around. He sees me watching and stretches out the ends of his scarf and moves his hips around as if he wants to dance with *me*! I shove my hands in my pockets and walk further down the platform towards the end. I wish I'd charged my phone now.

A boy in a cap says, 'She's cute!' I think I'm supposed to hear. I felt angry enough before, but now my neck and face feel all hot. How do they think that it's OK to make me feel like this? Now I have to stand here while they smirk at me.

This is the slowest three minutes ever.

I pretend to be really interested in the posters at the end of the platform. There's a philosophy course you can do that says it will give you answers to all the big questions you've got about life.

Then there's something called a Public Information Poster where the writing scrolls across on a loop. I read the same lines as they come around and around. They don't make me feel any better.

> This city is on high security alert . . . Make
> sure you keep your luggage with you at all
> times . . . Report any unusual behaviour to
> Underground staff . . . Beggars are not
> welcome on the London Underground or any
> other transport networks . . . Please report
> any begging activity to staff . . .

I look up the platform but I can't see any staff. One of the boys waves at me and whistles. Idiot!

Finally the train arrives and I step on to a carriage where there's a woman sitting with a toddler on her knee. I can't think of anything else to do so I unzip my hoodie and take the letter from Simon out of my dungaree pocket and read it again. Not that I need to – I know the words off by heart now. I've got this picture of what Simon looks like in my head. I can't wait to see if he's anything like the person I'm imagining.

The warning voices from the leaflets we got in Year Six fill my head: Where did they come from? I haven't even thought about them since we did that lesson. I wish I could get them out of my head now. They're not helping.

> **Always tell someone where you're going.**
> **Never visit a stranger even when invited.**
> **Never accept gifts from strangers.**

Always, Never, Never. My head's starting to really ache. Always, Never, Never – the words keep repeating in time to the rhythm of the tube as it speeds through the tunnels. The train comes out into the light of the station . . .

Simon Makepeace doesn't know I'm coming, but he's not *really* a stranger because he knew Nana Josie, so you could say he's more of a family friend than anything, and Krish did say he was a legend. All he wants to do is give back something that belongs to our family, and he was expecting Mira, not me, and she's an adult so . . . I wonder how old he'll be by now. I read the address again. It's not like I'm going to his house or anything. 'The Caring Community' sounds like an old people's home to me.

In the next tunnel the train slows, comes to a standstill, and a voice fills the carriage. It's like the man's holding his nose while he speaks.

'Apologies for the delay. We are being held at a red signal.'

Finally we move off again. At the next station a few

more people get on and now the carriage is about half full. Just as the doors are about to close, a family steps in. A mother, a father, a girl a bit younger than me and a little boy – a toddler. The mother has a handful of laminated notes and she places one, along with a packet of tissues, on the seat next to mine. Then she trails along the carriage, leaving the rest on empty seats.

The dad and the children stand by the door and watch the mother make her way through the carriage. The weird thing is that no one's reading the notes. Maybe they've read the poster and don't want to encourage begging, because that's what I think this is . . . but I can't stop myself from glancing down at the words, all written in capitals.

WE ARE WAITING FOR HOUSING. UNTIL THEN WE HAVE NOT ENOUGH MONEY TO FEED OUR CHILDREN. WE RELY ON THE KINDNESS OF STRANGERS. WE ARE ALONE. PLEASE SPARE SOME LITTLE MONEY. GOD BLESS YOU.

By the time I have finished reading I realize that the little girl is standing in front of me. She has cropped hair with a chunk missing out of the fringe, and she's holding out her hand. I can't believe she can look at me for so long with her huge brown eyes, unblinking.

I feel in my hoodie pocket.

The woman sitting opposite shakes her head and mumbles something under her breath about 'gypos'.

If Mum, Dad, Mira, Krish or Kez were here, I think I would leave it for them to decide what to do. I would take their lead. Why is this girl still standing in front of *me*? I wonder if she's got an instinct . . . I suppose even someone as young as her would get a feeling for wavering people.

I catch the eye of the dad holding his toddler's hand. He keeps looking at me for a second and then lowers his head and winces like he's in pain. Can shame actually cause you pain? I quickly look away and smile at the little boy instead, but he doesn't smile back.

I don't know where to look myself so I glance down at my feet. The little girl's foot taps on the floor. Her sandals are all worn and broken and her toenails are stubby and caked full of dirt. I can't stand it any more so I take a pound coin from my purse, give it to the girl and hand back the tissues. I think at least she can use them again. She runs back to her dad as if she's discovered treasure. He nods twice at the ground but doesn't look up. Now the mother is making her way up the carriage collecting the rest of the messages and tissues.

When she returns to her family the little girl points

to me and talks in . . . I don't know what language. The mother's face is stern. She pushes her daughter hard on the shoulder so that she stumbles towards me. She hands me back the tissues and I see that her eyes are full of hurt and tears. I think it's *me* who should be handing *her* a tissue.

The doors open and the family get off the train. As I put the tissues in my pocket the woman opposite catches my eye.

'Best not to encourage them, love. They're professional beggars. They're trying to put a stop to it, you know.'

I feel as if I've been told off. I'm glad there's only one stop to go. As I wait by the doors, a tall old man in a grey coat reaches into his pocket, smiles at me and slides out his packet of tissues just far enough for me to see.

It feels like I've been travelling for days by the time I get off the tube at Finsbury Park. I can't believe that Pari does this every single schoolday.

When I finally arrive outside I take a glug of air. You can smell the fumes in the atmosphere. I check the address on the letter and look around for a street map, but can't find one. I'm getting bustled around a bit as I try to work out who I can ask for directions when a tall boy with a guitar slung over his back knocks into me. He's about two heads taller than me, but I reckon he's about my age.

'Sorry! I'm always doing that! I should get a rear-view mirror!'

I smile at him but don't say anything. I can't say anything. *Ask him the way, Laila – why don't you ask him the way?*

I look at the network of roads, traffic lights and busy streets and realize I haven't got a clue which way to go. I'm about to turn around and go back home when someone taps me on the shoulder and I swivel around.

It's the boy with the guitar.

'Sorry! Didn't mean to shock you. I was just thinking that you might want some help?' He looks down at the envelope in my hand.

I turn it over, point to the address on the back and hold up the palms of my hands as if to say, 'I don't speak English and I don't know where I'm going.'

The boy frowns like he's a bit confused. 'Right! OK. I know that building. That's the one with all the solar panels.' He points straight ahead. 'It's near where I live. Near my home. I'll show you!'

'Where are you from?' the boy asks as we walk up the road.

I shake my head like I don't understand.

'Where's your home? Your country?'

'India . . . Kolkata,' I say, trying to do an accent that sounds a bit like Janu's.

What am I doing?

'My mum's best friend is from India. I really want to travel there one day.'

Why is he still talking to me? I'm sure he doesn't believe that I don't understand. We walk along in silence after that, but he keeps glancing sideways at me and smiling with his soft hazel eyes and sandy hair. I can't believe how stupid I'm being. I keep blushing every time he looks at me.

'This is the address you wanted . . . Funny, I've walked past here so many times and never noticed its name. This is it . . . The Caring Community.' He smiles at me and points up to the sign. When he smiles, his whole face lights up.

My face feels all hot. I know I'm blushing, so I look down and nod. I feel a bit rude as he walks away. 'Thank you,' I call after him as he continues up the road. He looks around and smiles at me again. Am I imagining it? I don't think any boy has ever looked at me like that.

'No problem, Mira!'

I turn the envelope over. I suppose he must have spotted the name on the front and thought it was me.

Well, what difference does it make? I'm never going to see him again.

I wait till he turns the corner, then walk up the pathway to the row of old brick cottages.

SEVENTEEN

'The Caring Community' seems to be a line of cottages all knocked together. The spaces where the doors used to be have been replaced by arched windows. In front of each one there's a rose garden where there are still a few red and white rose petals hanging on. There are onions too that someone's dug up, their brown strands lying on the grass. In among them are three huge pumpkins, including a Halloween one with a face cut out, collapsed now and drooping at the mouth.

I follow a pathway leading to a turquoise painted door in the middle of the row. There's an old-fashioned bell pull to the side of it. I ring it once. It chimes all through the corridor. I feel deep in my dungaree pocket for Nana Josie's chime. The bell sounds to the end of the ring and no one appears. I'm just wondering if I should pull it again when a tall woman wearing a bright orange wrap on her head opens the door. I suppose I was expecting Simon to answer . . . I get all muddled.

'I'm the Nana . . .'

Instead of giving it another go to get my words in the right order, I just stop. It's like I really have lost the power to speak English.

'I'm a grandmother, but I shouldn't think *you* are! Start again.' The woman speaks with a soft French accent. She has a kind look in her eyes.

'Sorry! I mean . . . My nana was a friend of Simon Makepeace. I've come to pick up a book from him.'

'Does this granddaughter of an old friend of Simon Makepeace have a name?' the woman asks.

'Laila Levenson,' I just about manage to get out.

'Levenson . . . Leven-son . . . Lev-enson . . .' She repeats my name as if saying it over again in different ways will spark her memory. It seems to work. 'Oh my word! Now I see it, Josie's granddaughter! But you're—'

'I'm Mira's little sister,' I explain.

And before I know what's happening, she reaches out, clasps my hand in both of hers and draws me into the hallway.

'I'm Hope. I shared a tent with your nana for a few nights . . . it was many years ago! She was so amusing. Somewhere I have a *dessin* . . . drawing she made of the two of us together . . .' Her voice is like a happy little bird practising its scales.

Hope's smile turns into a grin. She reaches out and touches my shoulder.

140

'Such a shame she had to go so early. She would have been welcome in our commune. But here in you, *je crois* . . . I believe, there is a little of her calling to see us. Same fire in those eyes, like Josie! I'm so happy you came. Simon's been bothered about returning that book to your family.'

The hallway is long and sunny with brightly painted doors leading off it into bedrooms. I follow Hope past the yellow, orange, purple and red doors. A piece of art is hung on the wall between each one. Hope taps a painting of a yellow poppy on a stony beach as she walks past. 'This is of Josie's hand.'

It does look like one of hers. I've never really thought about other people, outside of our family, owning Nana Josie's paintings. I stop and look at it. From the pale grey colours of the pebbles and that big sky, I guess it might be Suffolk.

The corridor opens into a room flooded with sunlight. It's something like a conservatory with a back wall painted in the same deep turquoise colour as the front door . . . well, what I can *see* of the wall, because it's almost completely covered in grape-vines. In front of the creeper there's a huge plant with knobbly bark twisting and turning in all directions and ending in fan-shaped branches that look like giant outstretched hands reaching towards the glass. I've never seen a plant that big before in someone's house. It's like a greenhouse in here.

'Simon's soaking up the sun, the sleepy old cat!' Hope ushers me into the room and as I enter I knock the wheel of a bike that's resting against a wall. It has flowers and little bells threaded through the wheel spokes just like Krish remembered. Hope steadies it as I pass.

'Simon's old bike,' she says.

'My brother remembered that.'

'Well, he won't be the only one. That bike has travelled!' Hope says.

I try to laugh but I'm so nervous it comes out sounding fake.

Maybe I have seen a photo of Simon somewhere around the house, because I feel like I've seen him before. In the centre of the room is a table with a thick half-melted candle in a vase placed on a mat in the middle. An old man is sitting straight-backed in a chair, completely still, with his eyes closed. His eyelids are the texture of scrunched-up tissue paper. He has bushy eyebrows that lift up like the wings of a baby owl. He also has a thick wiry beard, so it's hard to see his mouth, but it seems to be turned upwards in a faint smile. His hair is long and straggly, the colour and coarse texture of those little Border terrier dogs that Nana Kath's sister, Auntie Mairi, breeds. The ones Krish is always trying to persuade Mum and Dad to get. Not grey, not brown, but somewhere in between.

The man has a big forehead with a single deep line running across the middle from one side to the other. His nose is long and straight, his cheeks shiny and red, and he has a fan of fine lines around his eyes. He's wearing jogging bottoms and a navy-blue T-shirt with the words 'Free Tibet' embroidered in orange across the front. He has friendship bracelets on his wrist and what looks like a necklace made of painted seeds. I don't think I've seen anyone old dressed like this before. These clothes are more like the sort of thing Krish wears. And no shoes, no socks. His hands are resting palms upward on both knees, like he's waiting for something to drop into them. A pair of beaten-up old trainers are on the floor by the table.

'Meditating,' Hope whispers. 'Sometimes he sits like that all day, but I'm sure you won't have to wait that long!'

'I don't want to disturb him,' I whisper.

'No, no, you will not. It's not a problem. Just to have patience. He's not sleeping; he'll hear us in the room. It may just take him a little time to return to us. I'll prepare some tea while we wait.' Hope walks off in the other direction and leaves me on my own with the meditating man who is Simon Makepeace – the sender of the letter and Nana Josie's good friend.

This feels so awkward, standing here waiting for this stranger to open his eyes. I carry on looking around the room. It reminds me of a tiny section of the butterfly house Mira once took me to in London Zoo, and it's almost as hot too. I unzip my hoodie, sit down on an old church pew and wait for him to sense I'm here. I glance over at the bike and wonder why I ever thought it was a good idea to come.

The reflection of the sun through the glass roof casts a circle of light on the wooden floor. Simon's trainers are right in the middle of the sun-pool. I lean back and look up through the glass roof at the swaying branches of the tree outside. A few mustard-coloured leaves float down.

'Hello. I didn't hear you come in!' Simon's voice is slightly dry and crackly. He opens his eyes slowly, like he's trying to wake up after a long sleep.

'Josie?' he whispers, and presses his knuckles on the table, leaning hard on it to try to push himself up.

I stand too.

'Is that you, Josie?' he asks again. I wonder if the old man's lost his mind. I look down the corridor to see where Hope is. She could have told me he's confused. I wish she'd come back.

Simon's staring at me like I'm a ghost or something.

'I've come about Nana Josie's Protest Book - you sent my sister a letter,' I explain.

I place the envelope on the table between us.

'Of course!' He laughs and shakes his head. 'Sorry! I've been in a different space-time continuum!' He chuckles.

I'm not sure whether I'm supposed to reply or not.

'What do you suppose this means?' he asks. 'A few minutes before I started meditating, Josie was on my mind . . . she was holding this orb – a little ball of sunshine in her hand – and now I open my eyes and find you dazzling me!'

I point to his trainers in the middle of the sun-pool. 'It is sunny in here!'

Hope goes over to the candle and blows it out.

'Did you have a peaceful journey?' Hope asks.

Is she talking to me?

Simon shrugs and looks down at his trainers. 'My shoes were more peaceful than my head!' Hope laughs like she completely understands. 'My mind was full of the news. Maybe I felt my visitor coming!' He grins at me. 'I think when I've handed over the old book I'll be able to let it all go. My head was all over the place, leapfrogging from all the marches I'd be on if I could . . .' He looks at me for a while. 'So, you must be the younger sister, Lai . . .'

'Laila.'

'That's right! The little protester!'

'Sorry?'

'That's what Josie used to call you! It was her joke when I went to visit her just after you were born. I seem to remember you had a foghorn voice for such a tiny little thing! She told me, "I've got my replacement now, Simon! One protester on the way out, one on the way in!" That was the thing about Josie. She kept her sense of humour right to the end. I'm planning to do the same.' He looks at Hope. 'Not that it's hard to do when Hope's your right-hand woman!'

She smiles at him in a way that makes me think that they might really love each other.

'Come and sit down here!' Simon says, pointing to the chair opposite him. 'Sorry if I freaked you out, but it's uncanny how alike you are to Josie!'

'Everyone says that.'

Simon's grinning at me with his sparkly blue eyes. He has one tooth missing on the side of his mouth. You don't notice unless he smiles really wide, which he does now. His smile lines fan out from each eye like he's spent years laughing and smiling them into their grooves.

'Very pleased you got my letter. Where's your sister Mira then?'

'Gone off to college. She asked me if I would collect the book for her.'

Is it *always* wrong to lie?
Is it *always* right to tell the truth?

I half expect a lightning shaft to break through the skylight – 'Lai Lai Liar! Lai Lai Liar!' . . . But nothing happens, though the sun does go behind a cloud and the room darkens.

'What's she doing at college?' Simon continues.

'Art – she's at Glasgow,' I say.

Simon's eyes twinkle little stars of bright blue happiness.

'Josie had her down as an artist! And how about your brother . . . Krishna?'

'Krish,' I correct him. 'Music and Sport mostly. He's doing this outward-bounds apprenticeship in the Lake District. He plays the guitar and sings . . . makes up his own songs.'

'What kind of music's he into?'

'He calls it ambient. I don't really know. He's always got his headphones on!'

'*Ambient.*' Simon repeats the word really slowly, looking up at the leaves. He's tracking another yellowing leaf as it floats down and lands on the glass roof. 'And you, Laila . . . ? What are you into?'

'Not sure yet.'

'Fair enough. Your Nana Josie dreamed of being a dancer. Did you know that? She looked like a little ballet dancer too, a bit like you.'

I shake my head. I didn't know that. I suppose I don't know much about her . . . yet.

'My cousin Priya's a dancer; she's really good. She does Indian dance and contemporary . . . fusion stuff.'

'I'm liking these words . . . *ambient* . . . *fusion* . . .' Simon looks at Hope and laughs.

I can't believe how easy Simon is to talk to. He's

not like an old man at all. It's more like talking to Krish. It's the way he thinks and speaks, like talking's a game.

'How did you get here, Laila?' Hope asks as she pours the tea. 'Did your family drop you off? Are they waiting for you – perhaps they would like to join us for some tea?'

'Oh no! I came on my own . . . on the tube,' I say.

'Good for you. Not like your daughter, Hope, insisting your grandchildren get chaperoned everywhere.'

'I know they're – how do you say, Simon? – *mollycoddled* . . . but the world is different today.'

Simon purses his lips and raises his bushy eyebrows a couple of times. It makes me laugh.

'Not sure about that! Same world, different psyche,' he says, tapping the side of his head. 'I remember what me and my friends used to get up to when we were kids, claiming the streets on our bikes . . .'

'What's *mollycoddled*?' I ask.

'Hope's grandchildren!'

Hope pretend-scowls at Simon.

'Overprotected,' he explains.

'How old are you, Laila?' Hope asks.

'Thirteen.' My voice wobbles a bit. Even *I'm* not that convinced by the way I say it.

'You see, two years older than my Corinne.'

Simon's frown deepens . . . maybe he's doing the

maths. Then he winks at me. He totally knows I'm lying about my age.

He leans forward and looks straight into my eyes but doesn't say anything more. Adults don't normally hold your look the way Simon does. It feels a bit like that toddler on the tube sussing me out, but friendlier. There's a pause, as though he's waiting for me to say something. When I speak, my voice sounds weird, even to me. I realize that in our family it's not usually me who has to get a conversation going, mostly I just join in. I can't think of what to say, then I remember Mrs Latif's advice the other day that if you're stuck just ask a question. I wonder if that's why Mum always fires questions at me.

'When did you start meditating?' I ask.

'Now, let me see . . . I've been practising it for about thirty years, but it's only in the last ten that I've really got into it.'

I laugh. It's half nervous laughter, but the way he speaks does make me smile.

'Are you a Buddhist? My tutor was talking about the Dalai Lama. He's into meditation, isn't he?'

'He is! But I'm no Dalai Lama! I'd say I'm more of a searching Simon!' He smiles at me, as if that's an answer that makes sense. 'Now, if the existential questions are over, go and search out your Nana Josie's book. It's on a shelf over there in a Jiffy bag,' he says, pointing to the yucca plant.

Then Simon stands up slowly, like he's checking that every bit of his body is ready to hold him up, starting with his feet.

Hope stands too, getting ready to help him, but Simon shakes his head and pats the back of his chair as if to say, 'Sit down, I don't need your help.'

He holds on to the side of the table until he's balanced enough to carry on. It's like he's walking in slow motion. He doesn't turn back to me but raises his hand and touches one of the giant leaves of the indoor tree.

'Excuse me, I've got to pee. It'll take me about the same time to get to that bathroom over there as it used to take me to run five K!' He holds on to a thick stem of the yucca as he passes. 'You'll have to find your way through these branches . . . you know, Josie gave me this from a cutting. She had green fingers, your nana. She said it would flower, but I'm still waiting! Anyway, I've always been more of a leaf than a flower man. It was only in a little pot plant when she gave it to me . . . now look at the span of it!' Simon finally reaches the door.

I climb under and over the tangle of plant that's spreading its fan-shaped leaves across the roof. From this angle it looks like its branches really are trying to break through the glass.

I duck underneath a giant leaf finger and hold back

some grape-vines to find the shelf.

I pick up the Jiffy bag. It's heavier than I expected. I climb out back over the branches to find that Hope's gone, leaving me on my own to open Nana Josie's Protest Book.

EIGHTEEN

The words on the cover say 'Josie's Book of Protest'. It's written in her arty swirly handwriting. I wasn't expecting to feel so nervous about opening this. It's like I'm meeting my nana for the first time. I take the chime out of the silk purse in my pocket, hold it in my hand and turn to the first page. There's a black-and-white photo of Nana in a straw hat. Her hair is wound into long thick plaits. She must be about twenty years old. She's smiling at me.

I turn the next page. There's a card, it says Josie Levenson – it's an Anti-Apartheid membership card. In a little envelope stuck on underneath there are some small black-and-white photos and newspaper clipping of people on marches holding banners. There's one of Nana Josie in America on a Civil Rights march. It's hard to believe that not very long ago there was segregation in American schools. It's scary to think about. I peer at one picture. I think the tall woman with the floaty long dress might be

Hope. It's so weird to see old people when they were young. I pick out Simon in a crowd, pushing along his bike. It actually looks like the same one . . . Simon hasn't even changed that much, except in the picture his beard and hair are thick and sun-streaked, hugging his face like a mane. He's got the same playful expression in his eyes. I wonder if he's ever cut his hair.

I flick forward. The book is crammed full of articles and leaflets about marches, campaigns, protests and vigils . . . I've seen some of those on the news, people standing on pavements of flowers and lit candles. I love the way that Nana's arranged tickets and articles on each page, like she knew they were important. She's written a list of all the marches she's been on, and on one page there are lots of slogans. At the head of another she's written the lyrics for protest songs. I think Krish would like to read that page. Why did she record all these things so carefully? I suppose it's just that she wanted to keep a record, like people post things on Facebook . . . but actually not, because it feels like she always knew someone in our family would hold it in their hand eventually and maybe treasure it . . .

There's an article about rabbits that they test make-up on. Who could think up doing something like that? The rabbits' eyes are all swollen and it says here that some of them go blind – just so people can use make-up. Maybe if Kez knew this she wouldn't be so into her eyeliner and mascara. I'll have to tell her to check if they've tested it on animals. Maybe people don't think about this stuff. I never have before. There's all these pictures of how animals are slaughtered. I can't even look at them.

I turn another page and wish I hadn't, because there's a photo of Simon on his bike with flowers threaded through the wheel spokes and garlands around his neck, and apart from the flowers he's not wearing anything else. He's riding alongside a girl with curly red hair streaming down her back; wild and long like a cloak, covering her milky-white skin. She reminds me a bit of Kez. Apart from the hair and flowers, she's naked too. Behind them someone is holding a placard that says 'Naked Bike Ride – Campaign against Climate Change'. I suppose if you're wearing no clothes and you're riding a bike, you're definitely going to get your message across!

I quickly turn over the page as Simon makes his way step by steady step back towards the table. I feel like I should help him, but I know that when Kez wants help she prefers it if you wait till she asks for it and I suppose it might be the same with Simon.

'There you have it . . . Job done! One Protest Book handed over!'

Simon finally manoeuvres himself into his seat and turns the book towards him.

'I haven't looked at this for a long time. It doesn't help, poring over the past when you're trying to let go, but I don't suppose one last peek will do any harm!'

He balances a pair of glasses on the top of his nose and slowly turns the pages.

'The last time I looked through this was after your nana died. She didn't throw much away, did she? There's more than half a century of campaigning in this book.'

Simon pulls a drawer open on the table and takes out an envelope.

'Here – you can stick these in too if you want . . . a few things I've got involved in since she died . . . It all belongs together really.'

I take the envelope from him.

'You interested in all this?' Simon asks me.

I nod.

'Then take your time, look it all up . . . or the things that stoke you anyway!' He leafs to the end of the book. 'Ah yes! This was the very last march Josie came on with me. Against the Iraq War . . . and now, well, don't get me started.' Simon's voice wobbles. 'See, I shouldn't have looked!'

'I have a friend, Pari. She's from Iraq,' I say.

Simon nods. It's like he's waiting for me to say more.

'I don't know her very well yet. I only met her this term. I think her parents might have come here because of that war. I'm not sure though.'

'We were at the march against that war,' Hope says, and shakes her head. 'Not that it stopped them.'

Simon nods his head to his chest and closes his eyes.

I stand up because I think maybe he's getting tired and wants me to go. Hope walks over to Simon, places her hand on his shoulders and leaves them there.

Tears appear in the corners of Simon's eyes. 'I don't know where these are coming from!' he says, wiping them away with his hand.

I open the packet of tissues I got from the girl on the tube and hand one to Simon. He tilts his head to one side and smiles at me with his lips closed; his mouth's a small upward curve, part lost in his beard.

'Are you a crier then, Laila Levenson?'

I shake my head. 'Hardly ever.'

'I never have been either, but just recently I've been finding the tears flowing. It's a new one on me!' He looks up at Hope like she might have an answer. 'Maybe it's seeing all these apartheids now, all harder to fight against in their own way than the ones we fought, eh, Hope?'

She nods and now she looks like she's about to cry too.

Simon tries to pick up the Protest Book, but doesn't manage it. Instead he places it back down on the table.

'Too heavy for me to carry around now.'

Someone has painted a snake with orange-and-black markings on the back cover. Simon reaches out and runs his hands over the painting.

'Why's there a snake on the back?' I ask.

Simon shrugs. 'Not sure! Josie was into Eastern symbolism, Karma and all that . . .'

'We had a snake in our kitchen!'

Simon's tears turn to laughter. 'Just passing through, was it? Should we have a little meditation for Josie? Got a light, Hope?' He grins at her, like it's their joke. She nods, feels around in her pocket, takes out some matches and lights the candle again in the middle of the table.

Then Simon and Hope do nothing. They just sit and stare at the flame. I do the same but I feel like such a fake. This reminds me a bit of a vigil – well, it could be if I knew what I was supposed to be thinking about. After what seems like ages, the person who comes into my mind as I watch the flame tilting, shrinking and growing is . . . Pari.

I wish I'd said goodbye to Simon and Hope before they started this, because the two of them are just sitting there with their eyes closed and breathing softly. It would be rude to just leave, but how do I know how long they'll stay like this for? I'm starting to get worried about what'll happen if Mum and Dad find out I've actually not been at Kez's. I'm thinking about coughing or making a noise getting up, when a

157

bird sets off, making a bit of a racket. Simon opens his eyes and looks up through the glass roof to the almost-bare branches of the tree.

'Strong voice for something so tiny! Proper little protester, isn't it! I wonder if it feels a change in the weather.'

I remember Nana Josie's chime and think maybe Simon would like to see it. I take it out of my dungaree pocket, slip it out of the silk purse and place it in Simon's hands.

'Nana Josie gave me this when I was a baby,' I tell him. 'It was given to her when she was a baby too.'

Simon's examining it closely as the light falls in shafts through the glass roof and it glints in the sunlight.

'Ah! And there we have it. The orb of sunshine I saw in my meditation!' He shakes Nana's chime and then hands it back to me. 'It's like a little meditation bell. Give Laila the Banner Bag too, Hope.'

'Are you sure, Simon?'

'I am sure . . . Yes! And take her painted banner off my wall. Give her that too.'

Hope hesitates for a minute, like she's checking again that this is really what Simon wants.

He nods and she goes out into the corridor.

Simon grins at me, wide enough to see his missing tooth.

'Bye, Laila,' he says, and closes his eyes again.

I walk past Nana's yellow poppy painting and wait for Hope.

She's gone off into a room. She's taking ages. I'm about to call out and ask her if she wants some help, but just then she reappears with an old green canvas bag that's about the size of Krish's cricket kitbag. She's really out of breath.

'Sorry, Laila, the old catches are stiff and I had to unhook your nana's banner. It's been on Simon's wall for a while!'

The Banner Bag has worn leather straps dangling over the sides and it's got two closing locks in a brass colour. It looks a bit like an antique.

'You keep this safe, Laila.' Hope takes the Protest Book from me, places it inside the bag and attempts to close it. 'These fastenings are a bit rusty, but the straps will keep it safe,' she explains as she ties the leather bits up again. 'Will you be all right carrying all of this? It's quite heavy, what with your nana's banner and all our paraphernalia inside! If I had known, I would have cleaned out some of the old paint . . . placards too. Shall I help you home?'

'I'm fine.'

'I think you've inherited your nana's independent nature!' Hope says, opening the door to the rain. 'Well then, at least take my umbrella.' She picks an

159

orange umbrella from the stand by the door and hands it to me.

I thank Hope, press the button so that the umbrella opens wide, and I walk out into the rain carrying Nana Josie's Protest Book in the Banner Bag.

NINETEEN

It's still raining hard when I come out of the tube. I'm grateful for Hope's umbrella, but I wish it wasn't bright orange. I just want to get home without being noticed and hide this Banner Bag somewhere safe. I think I might have to leave it down the side of the house behind the bins when I get home, until the coast's clear to go back and get it. If I walk in with this, the questions will never end.

As I pass Kez's flat, Bubbe's standing in the bay window watching the road, probably waiting for Kez. She waves at me and comes to the door.

'Where on earth have you been, Laila?' she asks, looking down at the bag.

'Just out for a walk.' I feel terrible lying to her.

'In this rain? Your mum called around with your coat ages ago. She's been beside herself with worry. We all have. Just wait a minute.'

Bubbe takes her phone out of her pocket and texts Mum. She doesn't try and hide her message from me.

A text comes straight back and Bubbe tilts her phone so I can read Mum's message back to her.

'You'd better go and face the music, Laila. I told Uma I thought it would be OK. That you and Kez had a falling out . . .'

'Kez told you?'

Bubbe nods. 'She was upset about it. All friendships have their ups and downs, you know. Make sure you come and see me soon for a little chat. But you'd better hurry back now.'

'Bubbe . . . can I leave this here with you?' I ask, showing her Simon's bag.

She looks at it a bit strangely.

'What is it?'

'It's a Banner Bag. It belonged to my nana's friend. I'll explain later . . .'

She takes it from me.

'We can talk about this later. Just get home now . . . Your mum's been out of her mind with worry.'

'Don't say anything about this to Mum or Dad. It's important. Nor to Kez,' I plead.

'That puts me in a difficult position, Laila.'

'Please, Bubbe,' I whisper. 'I promise I'll come and

162

tell you about it. It's all about my nana.'

Bubbe shakes her head like she's going to say no, but then changes her mind. 'OK . . . for now! But I do want an explanation. I'll call Kez as well. She was worried about you too, you know.'

I run the rest of the way home and lean on the wall for a minute to get my breath back. When I stand away from it, a big piece of plasterwork falls off, making the crack in the wall look twice the size. I try to stick it back but I can't make it stay, so I throw the piece of wall into the garden and it crumbles to powdery dust.

Mum opens the door. I stand halfway up the steps and shake Hope's umbrella. What an idiot I am. I should have left this with Bubbe too.

Mum leaps on me so I nearly fall backwards down the steps. She's holding me in this really strange way like she half wants to hug me and half wants to kill me. She's squeezed so tightly against me that I can feel her breath coming in angry-sounding sobs. Then suddenly she lets go of me, wipes her eyes really roughly, like she's annoyed with herself for crying, takes a few deep breaths and sets her face into this blank expression. I've seen her do this before with Krish and Mira when she really wants to scream and shout but she holds it in and doesn't say anything. It actually freaks me out and I just wish she would get it over with and have a blowout. This must be off-the-scale bad because she just stands aside to let me in.

'Where's that come from?' she asks as I edge past, pointing at the dripping umbrella I've left leaning against the back of the door.

'Found it on a bench,' I tell her.

'That was convenient.'

She *so* doesn't believe me.

'Where have you been, Laila?'

'Just walking.'

'So you've been walking around for the whole afternoon in the rain and you found this umbrella and so you just kept walking . . . for – what's it been – nearly four hours?'

Mum lays a hand on my shoulder, leads me to the table and practically pushes me into a seat. I feel like I'm about to be interrogated. She sends a text to Dad and I hear one pinging straight back. She shows me his message on the phone.

I called the police. Told them she's safe. On my way back now.

Give her a hug and hello for me. Love you X

I feel really guilty. I hadn't really thought what would be going through their minds. Mum sits down next to me with her hands folded on her lap; the top hand

164

stroking the bottom one like she's trying to calm herself down.

'Well? I'm waiting.'

Is it *always* **wrong to lie?**
Is it *always* **right to tell the truth?**

Mrs Latif's voice echoes through my head. A bit of me wonders what would happen if I actually told Mum the truth, but I know that if I did, she would make me hand the Protest Book straight over to Mira and I wouldn't even get to read it properly. Mum's definitely going to ground me anyway.

'I had an argument with Kez and went for a walk. That's all,' I tell her.

She nods slowly.

'What was the argument about?'

'I don't know really . . . we weren't getting on, that's all.'

'So let me get this right. You had an argument and you went for a walk for hours on end and happened to find a nice expensive-looking umbrella along the way? Where did you walk to?'

'I went up Parliament Hill . . . I sat on Mira's bench and someone left the umbrella leaning against it. '

Mum's face softens a bit. I know she'll be wondering if I'm missing Mira and Krish too. It's frightening how good I'm getting at filling in the details.

'And you couldn't text me or Dad and tell us that?'

'My phone ran out of charge.'

Mum holds out her hand. I reach into my pocket and pass my mobile to her.

'Are you sure you didn't switch it off? Let me see.'

She plays with it for a bit and, when she realizes that it actually is dead, puts it back on the table.

'Can I go now?' I ask. I get as far as the first step of the stairs.

'No! Laila, I think you've been gone long enough – come back here right now!'

I carry on up.

'Have you got any idea how dangerous it is to go off on your own like that without telling anyone, without being in contact?'

Mum's stomping up the stairs after me. I manage to get to Mira's room and half close the door . . . I'm still holding the handle when Mum pushes it hard and makes me stumble backwards.

'You nearly made me fall!' I shout at her.

'We called the police, Laila. We thought you'd been abducted. If you weren't back in the next hour they were going to start looking for you,' Mum shouts.

'I'm sorry. I'm fine, Mum.'

'Well I'm glad about that, because I'm not!'

Mum takes a deep breath and sits on Mira's bed. She taps the duvet for me to sit down next to her.

'Please don't ever do that to us again, Laila.' Mum

sighs. 'What can we do to help you and Kez sort out this argument?'

'Nothing! You can't fix everything for me, Mum. Please can I just be on my own now?'

Mum nods and tracks around the empty walls of Mira's room. 'Let me know when you're ready to talk . . .'

She gets up off the bed, closes the door quietly behind her and walks down the stairs. When Dad comes in I tiptoe out to the landing and sit on my perch.

Mum's talking and talking. Dad's voice is raised. They sound like they always do when they try to convince me they're not arguing.

'It's not like Krish and Mira never went off on their own for a few hours without telling us, Uma. Remember when Krish ran off after Mum died? He was much younger than Laila and he didn't even have a mobile. She probably just needed a bit of space! It's all change for her too, remember.'

Dad heads for the hallway. I try to get up and creep back into Mira's room but Dad hears me as he comes up the stairs.

'Which bit of that did you hear?' he asks.

I shrug.

'Thought so!' Dad holds out his arms wide and crushes me in a hug.

'Dad! I can't breathe.' I try to pull away.

'Well, that's what you get for worrying us stupid!'

'Sorry!'

'You'd better say sorry to Mum too. You won't be allowed out next time unless your phone's fully charged. We've got to be able to trust you to tell us the truth.' Dad pauses and leans against the banister. He speaks a bit louder, I think so that Mum can hear him telling me off. 'And . . . you're grounded.'

'Till when?'

'Till you convince us you can be trusted again.'

'I never go anywhere anyway,' I say. But all I can think is: how am I'm going to get the Banner Bag and Nana Josie's Protest Book back from Bubbe . . . ?

'Well, you went somewhere today!'

'Think I'll go up and sort out a few things in my room,' I say after dinner.

Mum and Dad look really pleased, and they leave me to it till they come up to bed. Not that I've done anything except lie on Mira's bed and try to remember everything I read in the Protest Book. I wish that I had it with me right now.

'Night, Laila, sleep well,' Dad calls.

'Can I come in, Laila?' Mum knocks and peers around the door.

'I'm really sorry I worried you, Mum!' I say.

She comes over and hugs me.

'So what have you been doing up here all evening?'

she asks, pulling away from me and looking around the room to see if anything's changed.

'Hung up a few more clothes!' I say, pointing to the closed wardrobe doors.

'OK, well, it'll be good for you when you're properly settled in here.' She tests the mattress. 'This is a lovely comfy bed, Laila. Get a good night's sleep so you're not tired for school tomorrow.'

Without even asking me she takes hold of one arm and then the other, takes the cream off the bedside table and starts smoothing it into my skin.

'I think you'll have to wear gloves to stop the scratching. Or a onesie with hands in. I've seen them advertised.'

'What? A babygrow! Don't think so.'

She ignores me. I'm not sure if she's soothing me or herself, but I close my eyes as she does it and start to feel waves of tiredness spread over me. But there's only one place I want to sleep.

'I love you, Lai Lai,' Mum says as she kisses me goodnight.

'Love you too, Mum,' I whisper back.

When the house is quiet after Mum and Dad are in bed, I take my duvet and Nana Josie's chime with me and let the sound sing through me until I fall asleep.

TWENTY

'Ignore it, Uma, don't say anything,' Dad whispers. 'The more we make a thing of it, the longer she'll want to stick it out!'

'Stick what out?' Mum whispers back.

'Her landing protest!'

The smell of bacon comes wafting up the stairs. Dad never makes bacon sarnies in the week. I come down in my uniform and sit at the table.

'Here you go! Weekend breakfast on a schoolday! Can't be bad!' Dad places a sizzling bacon bap and a glass of orange juice on the table.

My stomach makes a hungry growl.

'Sounds like you need it.'

I sit and look at the plate, and even though the smell is driving me crazy, and my mouth's producing mad amounts of saliva, I can't get the slaughterhouse pictures from Nana's Protest Book out of my head.

'I can't eat this, Dad.'

'Why not? Come on, Laila. It's my cheer-you-up breakfast! Tuck in!'

'It's meat!' I say.

'And? You love meat.'

'Not any more. It makes me feel sick.'

'It's from free-range pigs. They'll have had a good life.'

'Before their throats were cut.'

Dad looks at me like he thinks I'm messing about.

'I'm not eating it. I'm vegetarian now.'

'Since when?'

'Since I read about what actually goes into slaughtering animals. Anyway, if everyone was vegetarian it would help with climate change. Do you know how much cows fart?'

Dad bursts out laughing.

'That's what happens when you eat too much rabbit food!' Dad jokes.

I give him my 'so not amused' look.

'That's it then. It's all over! Am I the only carnivore left in this house till the prodigal son comes home?' Dad moans.

'Looks like it!' Mum sounds pleased. 'What did I do with those case notes?' she asks, rushing around, trying to find a file for work.

'It's on the sofa in the living room,' I tell her.

'Thanks, Laila!'

I open the fridge to get some milk for cereal. All I

can see is *meat*. Minced beef, chicken and bacon . . . I inspect the bacon. It's bog standard. There's nothing on the packet that says anyone's made an effort to give the animal it once was a good life. I close the door and start rearranging the mini fridge magnets. The ones Mira and Krish used to write notes to Mum and Dad with when they went out. It takes me a while.

Thisfridgeisthesceneofanimal TORTURE

'You lied, Dad,' I say as I'm arranging the second 't' in 'torture'. There are only capitals left for 'TORTURE'.

'Lied about what?'

I point to the fridge. 'Nothing in there's free range, not even the eggs.'

'It usually is, isn't it, Uma?'

Dad's doing that funny 'talking between clenched teeth and raising his eyebrows up and down' thing to try to get Mum to agree with him.

'No! Don't you remember? Krish was eating so much it was getting too expensive . . . but I'm thinking if you're the only carnivore in the house, we might as well all go veggie! Great slogan, Laila!' Mum laughs as she reads the fridge letters.

'Thanks for the support, Uma!' Dad scowls.

'So you lied to get your way, Dad?' I say.

'Give me a break, Laila! I'm in the minority here. My only hope is Janu—'

'Not a chance! He's veggie too – he might even be vegan . . . I'd better check.' Mum laughs at the look of despair on Dad's face.

Dad places his forehead on the table, arms dangling by his sides, like his world has come to an end.

TWENTY-ONE

'Ready!' Miss Green shouts, and lowers the red flag.

I feel my legs judder and I'm off, arms and legs pumping fast, heart thumping. I glance to the side and see that Pari's keeping pace. She's only a bit taller than me, but she's light. She grins my way. I think it's a challenge!

We pull ahead of the others and sprint for the finish line, arriving at exactly the same time.

Miss Green clicks her timer. 'That was a competitive time. Like it or not, you two are definitely down for the school team!'

We both double over to get our breath back.

'Well done, Pari. Fantastic run. And you're –' Miss Green looks at me like she's trying to size me up – 'Krish Levenson's sister, aren't you?' She taps me on the shoulder as I straighten up.

I nod because I'm still too out of breath to talk. Pari catches her breath much faster than me.

'Thought so. You'll need to put in some training though, get your fitness levels up.'

'I don't think I've ever sprinted as fast as that!' I tell Pari, as we get changed.

'Didn't you race in primary?'

'A bit on Sports Day. But that was just in teams. They didn't do competitions really.'

'I don't get that! I like being able to win at something.'

At first I think she might be joking, but when I look at her she seems dead serious.

'This is the bit I hate though,' she says as we walk into the gym block. Pari holds her nose as she looks with total disgust around the changing room.

I suppose it does whiff a bit of sweat, but it's not that bad.

Bits and pieces of people's uniforms have fallen off the pegs under the changing hangers. Our things have been knocked off too, so we start sorting through them to find out whose uniform is whose. When I pick up Pari's blazer I see that someone else's name tag has been removed and a new one for 'Pari Pashaei' has been stitched into it with perfect, even stitches. I've made a real mess of mine. I ended up writing over Krish's name tag in black marker pen, which was a mistake because it looks like a mish-mash name now and you can't really work out any of the letters. If I lost it somewhere around school there's no way anyone would be able to read my name.

I hand Pari her crumpled blazer.

'It's got trainer marks all over it!' She grabs it off me, runs over to the sink and starts to dab at it with a paper towel.

'Who did this?' she shouts. I hardly recognize her voice. It's all sharp and hard. She turns and looks around accusingly.

'What's your problem?' Stella asks, and looks at Pari like she's lost the plot. 'Don't get up in my face. I didn't do it!'

'I don't think anyone *meant* to stand on it . . . clothes just get knocked off the pegs,' I say, trying to cool things down.

'They don't take enough care. Look here! Dirty footprints all over it . . . and on my skirt too. They always do it on purpose, just like in primary . . . I *have* to get this off!'

'Here – try this.' I hand her a tissue.

She rubs it hard but it actually looks worse now because the tissue fluff sticks to the sleeve.

'It won't come off!' Pari's scrubbing at it now.

'It's not that bad!' I say. I can't believe she's in such a state over her uniform. 'I don't care about mine. It's my brother's and sister's old uniform anyway,' I tell her.

'So? You should care. Everyone should take more

care!' She's shouting now and all out of breath, as if she's been running again.

'What's all the commotion? Everything OK in here, girls?' Miss Green pokes her head around the door.

'We were just practising something for Drama,' I say.

Miss Green looks from Pari to me and nods. 'Well, it was pretty convincing!'

Pari keeps her back turned away from me as she tries to calm down.

'Pari?' Miss Green walks over and places her hand on her back. 'Have a sit-down and take a few deep breaths.'

Pari breathes in and out slowly, keeping her head down.

'Better?' Miss Green asks.

Pari nods. 'You go on ahead, Laila,' she says quietly.

It's so strange, going from knowing Kez so well to then starting from scratch with someone new. The way Miss Green put her hand on Pari's back makes me think teachers know stuff about her that I don't. I wish she would trust me enough to let me in. I don't know why it is that you want to get to know some people more than others, but I really would like to be friends with Pari.

I wait outside the PE block. Miss Green comes out first and smiles at me. 'Pari won't be a minute.'

It's a lot longer than a minute! When Pari finally joins me, she won't look me in the eye.

'Sorry I got into a state. I get panicky sometimes,' she says. 'I just need to keep my uniform smart. I don't like to make more work for my mum.'

I have loads of things I want to ask, but I don't because I get the feeling that if I push her she'll clam up completely.

'Thanks for saying that thing about Drama . . . and for waiting for me,' she says as we cross the courtyard.

'Laila! Pari!' Kez calls out to us and I swivel around. At first I can't work out where her voice is coming from, and then I catch sight of her flame-red hair tied back in a ponytail as the platform in the minibus slowly lowers and I go over and wait for her to get off. She stretches out her arms to me and we hug.

'I was so worried about you. I should have told you . . . sorry we argued,' she whispers.

'Me too!' I whisper back.

'Bubbe says you're grounded now?'

I nod and check Kez out to see if Bubbe's kept her promise about the Banner Bag. I don't think she's told her.

Behind her, one of the PE teachers comes over to talk to Miss Green.

'It's an amazing facility, well worth the journey, and such a great atmosphere with them opening it up to all the schools on the same day. It's huge.' He's doing that thing of talking loudly on purpose so we can overhear. 'I've never seen anything like it!' he tells Miss Green. 'And Kezia and Selina here were in-spirational. Selina just ran her first two hundred metres.'

Kez raises her eyebrows at me and Selina and mimes 'OTT'.

I laugh. He *was* being a bit Over the Top enthusiastic!

Stella walks straight up to Miss Green. 'You said you would talk to the Head about it. Can I go with them next time, or not?' she asks.

'Just a minute, Stella.' Miss Green looks a bit annoyed with her for interrupting. 'Mr Bamford, could you go and discuss that plan in the office with Stella?'

'Was she being funny? Why would she want to come with us?' Kez asks.

'Right, well, you lot are all on my team radar then!' Miss Green announces, and goes off to help another PE teacher unpack equipment from the minibus.

'Selina . . . this is Laila, and Pari,' Kez says, introducing us all.

'Where did you go for PE?' Pari asks Selina, and they talk while Kez and me chat.

As we reach the school entrance Kez starts talking to Selina about physio. It seems like they knew each other before from there.

'Yeah . . . I'm going to the hydropool straight after

school today. My muscles are really tired after all that exercise!' Selina says.

'Mine too,' Kez says. 'Float with you later!'

I hang around in the park for a while after school, giving Kez enough time to go off to physio. Mum won't be back from work till five anyway so hopefully she won't find out if I go over to Kez's, and if she does I'll tell her I went to say sorry for putting Bubbe in a difficult situation at the weekend. Mum can't get too angry with me for that. Anyway, there's no way I can wait another day to look at the Protest Book again or see what else is in the Banner Bag.

On my way to see Bubbe I try to work out if I'm telling myself the truth. OK, so the letter was meant for Mira, and so was the Protest Book. I shouldn't have picked it up or read it, so I did lie about that, but I am going to come clean with Mira and give it back . . . though Simon did give the Banner Bag to me. He wanted *me* to have it. So it's mine to keep. I don't think I'm lying to myself.

TWENTY-TWO

Bubbe's neat steps click through the hallway.

'Oh, Laila – what a lovely surprise!' she says as she opens the door, reaching up a little to stroke my hair. She always does that; does it to Kez too. 'But Kezia isn't here. Didn't she tell you she's got physio?'

'Yes, she did . . . I actually only came by to pick up the bag.'

'Ah yes, your mysterious bag. Come in, come in. I'm glad of the company. Pull up a chair!' Bubbe orders.

'Actually, I'm grounded . . . I've got to get back before Mum gets home from work.'

'I'm sure Uma won't mind you spending a little time with me. I'll text her to let her know we're having our chat,' Bubbe says, tapping the table.

I sit down beside her. There's a candle lit in a glass jar and a plant next to it that I've never seen before. The candle looks like it's been burning for a long time.

'It's my Stan's yahrzeit, his anniversary,' she explains.

'Oh sorry, I don't want to disturb you . . .'

'No, no. I could do with the company. It's nice to have someone to share the memories with.'

'I like that little tree!' I say pointing to a bonsai tree like the one on the box I found Nana's chime in.

'Isn't it beautiful? Hannah bought it for me today,' Bubbe says. 'So delicate and old-looking! She probably thought it looked a bit like me!' Bubbe laughs. 'Oh, look, it's still got the tag on – what does it say? I can't find my glasses anywhere.'

I read the little square tag for her:

May this bonsai tree bring harmony, peace, order of thoughts, balance and all that is good in nature. This evergreen bonsai is easy to care for. Give it light and space. Keep out of draughts. This specimen is from the Chinese Elm family (*Ulmus parvifolia*) – the tree of harmony. The Elm symbolizes inner strength, intuition and wisdom.

'Well, that's a bit of a tall order! I've never been very successful at growing things, but I'll give it a go.' Bubbe laughs. 'Here's hoping! Talking of harmony, I was hoping to have a little word with you, Laila. I don't want to interfere between you and Kezia, but I'm going to say one thing and get it out of the way . . . clear the air.' She wafts her hands around her head, as if to get rid of smoke.

'We're OK now, Bubbe.'

'I'm pleased to hear that – but as I explained to Kezia, if she'd only talked through her decision about the tutor groups with you in the summer, there would have been no need for all this tension. You girls are growing up so fast . . . it happens in every friendship. You have to be honest, try to understand what the other person's going through and take the people you love with you.'

Kez would call this one of Bubbe's 'lectures'. She can go on a bit – but it's Bubbe, so I don't mind. 'Really, everything's fine now, Bubbe,' I reassure her. 'Can I have the bag now?'

She nods, goes into the hallway and pushes a button on the wall, which is actually a hidden cupboard. It's so smooth the way it slides back.

'I tucked it under there behind all the shoes . . . I've thrown a coat over it.' Bubbe points it out for me.

I bend down on my hands and knees to get hold of the handle. 'Thanks for not showing it to anyone,' I say.

Bubbe nods and inspects the bag again like she really wants me to tell her about it.

'Right! Well . . . I've kept my promise,' she says.

I carry the bag through to the kitchen.

'Put that down on the chair for a moment. You'll

have a cup of tea and a slice of strudel with me while we chat. It was always Stan's favourite.'

Bubbe brings a dish with a tea towel over it to the table, cuts us a slice each and hands me a plate. It's so delicious the way the apple squidges out of the thin pastry. Bubbe laughs at the mess I'm making, pulls open a drawer in the table and hands me a serviette.

'Good, good – glad it's being appreciated.'

I glance down at the newspaper clipping that's open on the table. It's a brown colour, like it's been tea-stained.

'I was just about to read Stan's obituary. I get it out every year,' Bubbe tells me. 'But I can't find where I've put my glasses down. I should keep them around my neck really.'

'What's an obituary?' I ask.

Bubbe thinks for a moment.

'You could say it's a little potted story of a person's life.'

'I can read it to you, if you want,' I offer.

'Thanks, Laila. Let me get you a drink and then I can give it my full attention. What would you like? Apple juice?'

'Tea, please!'

'Tea!' Bubbe sighs. 'You girls are growing up so fast . . . I don't know. Still, I'm the lucky one, living long enough to see Kezia's bat mitzvah.' Bubbe switches the kettle on and nods that she's ready for me to start reading.

'Stanley Levi Braverman (1930–2000), beloved husband of Dara Braverman and father of Hannah, both of whom survive him, died peacefully on 15th October 2000.

'Stanley was a child of the Kindertransport. He arrived from Germany, aged nine, in 1939. He lived in a hostel for several years before being adopted by Dr and Mrs Feinstein of Manchester. From an early age he was a promising student with a passion for social justice. After finishing his schooling in Manchester he moved to London to study Law. At a dance in Camden Town, North London, he met his wife Dara, who was studying to be a teacher at the time . . .'

I pause. Bubbe's standing over by the kitchen counter staring out of the window. 'Carry on . . .' she says. 'The best is to come!'

'. . . They discovered that she was also one of the Kinder. They married in 1956 and had one child, Hannah, who was born in 1966. Stanley and Dara are respected members of the North London Reform Synagogue. Our thoughts are with the family at this time.'

Bubbe keeps her back turned away from me for a while. 'He was a treasure of a man, my Stan.' Then she turns around. 'He'd have loved you and Kez; he would have felt much nachas for you both.'

'Nachas?' I ask.

'Yes, very proud he would have been of his family.' Bubbe smiles and holds out her hand for me to give her back the newspaper clipping, then she places it carefully into a silver box with the initials SLB engraved on the top.

'That's kind of what this bag is, Bubbe. We had a letter from an old friend of my nana's to pick up some of her things. I shouldn't have gone but . . .'

I wasn't planning to tell Bubbe the truth about the letter and going to collect the Protest Book and how Simon gave me the Banner Bag. I wasn't going to say anything, but Bubbe has that way about her, of making it easy to talk. She sits quietly and listens. It feels so good to tell Bubbe everything.

'That's why I needed to hide it at yours, because no one else knows about this,' I say as I finish. 'Are you going to tell Mum where I was?'

'You can tell her when you're ready,' Bubbe says. 'Though I can't pretend I'm not intrigued to have a look at the Protest Book myself when you're ready to show me! Your nana and I were about the same age, I think. You never know, we might have been on some of those marches together.'

Bubbe looks over at Stan's silver box.

'No, Laila, you hold on to your nana's precious things. You'll find a way to tell your family what happened when the time's right.' She taps my hand. 'Now, don't tell anyone this or they'll think I'm losing my marbles, but sometimes when I'm looking through Stan's old things I feel like he's actually here sitting with me, drinking tea and listening to the radio . . . nothing ghostly, just companionable, you know?' Bubbe laughs. 'It's silly, I know.'

'I don't think it is,' I say.

'So, tell me, Laila!' she says, changing the subject. 'How are you getting on at school? Kezia tells me you've made a new friend.'

I nod and keep my lips sealed.

She waits for a minute to see if I want to tell her anything else about my new friend, and when I don't she nods and carries on. Bubbe knows me as well as I know Kez. Sometimes I don't need to say anything and she gets what I'm thinking . . . 'You know, the bat mitzvah really does take a lot of time to prepare for and Kezia's committed to doing it as well as she can, but it'll all be over by December and you can spend more time together then.'

'I don't think I really get the bat mitzvah thing. I didn't even know she was religious before this.'

Bubbe folds her hands together. I follow the candle flame flickering this way and that, and for a moment I worry I've insulted her.

'How can I explain? It's this feeling of belonging to something beyond yourself – I think Kezia really needs that at the moment. There's this saying in the Shabbat prayer, let me see if I can translate it . . .' Bubbe mumbles it to herself in Hebrew. '*First you must find who you are and then you can start to see how you connect to your community* . . . The way I see it, a bat mitzvah gives you this . . . compass to help you on your way. At your age it's quite natural to question where you belong in the world, and I think Kezia is just waking up to what's ahead of her – but she's not the only one, is she, Laila?'

Bubbe looks over at the Banner Bag on the chair and holds on to my wrist.

'And then of course there's the getting dressed up and the party afterwards! Oh my goodness, now that's quite something! I never had one myself. There were only bar mitzvahs in my day, for the boys.'

'That's a bit sexist!' I say and it makes her laugh.

'Well, times change, Laila . . . at least I thought they had.'

Bubbe holds her hands in the air as if to say, 'Just a moment –' as if I've been the one chatting on, not her.

No matter where you are in a conversation, if there's something she's really interested in on the news, Bubbe stops to listen. She goes over to the radio, turns up the volume and leans against the counter while she listens. Right now a politician's being interviewed.

'Listen to the language they use! Quotas, swarms . . . as if people are insects – or vermin!' She holds on to the delicate gold necklace that she always wears as she concentrates.

The presenter is now interviewing a boy called Amit – his voice sounds so sweet and young.

> *I am ten years old. I make this journey on my own. My feet always hurting from walking so far. Nothing in my home is left. All is destroyed with shelling. I don't know where is my mother, where is my father, my sisters . . . We have no clean water, not enough food, and here are some not good people, you know? Please, give us some safety. Make your hearts open. How can you close your borders to us? We are only children. If you turn your backs from us, we will die. Once already I have died to lose my family. Now we die a second time.*

The reporter goes on to talk about something else, but Bubbe stares silently at the flickering flame of the candle for what seems like ages. Then she turns off the radio, walks over to a shelf and takes down two photos. I remember she brought them into an assembly talk she did when we were in Year Six. She places them gently on the table.

There's a black-and-white photo of a little boy

wearing shorts and a really tall girl with long, thick bunches who looks a bit like Kez.

'Stan and me. We didn't know each other then . . . but he was sure he remembered me from the train. Peas in a pod, he used to call us.'

'But you look so tall!' I say.

Bubbe straightens up and sticks her chin in the air, like she's trying to remember what it felt like to be tall.

'Maybe that's why he noticed me! I was tall when I was ten, Laila. People used to think I was a really tall girl, but that's about as far as I got!' She laughs.

You can still see the little girl in Bubbe's face, even through all her lines and wrinkles.

'What colour was your hair?' I ask.

'I suppose you would call it chestnut. Like Kezia's before she dyed it. Mine was quite a mane too!' Bubbe touches her shoulder as if she can still feel curls there.

'Stan had this story he used to tell people: he swore that we sat opposite each other on the train from Harwich to Liverpool Street. Remember the statue I took you and Kezia to see?'

I nod.

'Sometimes Stan and I would go and sit on that platform we stepped out on to. I don't think he can really have remembered me . . . I didn't remember him. But he said I was crying so much I wouldn't have. It's true that I did cry all the way. That little boy's voice –' she nods towards the radio – 'took me right back there. That's the strange thing about parting. I remember it like it was yesterday.' Bubbe looks over to my bag. 'Do you remember my little suitcase I brought into school when I came to talk to you?'

'Yes.'

'You wanted to know what was inside . . .'

'You said memories. I remember that.'

Bubbe smiles. 'Would you like to see what I keep in it?'

I nod.

She goes through to her bedroom. I look at the photo of ten-year-old Bubbe, holding the suitcase. She looks so frightened.

Bubbe returns with the little leather suitcase she let us hold when she came into school. She puts it on the table, opens the clasp and takes out a pair of little shoes.

'People might look at these –' she points from the Banner Bag to her suitcase – 'and see two old bags!' She's joking, but I don't feel like laughing and I don't think she does either. 'They say you shouldn't put new shoes on the table . . . but these are pretty old. We didn't come with much, but these are the shoes I arrived in, Laila.'

They are plain little black shoes with silver buckles. They look a bit like tap shoes.

Bubbe bends down, slips off her shoes and tries them on.

'They still fit! Your feet are so tiny!' I laugh.

'Do you know the strangest thing, Laila? They never grew at all from when I arrived. Not even half a size! Look – I'm still being carried around on my ten-year-old feet!' Bubbe takes the shoes off and puts them back in the case. 'I don't get them out much.'

When I look down at Bubbe's tiny old feet it makes me feel so sad. Like a bit of her could never grow properly again after she was forced to leave her home.

TWENTY-THREE

I block the door with a chair and pull the Banner Bag out from under the bed.

Its leather ties are stiff and it smells a bit damp too, like it's been in storage for a long time. I have to press the catches really hard to get the bag to open. I carefully lift out the envelope with the Protest Book inside. The bag seems to have lots of separate compartments and there are old cobwebs in the folds of the yellowing canvas and a few paint stains. On one side there are sections containing paint bottles. I take them out. There's a blood-red colour, a dark blue, a nearly empty bottle of black, an orange and a turquoise. The turquoise paint bottle hasn't been opened yet, but all the others have been used and have crusted-up paint inside. There's another section for paintbrushes, thick ones and thin ones too. In the bottom of the bag is a roll of old ripped sheets and a pile of bamboo poles about the same length as my arm. There's one huge sheet that's all bright colours.

I carefully take it out and unfold it over Mira's carpet. This must be the banner Hope was taking down off Simon's wall.

I hold my breath as I unroll it like a precious scroll. It's my Nana Josie's painting, and this sea of bright-coloured faces wearing clothes of every colour of the rainbow holding up banners is for me. I know it is. I can feel it. In turquoise letters across the back of the sheet is written 'Women's March'. In the background you can't tell the features of the faces – it's just hundreds and hundreds of people – but at the front there are three people I recognize even though they're so young. It's Nana wearing a yellow skirt reaching down to the ground, Hope with a massive wild tangle of Afro hair and Simon pushing his bike with flowers in the spokes of his wheels. They look like proper hippies all marching barefoot.

I can't believe I've got this painting of Nana's and the paint she actually painted it in. I wonder if paint goes off. I twist the lid of the turquoise paint; it's really hard to open and I have to use every bit of strength to get it to budge. It does smell a bit stale.

'Laila, I'm home!' Mum's voice makes me jump. She's climbing the stairs now.

I quickly scoop up the paints, the banner and the Protest Book and push them under my bed.

Mum calls through the door, then the knob turns. 'Why are you blocking the door?'

'Just hang on a minute, Mum.'

I pull the duvet over so that it covers the gap at the bottom of the bed and then I unwedge the chair from under the door knob.

'What's going on?' Mum asks, sniffing the air.

'I was just getting changed. I need a lock on this door!' I say.

'We don't do locks in this house, Laila.'

'I might as well sleep on the landing then!'

Mum's nose is still twitching. 'Do you think it smells a bit damp in here?' She goes over and opens the window. 'How's your eczema . . . any better?' She takes hold of my arm.

I wish she wouldn't just grab me, like my body belongs to her. I shrug her off and pull my arms away from her inspection.

'I've brought you some colour charts to look at. How about a mauve?' Mum scans down the shades of purple.

I pretend to shove my fingers down my throat.

'Not mauve then! What about something more neutral?' She hands me a chart of creams and whites.

'Mum, I keep telling you, I'm not bothered about getting Mira's room decorated.'

'That's the whole point, Laila. It's not Mira's room any more. You need to make it your own, and it would be so much easier for me if we could get it done before Janu visits.' Mum rubs at a stain on the carpet. 'We could maybe get you a rug. This carpet's looking pretty ropey with all Mira's art stains! I don't want Janu to think we live in a mess.' Mum sighs.

'He runs an orphanage for street children, Mum; I don't think he'll care how my room's decorated.'

Mum knocks against something with her foot, then feels for it under the bed.

Well, I suppose this is it. I'll have to tell her everything.

'What's this?' she asks, picking up the bottle of turquoise paint.

Maybe she hasn't seen the Banner Bag.

'Kez gave it to me . . . I like the colour!'

'If you like that . . .'

Mum scans down the blues and turquoises on her charts.

'You know, this deep turquoise was one of your Nana Josie's favourites too! Lots of her paintings are in this and gold. It might be too much for all the walls, but maybe one would work in this colour.'

Mum looks happy, as if me liking the colour turquoise is somehow progress.

The phone rings and we bump into each other in our race downstairs to pick up the phone. I get there first. It's Mira. Mum's doing that thing that Nana Kath does – and Mum says she hates – of telling me to ask questions at the same time as I'm talking.

'Mum wants me to tell you that Janu's coming next

Sunday. She needs to know which of the weekends you'll come home to see him. It's in half-term,' I tell her as Mum carries on talking in my ear.

I want to tell her about Nana's beautiful banner painting. But how can I do that without letting on that I've got the Protest Book too?

'She says she doesn't have half-terms, Mum.'

I tell Mira that I'll call her on my mobile later because even she can hear Mum talking right in my ear!

'You get annoyed with Nana Kath when she does that!' I say as I hand the phone over to her. But the truth is I feel so strange talking to Mira. Since Mrs Latif asked that question about lying, it seems like I haven't stopped. I really want to tell Mira the truth about everything that's been going on. It's hard to be close to someone when there's too many lies between you, and I hate feeling so far apart. But I just want to have a chance to take it all in before I own up to having the Protest Book. I think Bubbe understood that. I want to sit with Nana Josie's Protest Book for a bit, just me and her and all the things she cared about.

I sit on the carpet, take the Protest Book out of the Banner Bag and start to read about all the marches Nana Josie went on. There are pages of them! And it's not just marches – there are letters and campaigns and petitions too. There are even letters from prime ministers. Well, secretaries on behalf of prime ministers. Margaret Thatcher and Tony Blair mostly . . . There are quite a few from Glenda Jackson, who I thought was an actress but turns out she used to be an MP . . . she must have been a good one, I think, because she wrote all these letters back to Nana explaining things. Most of the official letters that the politicians and organizations sent back are quite boring really. Just standard ones like they'd send out to everyone. It's strange that they write in such good English – the kind of letters you're supposed to learn how to write. But even though they use the right words, most of these letters don't actually seem to say anything. I suppose they would just reply by email now. It would be much more interesting if there were copies of the letters that Nana Josie sent to them.

I read through page after page of newspaper clippings. I can't really take in all the information. I make a note of the campaigns so I can research the things that mean something to me, like Simon said I should. Soon I will have to give this back to Mira and she might be angry with me for not telling her about it and take it away with her.

- Women's March
- March on Lincoln Memorial - 1963 - Nana actually heard Martin Luther King's 'I Have a Dream' speech
- Anti-Apartheid movement (ANC - National Membership Card) - Meetings where Simon and Hope said they used to meet together
- 'Not in My Name' (Banner Nana used for lots of things)
- Greenham Common
- CND
- Animal Welfare
- Anti-Arms Trade
- Anti-Vivisection
- Free People of Tibet (Vigil outside Tibetan Embassy, London) - Photo of Nana and Simon sitting holding candles
- Naked Bike Ride for Climate Change (That photo!)
- Bhopal Medical Appeal (Simon's marathon fundraising runs)
- Iraq Anti-War March
- Refugees Welcome March (Simon's last one)

There are lots of other local campaigns too that I don't write down, but they're kind of sweet, like 'Save our local oak tree'! I like the picture of Nana and Simon and some other people linking arms together around the tree. I actually think I've walked past it on Hampstead Heath near the ponds – so that's proof their protest actually worked.

TWENTY-FOUR

I'm walking along the pavement thinking about the different protests Nana was part of. The oak-tree protest worked and so did some of the really big ones that people all over the world fought for, like the Anti-Apartheid movement and the Civil Rights marches. But lots of the other things Nana was campaigning against are still happening. Was it really worth them doing all that marching and protesting when it hasn't changed anything? I wonder if Bubbe and Nana *did* ever go on the same marches. I can't get the picture of Bubbe listening to the refugee boy on the radio out of my mind. Now she's told me her own story I can see why she gets so sad when she sees all those children . . .

Someone sprints up behind me and taps me on the shoulder.

'Sorry, didn't mean to shock you!' Pari's really out of breath. 'Thought I was going to be late. Had to catch the bus from the tube.' Something glints on the side of her head.

'Like the scarf jewels!' I say.

'Oh, thanks! Mrs Latif told me where to get them!' Pari says, turning her head so I can get a closer look at the little diamond flowers. 'She's not sure they're allowed in school, but I said if earrings are allowed then scarf rings should be . . . She said she thinks that's right and that she'd make the case for me if anyone tells me to take them off! We got lucky with our tutor group, didn't we?' Pari smiles at me.

I don't think she's only talking about Mrs Latif. 'We did!' I say.

We walk the rest of the way into school together, past the Unfriendship Bench.

'Where do you live?' I ask.

'Finsbury Park. It took ages to get here this morning, there were so many delays.'

'I went there not long ago. A friend of my nana's lives in a place called the Caring Community – do you know it?'

Pari shakes her head. 'It doesn't sound much like where I live.'

I'm not sure if she's being sarcastic. Pari has one of those faces that's quite hard to read unless she's actually smiling, laughing or in a state. She kind of keeps it in the same constant expression, like she's trying to control what she gives away and what she keeps to herself.

'You're so lucky to have a grandmother,' she says as

we walk into Mrs Latif's class and sit down next to each other.

It's too long to explain to her that the Nana I was talking about isn't alive . . . but it gets me thinking. Pari doesn't really know anyone in my family, so what harm would it do if I told her about going to see Simon and picking up the Protest Book?

'Do you have any grandparents?' I ask as we get our planners out.

She shakes her head.

'It's just my mum and me and—'

'Settle down now, class,' Mrs Latif says.

'I like her outfit!' Pari whispers.

Mrs Latif's wearing an embroidered tunic dress, leggings and golden pumps.

'Reading books out!' she orders, as she looks up and down at our desks and types the register into her computer. I think she's memorized all of our names.

I put my hand up.

'Sorry, I've forgotten my book.'

'I'll let you off this once, Laila, but you are expected to have it in school every day.'

She looks in her bag.

'Here – you can borrow this. I finished it on the bus on the way here. I nearly missed my stop! This young woman is a total inspiration.'

Mrs Latif puts *I am Malala* down on my desk. 'You haven't read it, have you?'

202

I shake my head.

'Right then. Half of you –' Mrs Latif reads a list off her screen – 'Carlos, Nita, Lara, Stella, Chirelle, Christopher, Lycette, Owen, Carmel, Rikesh, Pari, George, Nathan, Omar, Kelly, Milena . . . please take your books and make your way to the library for your reading assessment.'

Pari hangs back so she doesn't have to walk with Stella. She makes a worst-luck face that we're not together as she follows Milena out.

Mrs Latif taps me on the shoulder.

'Hello! Laila! Didn't you hear the bell?'

I look up to see the last person's on their way out of the classroom.

I'd completely forgotten I was even in school I'm so wrapped up in this book. I can't believe what I'm reading; how brave a girl my age can be. It seems impossible what she went through just to have the right to go to school. I want to go home to my perch right now, curl up and read the rest of the book. While I'm reading I keep thinking about the things in Nana Josie's Protest Book. Simon's voice and Bubbe's are floating around my head . . . Why are people's lives so different? Why can't there just be some things that all humans should have? I keep thinking about Bubbe and Stan when they were children, and that boy I heard on the radio at Bubbe's, Bubbe's frightened-little-girl eyes, and the expression in the eyes of the girl selling tissues on the tube . . . and Pari.

'That's how I felt when I read it,' Mrs Latif says. 'I couldn't put it down. Do you want to borrow it?'

'Can I? Yes, please, miss!'

'Please make sure you bring it back to me though. It's one for my children's shelf!'

'I didn't know you had children, Mrs Latif?'

'I haven't yet, Laila!' She laughs. 'But I hope to . . . If I do, and when she or he is old enough, I will definitely give them that book to read. Now, you'd better get on . . . you've already got one "late" registered – you don't want another!'

I meet up with Pari outside the library at morning break.

We go into the toilets together and Kez is there. We're side by side washing our hands.

'Everything all right?' she asks.

'Still grounded!'

Kez and me are at the dryers now but Pari's still at the sink washing her hands when Rebecca peers around the door. 'Coming, Kez?'

Kez looks a bit torn but she goes anyway. 'Yes . . . see you guys later!'

When Bubbe described what was going on between me and Kez it sounded so normal – so how come it feels like I'm being pulled in two all the time?

'Why are you grounded?' Pari asks.

'I went off without telling anyone.'

'Where to?'

'I took the tube to see my nana's friend in Finsbury Park.'

'So, what's the problem?'

'I didn't tell anyone I was going. Anyway, I'm not allowed on the tube on my own.'

'Why not? I take it every day.'

Being with Pari makes me think I'm that word that Simon used – *mollycoddled*. Why should I be grounded for doing what Pari has to do every day?

As we walk along the corridor through the break-time crowds, all the chatter sounds like thousands of pent-up stories ricocheting off the walls. If I tell her in the middle of this din, mine won't be heard by anyone else. Pari leans in close to hear me better. I tell her about Nana Josie and going to pick up her Protest Book and the Banner Bag with her beautiful painted banner in it . . .

'I went on a march once with my dad, when he lived with us,' Pari says.

'What sort of march?' I ask.

'I can't remember – I was really young. I just remember being carried on his shoulders and people singing a song about peace . . . "Give peace a chance"? Something like that.'

'Want to come back to mine sometime and see

205

Nana's Protest Book and her banner?' I ask.

Pari smiles at me like I've offered her something incredible.

'I'll ask my mum. She sometimes needs me to help her out. I'll have to see. Where do you live?' she asks.

'Just across the road from school.'

TWENTY-FIVE

I'm lying on Mira's bed reading the Malala book when Mira finally calls.

Mira: Hi, Laila! Sorry I missed your call. Everything all right at home?

Me: Yeah, I suppose. I'm grounded – did Mum tell you?

Mira: Ah yes, we had a first family phone conference about that! What made me laugh was Mum going on about your orange umbrella, as if that was evidence of something!

Me: Yeah, I don't know why she keeps going on about that. I only went for a walk, but she doesn't believe me.

Mira: Should she? Who did you walk with? There's no one you want to tell me about?

Me: No.

Mira: So, how are things with you and Kez now?

Me: Oh fine. She's got all her bat mitzvah stuff to

207

do. I haven't seen much of her. How's your
college? Have you finished the painting of
me? . . . What are you laughing at?

Mira: You never used to talk to me like this.

Me: Like what?

Mira: I don't know really.

Me: Is the painting you're doing of me a baby
painting? Let me guess . . . baby me on the day I
was born?

Mira: You'll have to wait and see! Tell me
something else.

Me: Pari – this girl in my tutor group's coming over
next Friday.

Mira: That's good. What's she like?

Me: Nice, I think! I don't really know her yet. I'd
better go actually – I've got loads of homework.

I hear this strangled sort of sound on the other end of
the line.

Me: Are you OK?

Mira: Please don't go, Laila. Mum says you're
redecorating my room turquoise.

Me: No! That's what she thinks . . . but I'm not.

Mira: You should move in, you know. It's sweet you
keeping it for me, but it's mad sleeping out on
the landing . . .

I can hear tears in Mira's voice. For the first time ever
I feel like she actually needs to talk to *me*.

> Me: What's it like in Glasgow?
>
> Mira: I love the city, people are really friendly, but
> the course is hard, though I'm learning loads . . . I
> just didn't expect to miss you all this much, and
> with Jidé being away too . . .
>
> Me: Is he doing all right?
>
> Mira: Yes. I managed to skype him the other day.
> He thinks he might go and work there when
> he's qualified. He says there's so much for him to
> do.
>
> Me: You would really miss him though.
>
> Mira: I would. I miss everyone.
>
> Me: Even Mum and Dad?!
>
> Mira: Even them!
>
> Me: Krish?
>
> Mira: He came to see me at the weekend, so I've
> had my fix of him! I miss *you*, Lai Lai.
>
> Me: Miss you too, Mimi. Why don't you come
> home when Janu comes? For a weekend?
>
> Mira: I can't, Laila.

Mira blows her nose really noisily.

> Mira: I think this is what homesick feels like!

Mira would never believe it if she could see me crying too. I'm glad I'm in her room with the door closed, because if Mum or Dad came upstairs now they would definitely try and talk things through and that's the last thing I need. Even though I'm at home all the time, I think *I* might be homesick too – for how it used to be.

Before I go to sleep I ring Nana's chime loads of times. The sound relaxed me before but it doesn't work this time, so I open the Malala book. How could anyone shoot a little girl just because she wanted to learn something?

Mum peeps around the door.

'It's so late, Laila! Get some sleep now.'

I lie on Mira's bed for a while and listen to Mum and Dad moving around in their loft bedroom. When they're quiet I sneak out to the landing. Even with the new cream, my arms are so itchy, but there's no way I'm wearing the gloves Mum's trying to make me wear at night to stop me scratching in my sleep.

I stare at Mira's painting of a woman in the mist walking with her dog by the sea. I like the way she's made everything look floaty like a dream.

'Laila! What on earth are you doing standing out here? It's the middle of the night! Laila, are you awake?' Mum takes me by the shoulders, leads me to Mira's room and stands over me till I get into the bed. I stay there but I can't sleep for the rest of the night.

'What was going on with you last night, Laila?' Dad asks as he hands me my tea at breakfast. 'I don't know if I can deal with another sleepwalker in this house. It was bad enough with Krish. If I'd known moving rooms would unsettle you so much I never would have dismantled your old high bed. You could have stayed put. We were going to let Mira decide how she wants to arrange that room, but just tell us if you need to move back in. We can always buy you a new bed . . . a low bed, if you want.'

I'm only half listening because I'm looking up a website about Malala.

Dad raises his voice. 'Laila, please don't ignore me . . .'

'I'm not moving back. Sorry, Dad. I don't know why, but I sleep better on the landing.' I manage to get the words out through my yawn.

'Seems like it!' Dad shakes his head.

TWENTY-SIX

Mr Rivera stands by the door of the music block as we
file in. He's wearing a spotty mustard-yellow waistcoat
today. Me and Pari have voted him and Mrs Latif the
best-dressed teachers in school.

We usually file into Mrs Latif's class in an orderly
queue, but I'd say the way we enter the music room is
more of a scrum. Mr Rivera is about the same age as
Mrs Latif but he only started teaching this year. I like
the teachers who didn't know Mira or Krish so I don't
have to have one of *those* conversations while they ask
me how they're getting on at college and what they're
doing now. I suppose it's nice that they care though.

'Settle down now, Seven Dials. Can you all sit at
the mini keyboards in pairs?'

Mr Rivera has to repeat the same instruction a few
times before everyone is finally seated. A few of us are
still squabbling over chairs.

'Oh, come on! How long does it take you to follow
a simple instruction? This is the thing: there are fifteen

keyboards and thirty-one people in this class. It doesn't take a mathematical genius . . . One group will have to work as a three.'

Stella's standing in the middle of the room on her own. She's pursing her lips together. They're a bit dry and cracked and her bottom lip's bleeding a bit.

'You want to sit with us?' Pari asks, so quietly that I'm amazed Stella even hears.

Stella pauses for a moment and then pulls up a chair, leaving a space between her and Pari.

'Did you complain to Mrs Latif about me?' Pari comes straight out with it.

Stella locks eyes with Pari and you can sense a bristling tension between them, as though they might have a fight or something. I feel like getting in between them both, like a referee. Pari turns to Stella and nods calmly.

'I told her I was sorry. I said I would say sorry.'

Pari looks Stella straight in the eye.

'For what?' Pari challenges.

'I don't know, saying stuff that upsets you about immigrants and stuff. I'm not the only one who says things . . .'

'And are you sorry?' Pari cuts in.

'I said so, didn't I?' Stella's picking at a thread on the crest of her blazer.

'That's not actually being sorry though, is it? You know that thing Mrs Latif asked about truth and lies?'

Stella nods. 'Well, I don't want you to say sorry if you're not,' Pari whispers, as Mr Rivera explains the lesson.

'That's a bit more peaceful . . . Now, I'm going off-piste here with you, Seven Dials, because I want to see what you can do as composers. I'd like everyone to think of a title. Here, I've thought up the kind of thing I'm after . . .' He looks behind him at the PowerPoint on the screen.

Misty Morning
Sunflowers
Wild River
Hurricane
Flood

People look a bit blank.

'Or perhaps something man-made.' He starts writing on the whiteboard.

Turbine Hall
Factory
Tube
Train
Bus

'I don't understand,' Carlos says.

Mr Rivera switches into Spanish with Carlos. I

can't believe how fast they talk.

After a few minutes Carlos looks happier. 'OK, I get it,' he says at last, switching back to English.

There's a general rumble of people starting up conversations and Mr Rivera has to shout over it. 'I, for instance, could compose something called "Seven Dials Music" that would blow most people away – a deafening postmodern discordant affair!'

Mr Rivera chats to someone for a few minutes and the volume in the room gets even louder. I swear some people only ask him questions to distract him.

'His class does my head in! Next time I'm bringing earplugs!' Stella says.

'Everyone clear about what they're doing now?' Mr Rivera shouts over the din. 'Title first, then you can start on the music and add vocals afterwards if you want . . . No more than three-minute compositions. Oh, yes, I forgot this bit. Keep the titles to yourselves. We're going to play a guessing game afterwards and see if we can match the list of titles to your compositions! You can add some percussion instruments if you want . . .'

Hardly anyone's listening to him now. It's only because he's standing right by us that we can hear. 'Zane, if you're going to use the bongos it has to be because it's integrated into your idea, not just to make a racket!'

Stella winces. I think she really has got a headache.

'Are you OK?' I ask her.

'This is why I like Mrs Latif's class. I hate noise! It stresses me out.'

I've never thought about it before, but what I'm realizing is that people aren't just one thing or another. I thought working together in a group with Stella would be a nightmare, with her mouthing off, but she's actually really quiet, just trying to listen most of the time.

'You come to school on the underground too, don't you?' Pari asks Stella.

She nods.

'Why don't we do something around the tube journey to Finsbury Park?' Pari suggests. 'At least we've all done that.'

'Do you come in on the tube too then?' Stella asks me.

'No – but I've done that route.'

We try a few things out to get the atmosphere of a tube journey. It's really hard.

'Some days it's funny if someone's clowning about, but mostly it's just boring!' Stella says. 'Everyone pretending they're in their own little world. We could start with a steady rhythm to set it up, maybe? I don't know . . .' She plays the same five low notes over and over.

'That's good, and then there's all this stuff going on underneath . . . people behaving one way, but

216

really thinking all sorts of other things,' Pari says.

'Yeah!' Stella nods.

'What sort of things?' I ask.

'You know, like –' Stella wags her finger:

> Don't get too close to me
> Don't cramp my space
> Don't get too close to me
> Don't get up in my face.

Pari laughs. 'That's good. I know what you mean. We could travel in together sometimes if you want.'

'Yeah, OK.' Stella looks a bit surprised, but a faint smile spreads across her face.

The school-counsellor man comes in and goes to talk to Mr Rivera. He looks at Stella but she's already getting up.

'I've got to go. I don't usually mind missing migraine . . . I mean music,' Stella jokes, 'but I was actually getting into that.' She nods towards the counsellor to say she's coming.

'Thanks, you two,' she says as she walks away.

'What for?' Pari asks

Stella shrugs. 'You know. Not shutting me out.'

'Why don't we carry on with it together later?' Pari asks.

Stella's face looks completely different when she smiles. I suppose everybody's face does, but Stella hardly ever smiles so you really notice it when she does.

'She's all right, isn't she?' Pari says after she's gone.

I nod. What I'm thinking is that Pari is much braver than me. I would never have asked Stella to sit next to us. I probably would have avoided her all through school. If Pari hadn't faced up to her we would never be working together on this or anything. Now it feels a bit wrong carrying on without her because she's the one who actually came up with most of the ideas so far. I'm sorry she had to go. I have to lean in quite close to the keyboard to hear Pari practising what we've done so far. She looks like she wants to tell me something, but she gives me this sideways glance, like she's trying to weigh up whether to trust me or not.

Pari leans in close. 'You know what Stella was saying about people hiding what they're really thinking? She's right. Sometimes I get this look from strangers like they're suspicious of me or just don't like me because I'm Muslim. Mum thinks I should stop wearing my headscarf and she doesn't like these –' she points to her sparkly scarf jewels – 'She says I shouldn't draw attention to myself.'

'That's not right! Why don't you tell Mrs Latif?'

'What can she do about what goes on out there? She can't have a word with strangers like she did with Stella. People outside of school don't have to say sorry, do they? Anyway, it's just a feeling. No one

218

actually *says* anything. But Mum thinks everything's getting much worse for us here now. No one trusts anyone else.'

'I'm sorry!'

'It's not your fault.'

We practise what we've done of the music so far. Pari thinks Stella's right; it's too even and steady. We really need to ramp up the tension.

I'm playing some chords, trying to work out what exactly the feeling was underneath the surface on that tube journey when the family got on to sell tissues. I go right to the top of the keyboard and play high chords, quietly at first, then faster and getting louder . . .

'That's more like the feeling!' Pari says, tapping at her chest like it's got her heart beating faster. 'Then we should go back to something flatter for the end but keep some of that in too, so you can still hear it. Like once you've tuned into it, it's just there all the time? I don't know . . . that's how it feels.'

I think I know what she means. It's a bit like Nana's chime, which you can hear ringing through you even though the actual note finished ages ago.

'Packing-up time!' Mr Rivera shouts, and people start to get up from their desks. He stands by the door, blocking the exit so people can't leave before he's finished telling us about our homework.

'. . . So get together and carry on working on this. I

realize this is quite an advanced task for Year Seven, but it's a good challenge, and I have every faith in you. This is your assessment project, so you have five lessons to perfect it. Does everyone know which days the music studio's open? If you don't, familiarize yourself with the practice times; they're –' Mr Rivera opens the door and shouts after us as we flood out – 'on the noticeboards to your right!'

TWENTY-SEVEN

'I know I'm grounded, but can I have a friend back next Friday? Pari's asked her mum and she says it's fine.'

Mum and Dad do one of their totally obvious non-verbal conferring looks over the dinner table.

After thinking about it for what seems like ages, Mum nods.

'As long as you're at home, I suppose it's OK . . . a new friend, is it?' Dad asks.

'Yes.'

'That's good!' Mum beams.

I wonder if they thought I was incapable of making new friends.

'How's Kez getting on with all her bat mitzvah preparations?' Mum asks.

I wish they would stop asking me about Kez all the time. It just makes me feel guilty and confused about everything all over again. We don't even text much any more.

'Fine.'

'Oh, she's doing all that, is she?' Dad asks.

'Why do you say it like that, Dad?'

'No reason . . . just didn't know Luke and Hannah were practising, that's all!' Dad shrugs.

'Practising what?' I ask.

'I just meant I didn't think they were religious.' Dad shrugs and picks up his phone.

'You don't have to be *really* religious to have a bat mitzvah. It can be like cultural too . . . being part of what other people do in your community. Kez says it's like a way of saying you're not a kid any more.'

Dad's tapping out a text message.

'Like a way of saying you're not a kid any more!' I repeat a bit louder.

'Sam!' Mum glares at Dad because she hates people being on mobiles at the table. Dad looks from Mum to me, as if he's trying to catch up with what's going on.

'Ah well, good for Kez, if that's what she wants.'

'Maybe *I'll* have a bat mitzvah,' I say.

'You can't! Not unless your mum's willing to convert!' Dad jokes.

'From what to what?' Mum laughs, batting Dad over the head with a tea towel. Dad grabs Mum around the waist. They're actually having a sort of play fight! Gross!

I leave them to it and go up to my perch and listen

to them messing around. Some families would be pleased if their child said they wanted to get religious.

I wedge the chair against the door, pull the Banner Bag towards me, get out Nana's painted banner and unroll it over Mira's carpet just so I can see it again. I wish I could put it on my wall, but then I would have some explaining to do. Mum and Dad might even think Nana's banner should be for Mira. The Protest Book yes, but this banner . . . I know Simon really meant me to have it.

I open Dad's laptop and type in 'Tibetan vigil'. I look through a few articles and find a photo of Simon and Hope standing outside the Chinese Embassy. Hope's so beautiful and tall. She isn't stooped forward in this picture. I flit around a bit, typing in the campaigns that Nana Josie and Simon were a part of, but then decide I should go through the list one thing at a time, because once you start reading about this stuff it gets really complicated. It's like Mrs Latif says . . . even if you start out by thinking this or that is right or wrong, and you know what side you're on, the more you read about it, the harder it gets to be certain. Though I think there are some things that just are right or wrong, whichever way you look at them. Like not letting a girl be educated, and shooting her just because she stands up for herself. That's wrong whatever way you look at it.

The last words written in Nana Josie's Protest Book

look like they were written after everything else. They're in pencil . . . like she just thought of something and wrote this . . . and the writing is really shaky.

I'll never forget my first march or painting my first banner.

I google marches in London. . . there's another one tomorrow. It's a Women's March. I feel like I've been going around with my eyes closed. I didn't know about any of this . . . It says here that the last one was for people all over the world marching for Women's Rights. I flit around from site to site, looking up different protests.

I find a clip of Martin Luther King's speech. It's so strange to think that Nana was standing in Washington listening to him when he gave it. What he says and the way he says it make you wonder how anyone could ever be racist again. His dream did come true, but maybe that's the point of all the things Nana and Simon did. I think it's what Malala's saying too. People have to keep dreaming, otherwise they forget. I don't care if I'm grounded. I've got to find a way of going on that march tomorrow. I look down at Nana's beautiful banner. I'm going on that march with my nana!

I tie some bamboo sticks to the ends of the sheet and secure them with the little elastic ties at the top.

It's too big for one person to hold, but I'm taking it anyway.

I unwedge the chair when I hear Mum and Dad come up to say goodnight.

'Night, Laila!'

'Night!'

'At least she's *starting* to spend a bit of time in her new room now,' I hear Mum say as they walk up the stairs.

I tuck Dad's laptop under my perch in case I want to look up anything else and settle down with the Malala book. I think I'll finish it tonight. I've never read half a book in a night before. Mira's always been the one that reads for hours. She said it would happen to me one day too, but I never believed her.

I don't know what time I actually fell asleep, but it must have been around 4 a.m., because the last thing I remember is hearing a bird singing. I thought it was weird that it was singing through the dark . . . but maybe it was almost morning when I wrote this in my reading record:

> **Themes:** A girl can change an unfair world. Adults should listen to children. Adults should protect children. All children should have access to education. Children can see what bad things adults do. Children can change the world.

Comments: This is the best book I have ever read. One day I would like to meet Malala Yousafzai.

My favourite quotes: 'One child, one teacher, one book, one pen can change the world.'
'When the whole world is silent, even one voice becomes powerful.'

TWENTY-EIGHT

'Massive march in town today,' Dad says, turning up the radio. 'Traffic will be terrible. I'd better set off now! I need to get that garden wall sorted before it falls on someone!' He ruffles my hair as he grabs his keys.

'We haven't got much in food-wise for tonight,' Mum says.

'I'll get something for dinner on the way home . . . should be back by seven at the latest! See you later!'

'I'm afraid I'm going to have to go into work today, Laila . . . to set up my new office. You want to come and help me?' Mum asks.

'I'm grounded!' I remind her as I tuck into a piece of toast to stop myself from smiling.

'Yes, but you could come with me if you want.'

'It's OK!' I say. 'I've got loads of homework to do.'

Mum smiles at me, like she thinks I'm getting back on track. Now she's listening to the radio – someone's talking about the Women's March.

'Families, men, women and children are all welcome, as on previous marches. We are taking to the streets to remind the powers that be that we march for the protection of our rights, our safety, our health and our families. We recognize our vibrant and diverse communities are the strength of our country . . .'

'If there's another march, let's go together,' Mum says, tutting at herself. 'If I wasn't working . . .'

'OK!' I say taking a sip of tea and trying not to sound too interested. 'What time will you be back?' I ask.

'Fiveish! If you get bored, you know where I am. Give me a call and you can come over and help.'

I watch Mum cross the road and then I race up the stairs. I take Nana's painted banner from under the bed and roll it up into a scroll as small as it will go. I get two black bin bags and cover it up. Dark clouds fill the sky so I grab hold of Hope's umbrella too. I've planned how to get to the start, but I don't even have to follow my own instructions because as soon as I walk out of the door I see groups of people heading for the tube: whole families, people pushing prams, groups of women and girls, some boys too. There's a man carrying a newborn baby in a sling, walking arm in arm with the mother. The baby's so tiny you can only see its little yellow hat. The pavement's pretty crowded so it's easy to duck behind some people as I walk past Kez's flat. Bubbe's in the window watching people pass. She's put a sign up:

TOO OLD TO MARCH.
NOT TOO OLD TO PROTEST!

She's waving at people as they pass, and some of them wave back. I really miss Bubbe now Kez and me don't see so much of each other.

I have to wait for two tubes to pass before I can squeeze on. But no one seems to mind that much. Maybe because most people are here for the same reason, travelling in the same direction. Some have banners sticking out of their bags, and the weird thing is that total strangers are actually talking to each other, laughing and joking. A girl with purple-dyed dreadlocks holding a guitar starts singing a folky song. She has a crackly sort of voice . . . it's not that good. I wonder if the boy who showed me the way to 'the Caring Community' sings as well as plays the guitar. This girl sounds like she cares about the words she's singing. I think she might have written this song herself . . . because the chorus is something about:

'*I can have purple hair, why should you care!*'

At the end of the song, a few people clap. A lot of us change at Finsbury Park. I can't believe that this is the same underground journey I took to see Simon. I have never felt less on my own than right now. I wish Simon could see me. I wonder if Hope will be on the march today.

It's not raining when we come out of the tube, but it is windy. Everyone's gathering in Victoria Park. There are some speakers – a politician I sort of recognize – but I don't really listen because the voices are a bit distorted through the speakers. I just take in the atmosphere and all the banners with different slogans written on them. Standard ones printed by organizations, some written by hand, some that make me laugh and others with quotes and lines from poems.

'UNTIL THEY BECOME CONSCIOUS THEY WILL NEVER REBEL, AND UNTIL THEY HAVE REBELLED THEY CANNOT BECOME CONSCIOUS' #1984

MEN OF QUALITY DON'T FEAR EQUALITY

'IF THE SOUL OF THE NATION IS TO BE SAVED, YOU MUST BECOME ITS SOUL' – CORETTA SCOTT KING

SPEAK OF ME WITH LOVE NOT HATE

HERE FOR MY TRANS SISTERS

OUR RIGHTS AREN'T UP FOR GRABS AND NEITHER ARE WE

I AM WOMAN – WATCH ME FLY

KNOCK DOWN WALLS OF HATE AND LIES

MY BODY IS MY BORDER. HANDS OFF.

REFUGEE CHILDREN ARE MY CHILDREN

MOTHER NATURE WEEPS

GIRLS JUST WANT TO HAVE FUN-DAMENTAL HUMAN RIGHTS

NOW YOU'VE PISSED OFF GRANDMA!

I laugh out loud at that one, and the old black woman carrying it, surrounded by lots of young people who are holding a banner together that says:

AND TAKE IT FROM US – YOU DON'T WANT TO PISS OUR GRANDMA OFF!

I hold Nana's banner under my arm. I suppose in a way I'm marching with my nana too.

People start to move out on to the road and raise their placards in the air.

A girl about my age is walking ahead of me carrying these words:

I'M A MUSLIM WOMAN.
I AM THIRTEEN YEARS OLD.
MALALA WAS TWELVE WHEN SHE
CHANGED THE WORLD.
HOW OLD WILL YOU BE?

I would like to catch up with her, but I'm struggling a bit to unroll Nana's banner. As I do, I drop Hope's umbrella and it's hard to pick it up because everyone's moving slowly forward. I get caught up in all these marching feet and nearly trip over. Then this woman pushing a pram grabs it for me before it gets trodden into the ground.

'Thanks!' I say.

As she hands it to me the sky brightens and a glimpse of sunlight shoots through the clouds. I think of Simon sitting in his conservatory sunning himself.

'What have you got there?' the woman asks, as I try to unroll Nana's banner. 'Here, let me help you!'

She whistles when she sees it.

'That's a beauty!'

The little girl in the pram starts squealing when she sees it and strains to get free from the straps keeping her in.

'You want to help hold your first banner, Fliss! Why don't you put your umbrella in the pram? Doesn't look like you'll be needing it,' she says, looking up at the sky, shrugging off her own raincoat and tucking it into the back of the pram. 'I'm Jackie . . . this is Fliss. Why don't we help each other out? How about I have Fliss on my shoulders and we can carry one side and you take the other!' She lifts Fliss on to her shoulders and she grabs the bamboo pole. When her mum tries to hold it with her, the little girl squeals again.

'All right, all right!' Her mum laughs.

Proper little protestor! Nana's words about me float through my mind.

'Thanks!' I laugh at Fliss, who is already wrestling her mum's hands off the pole. 'I'm Laila.'

'How long did it take you to paint this?' Jackie asks.

'My nana painted it for her first march.'

Someone nearby has started up a chant, so Jackie has to lean in to me so that I can hear her. The banner folds, making a little enclosed tent around us.

'Where's your nana now?' she asks gently.

'She died. I didn't really know her but she left me this!'

Jackie holds the banner higher and shouts over the chanting, 'Her spirit's not dead then, is it?'

Someone's brought a tabla and starts up a drum beat that makes me think of Priya's music. I take in all the colours of the crowd, and we just march along for a while laughing at Fliss because she looks so happy high up there holding our wonky banner . . .

'Queen of the castle!' Jackie laughs.

The chanting comes in waves. It lulls, and then builds again, surging over the crowd. Now, as we turn a big bend in the road, it settles down, and there's just a few whistles going off here and there . . . . A few people take photos of Nana's banner.

'Is this *your* first march then?' Jackie asks.

I nod.

'Fliss's too!' she says, looking up at her little girl holding tight on to the old bamboo sticks of Nana Josie's banner.

'Sorry I was so long! It took forever to sort everything out,' Mum says as she walks in the door and looks up at me snuggling on my perch like I've been there all day long! I can't stop grinning to myself. What I love most about the march is that nobody here knows I was there. I ring the chime . . . except for maybe somewhere out there . . . Nana Josie.

TWENTY-NINE

The week since the march has gone so fast. In lessons I've been replaying things in my mind, trying to make sense of how I came to be on that march. What made me go? I thought I would tell Pari about it, but somehow the time never feels right. I like the feeling of having all these thoughts, sounds and pictures whirring through my mind that just belong to me and all those strangers. It makes me feel like I'm part of something much bigger than me, like Bubbe said Kez doing her bat mitzvah makes her feel. Every time I think of myself on the Women's March holding up Nana Josie's banner with Jackie and Fliss, I feel a bit stronger.

I can't even explain to myself the feeling it's left me with . . . like something's building inside me.

'Laila, have you seen my laptop?' Dad calls up the stairs.

'Sorry! I borrowed it last night,' I say, bringing it down to him.

'Then it's no wonder you couldn't sleep. You know the rules about screens after eight o'clock.'

I ignore him and open the fridge door to find a half-mangled chicken sitting on a plate. I want to heave.

'What should I make you and your friend to eat tonight? What's her name again? Are you still veggie?' Mum asks.

'Her name's Pari. Why wouldn't I be? Are *you* still vegetarian?' I point to the slogan on the fridge door. 'And Pari's vegetarian too.'

'Ah . . . that explains it!' Dad chips in.

'What? I do have a mind of my own, you know, Dad!'

'Yep, receiving loud and clear! I seem to remember Krish going vegetarian except for bacon sandwiches and chicken . . .'

'Well, Mira's a proper vegetarian, and she's stuck to it,' I argue.

'That's true,' Dad admits. 'I blame you, Uma, for indoctrinating the girls!'

Mum pulls a face at Dad.

'It's got nothing to do with Mum!' I scowl.

I actually really do miss bacon and chicken, but there's no way I'm going to tell Mum or Dad that. It's so annoying that they think I can't make up my mind to do something and then stick to it.

Mum starts chopping onions and garlic. She's been

doing this nearly every morning since she started work. She's got this new pot that she plugs in at breakfast time and it cooks slowly all day. She loves it because she's discovered a way of cooking that doesn't set the fire alarm off! I like it too, because when I come in from school really hungry, the smell hits you as you walk in, and even if no one's in, it smells like home – especially now it's getting dark and cold. Mum's not really the best cook in the world, but the things she makes in this slow cooker are always delicious. But right now, the smell of dinner cooking is putting me off eating anything. It's like setting the day off in the wrong order. Garlic and onions for breakfast. Puke!

'You and Pari can help yourselves when you come in. I'll be back after my meeting. Vegetable casserole tonight, and you can warm some pitta breads, grate a bit of cheese if you want. There's some yogurts for afters. Will that be OK?'

'Can't we just have pizza or something easy? She might not like casserole.'

Mum ignores me and carries on chopping.

Dad turns on the laptop, shakes his head and taps the recorded time that I turned the computer off. I wish he wasn't so on top of all this stuff. I know he's always checking my browsing history.

'2.56 a.m!'

I can't believe it! I only started reading after that.

No wonder I feel so tired. I can't have slept for more than two hours.

'Nearly 3 a.m! No wonder you're so bad-tempered, Laila. Take a look at this, Uma . . .' Dad presses a link to the video I was watching last night about Simon's last march against climate change.

'How are you going to get to sleep with all that whirring through your brain? You can't function like this, Laila. And being on a screen watching *anything* before you go to bed is not going to help. From now on you're not allowed the laptop in your room at all.'

'My eczema's keeping me awake,' I say.

Mum turns my arms over. They're all red. In the bit of time I did sleep I must have been scratching away.

'Why aren't you wearing those gloves I gave you? We'll have to go to the doctor.'

Mum switches off the clip of the march and leans in to whisper in Dad's ear. Maybe I *have* got supersonic hearing like Krish always says, because I can hear every word she says.

'We've been here before, Sam.'

Mum sits down next to me at the table. There's no escaping now.

'Where did you say your friend was from?'

'What's that got to do with anything? Her mum's from Iraq, I think.'

Dad taps the top of the computer. 'And what about her dad?' he asks.

'How would I know? I'm not bringing Pari back if you're going to get all up in her face.'

'We're looking forward to meeting her,' Mum says, placing what I think is supposed to be a calming hand on my shoulder.

I just wish they wouldn't ask me so many questions.

'I'll be back by five. Help yourself to the casserole. Now try to eat some toast, Laila.'

'Not hungry!' I get up from the table and stomp up the stairs.

'Get up in her face?! Oh hell. Second's out; round three . . . !' I hear Dad say.

I wait on the top step to see if there's anything else . . .

'She's reminding me of Mum more and more every day . . . and it's not just a passing resemblance.'

I turn and look at the black-and-white photo of Nana Josie smiling out at me.

'Ever since she found that chime!'

'Don't let her hear you saying that, Uma! She'll never sleep!'

THIRTY

'Come on, team!' Miss Green shouts. 'Put a bit of effort in!'

My legs won't work today. They're all achy and heavy and I feel a bit like I could fall over. Pari wins the trials easily.

'Great run, Pari,' Miss Green shouts.

I wanted it to be me and Pari up front, just like last time, so we could go through to the finals together.

'What happened, Laila? You OK?' Miss Green asks.

'I didn't sleep much last night,' I explain.

'Well, we all have off days,' she says, and carries on with the others back to the changing rooms.

When Pari gets her breath back she comes and sits next to me on the bench. She's brought a special bag and folded all her uniform up in it so there's no chance of it getting trampled again. She doesn't say anything but keeps looking at me and checking to see if I'm OK.

At the end of afternoon registration Mrs Latif calls me over to her desk.

'Laila, I've had a few reports from teachers today about how tired you look and Miss Green told me that you weren't on form in PE. Are you unwell? Is something bothering you?' Mrs Latif looks down at my arm and I suddenly realize I'm scratching again.

I shake my head.

A spot of blood in the crook of my arm seeps through the white cotton of my shirt.

'What's that?' Miss Latif asks.

'Oh, it's just eczema . . .'

'Can I see?'

I unbutton my cuff and show her my arm. A crack's opened up in the skin and it's bleeding and weeping.

'Ooooh, that is nasty. Do your parents know about this?'

'Yes, but it's got worse. I forgot to wear my gloves last night. Mum's making me an appointment at the doctor's.'

'Is this the reason you couldn't sleep?' she asks, letting go of my arm.

I nod.

'Well, if there's anything worrying you at school just let me know. Make sure you have a restful weekend at home.'

'What did she want?' Pari asks when I get back to our desk.

'Thinks I look tired!'

'You do!' Pari says. 'Sure you're still feeling up to me coming over to yours later?'

'Yeah!' I say.

'I need to use the computer first though. I've got to get that history homework done. Can you give me your address and I'll come over as soon as I've finished.'

'You can do the homework at mine,' I suggest.

'Sure?' she asks, like doing her homework is more important than coming to mine.

'Sure!'

But I do think it's a bit weird because there is no way I would *ever* normally do my homework on a Friday night. Afterwards, in the middle of Maths, I start to wish I *had* told Pari to come over later, because now I've got this nagging worry about us bumping into Kez on the way out of school – which is stupid because we've said we're going to be honest with each other. I don't even know why I keep feeling like this – why *shouldn't* I have Pari back to mine? Kez knows so many people I don't, but still. If she sees me going home with Pari I know I'll feel terrible, like I'm replacing her or something.

I walk out of the school gates with Pari, silently chanting as I pass the Unfriendship Bench . . . 'Please don't let us bump into Kez. Please don't let us . . .' If I'm looking for her I never see her.

'Hi, Laila! How's it going?' Kez comes up parallel to me and touches my arm.

I jump. 'Fine!'

'Hi, Pari.' Kez smiles at her. 'Going to the tube? I'm off that way! We can go together if you want?'

'Thanks, but I'm going back to Laila's.' Pari's voice sounds a bit weak, like she gets it too that this feels awkward.

I can hardly meet Kez's eyes.

'That's great!' Kez's voice is a bit too shrill for me to believe her. 'OK then. I've got to go now anyway . . . Have fun!'

There's the tiniest pause before Kez turns and heads for home, and in that pause I know that seeing me and Pari together has made her feel all mixed up too.

'Sure you still want me to come back?' Pari asks as we cross the road. I've been so busy thinking about Kez that I realize I haven't said a word to Pari.

'Course!' I feel around in the bottom of my bag for my keys and we head up the path.

Pari runs her fingers over the stained-glass windows, following the patterns on our front door.

'Is this safe? Couldn't someone break it?'

'Why would anyone want to do that?' I ask.

'No reason!' Pari shrugs.

I look at her and then back at our door for a moment before I open it, and I suddenly wish I hadn't asked her round. This is nothing like when Kez used to come back and we could easily guess everything that was on each other's mind.

It's too late now though.

'Dump your things over there,' I say, pointing to the pile of shoes and bags spilling out of a rack stacked to bursting under the stairs.

Pari places her backpack and coat neatly in the corner and goes to take off her shoes.

'No need . . . unless you want to!'

She carries on unlacing her shoes, then squeezes them into a gap on the shoe rack.

'How many flats . . . ?' Pari looks up the staircase to the skylight in the hallway that leads to Mum and Dad's room in the loft. 'I mean, how many people live here?'

I never ever used to feel embarrassed when Kez came over . . . well, only about the mess, but having Pari here's making me look at everything in our house as if I'm seeing it for the first time. At a guess I would say there are about forty pairs of shoes, trainers, boots, slippers and wellies under the stairs. Some are Mira's and Krish's old ones, some are Mum's and Dad's – there's even a pair of Grandad Bimal's shiny black work shoes that Mum keeps because she likes to see them every time she comes in.

'Five of us . . . usually – but my brother and sister are away at college.'

'I know where to come if I need shoes!' Pari jokes.

I open the door into the kitchen and am hit by the smell of Mum's casserole.

As Pari stands up, her stomach makes a growling noise.

'Where did that come from?' She laughs. 'Sorry but something smells really good in here.'

'I told Mum we could have a pizza, but she wanted to cook for you.'

We go through to the kitchen and I take the lid off the slow cooker. Steam sweats my face.

'I'm always having pizza. This smells great!'

'Mum leaves the food ready because she's sometimes not back till later,' I explain.

'Does she do night shifts then? My mum used to work those,' Pari says.

'No, I mean she'll be back in about an hour,' I say.

Pari is scanning our kitchen, peering around the shelves and through the doorway. I can see from her expression that our house, with its mess, grubby walls, and its fraying old carpet is more like a palace in her eyes.

'You should see Kez's place!' I say. 'It's really . . . modern. They've made it so Kez can get around anywhere in it.'

'That's good,' Pari says.

I get the feeling she's only half-listening.

Every single thing that comes out of my mouth sounds wrong. It was better when we were at school. We're more the same at school.

'*This fridge is the scene of animal torture . . .*' Pari reads out my fridge-magnet sign. 'Who wrote that?'

'I did!'

I tell her about becoming a vegetarian because of reading how animals are slaughtered in Nana Josie's Protest Book, and how no one needs to eat meat because it's really expensive to produce and it's a waste of the world's resources. 'I didn't realize cows cause so much pollution with their wind,' I say, pointing to my backside.

Pari laughs and her stomach starts rumbling again.

'We can eat now if you want.'

'I think I better had.'

So I take two bowls out of the cupboard and ladle some of the vegetables in.

I grab cheese, a grater and some bread and carry them through to the table.

'I'll just wash my hands,' Pari says, and picks up the soap by the sink.

I grate some cheese into both bowls.

After what seems like ages Pari comes to the table. She picks up her spoon and eats mouthful after mouthful of casserole without saying a word. Occasionally she looks up and smiles, but then carries on eating until her bowl is completely empty.

'Your mum's a good cook!' she says, leaning back in her chair.

'Tell her that! She'll be your friend forever!'

We clear up the dishes and Pari points to the magnets on the fridge again.

'You know, you shouldn't make those sorts of jokes.'

'I wasn't joking,' I tell her. 'I'll show you the pictures of what they do to animals. It's disgusting how they're treated, crammed into trucks so they can hardly breathe . . . it *is* torture.'

Pari nods, but she's got this expression in her eyes that's half annoyed with me. 'We don't eat meat either, but it's disgusting how *people* are treated too.'

'I'm not saying it isn't . . .' My voice trails off.

I don't really know what to say to Pari. It felt like we were getting closer at school, but now she's come home we seem further apart.

'Should we do our homework then? Get it out of the way?' she asks.

'I'll go and get Dad's laptop. You can use that computer over there if you want,' I tell her.

She walks over to the table and sits down.

Why study history? is the theme of our homework.

'If the history teacher doesn't know why we should learn about history, I don't see how *we're* supposed to!' Pari laughs.

I think she's trying to lighten the mood.

We've been told to answer the question by drawing a mind map. You have to write loads of words and pictures in thought bubbles on a page like a brainstorm, and then, when we get back to class, we have to talk about it.

We look through the websites it tells us to visit to help us make our mind map. Then after that we have to come up with a symbol that means something to us about history.

I can't think of one, but I make a list of reasons I think we should study history, while Pari writes on the computer.

Mine's just a summary of what I've read on the websites. It's pretty boring. I don't think I've got more than I would have come up with if I hadn't looked anything up.

To learn lessons from the past

To learn about ordinary people and great leaders

To learn how old and modern problems have happened

To learn lessons from history

To learn why people behaved the way they did in different times

To learn about our ancestors.

Then we have to write about moments in history we've heard about that have affected our own family. I write:

> Holocaust
> Indian Independence
> World War One
> World War Two
> Women's March

I want to write something about reading Malala's book because that has really affected me, but I don't think that's the sort of thing you're supposed to put.

I'm sure there are loads of others, but I can't really think of anything big to write about after that. But then I get to wondering how long something has to be in the past to be history. Is it yesterday . . . or does it have to be properly in the past? Nana Josie's my family, and even if the stuff she wrote about in her Protest Book is not that old, it's still history.

Pari's eyeing the art materials Mum's tidied away into pots by the computer table.

'Mind if I use some of these?' she asks.

She sits down next to me at the table and starts doodling with them.

'What's yours going to be?' she asks me.

'A banner.' I think about telling Pari about the Women's March, but I'm not sure I know her well enough yet. She might think I'm a bit strange, just going off like that on my own.

'Good idea,' Pari says – but I get the feeling she's so enjoying trying out the coloured Sharpies and watercolour pencils that she's just being polite to keep the conversation going so she can use them for a bit longer. 'What's it going to say, your banner?'

'I haven't decided yet. Want me to print out your worksheet?'

'Thanks!'

She takes her time to write her name in an italic Sharpie pen at the bottom of the page, doing big swirly Ps.

Pari Pashaei

Without looking up at me she says, 'Sorry if I'm not being much fun. I don't have a computer – or any of these colours – at home, you see.'

'I don't mind! My parents are going to love you! I'll be the first person in this family ever to do their homework on a Friday night! It'll be like a Levenson Revolution!'

Pari laughs.

I type my name on my work, press PRINT and watch it inching out of the printer. Page one falls to the floor and page two starts to emerge.

'You've done loads more than me!'

'Mostly stuff from my nana's Protest Book. I'll show you when we go upstairs.'

'Does she live here then?' Pari asks.

'Oh, no, she died a long time ago.'

Pari gives me this strange look.

'Right! So, it's not really your stuff then?'

'It's my family stuff . . . mostly.'

Pari looks a bit doubtful.

'Do you think I've done it wrong?' I ask her.

She holds out her homework to me.

'I don't know. This is what *I* put.'

I read through Pari's list. It does seem different to mine. More personal.

> Stop war
> Stop religious hatred
> Stop torture
> Make people understand each
>   other better
> Iran/Iraq war
> 9/11
> Terrorist attacks anywhere,
>   everywhere
> Refugee status
> Syria

I feel a bit stupid. Like my list is homework and her's is actually her life. I get that if you're involved in things it feels different. I have a picture of myself holding Nana's banner, walking with Jackie and little Fliss. I don't think I'll ever forget my first march, just like Nana said she always remembered hers. Maybe that's the difference between mine and Pari's lists. *Everything* she's written seems to be more personal.

'Can I use these before we go up? Do you mind?' Pari asks, opening the box of charcoals I got last Christmas from Mira. 'The other colours aren't right for what I want to do,' she explains.

She draws a man's face on one side of the page and then folds the paper over so it prints an identical fainter version on the other side. She completely smudges out that side so it's like a shadow of a person. You can *just* work out that it was once a face.

'What's that?' I ask.

'It's what happens when half of who you are gets wiped out,' she says, without looking up.

I want to ask her more, but she looks at me and folds the paper over to cover up the face of the shadow man. Now she's doing that little smile that's not really a smile at all. It says, 'Don't ask. I can't say.'

'Can I see your room?' she asks.

As we walk up the stairs Pari pauses to look at all the photos on the landing.

'What's this room?'

'The landing.'

Pari looks blankly back at me.

'It's a passing-through place,' I explain.

'But there's a seat . . . like it's a waiting room.'

Maybe Pari's right. It is a kind of waiting room. The problem is I'm not sure what it is I'm waiting for.

'That was my old room –' I point to the door ahead – 'and this is my sister Mira's room,' I say, opening the door. 'It's supposed to be mine but I haven't moved in properly yet.'

'I would love to have a sister,' she says, walking over to the window and looking out at the garden below. She scans all the empty ghost frames around the room. 'Is this whole bedroom going to be for you? You won't share it with anyone?' she asks.

I don't think I've ever felt this uncomfortable before. I shake my head, rummage under the bed and pull the Protest Book out of the Banner Bag . . . I think about showing her Nana's banner, but I'm not sure about anything now she's here, so I fiddle around trying to close one of the catches while I try to work out why this tension seems to be growing between us, not getting less.

'This is the book I was telling you about.'

I carry it out to the landing and we sit down on the sofa and look through it together.

'I see why you wrote so much for homework now!' she says, carefully turning the pages till she gets to the end. She pauses for a long time on the final page. It's

Nana and Simon's last march that they went on together, where they're holding a banner that says:

NO BOMBING IRAQ
NOT IN OUR NAMES

'That was the last protest my nana went on before she died,' I explain.

Pari stares into the picture. Nana Josie hardly looks strong enough to hold up the banner.

'Was she ill?' Pari asks.

'She was dying, but she was determined to go on that march.'

'She must have really understood,' Pari says, passing the Protest Book back to me.

When I watch the news it never feels like the world is all connected up like this. Nana Josie and Simon marched against a war that was happening to Pari's family.

I take the chime out of the cushion cover and hand it to Pari.

'My nana gave me this before she died. It was hers when she was a baby,' I tell her.

She rings the chime and puts her head on one side to listen. 'It sounds like someone crying,' she says.

I feel a bit shivery and light-headed. It's Mira and Mum who have all these spooky ideas about stuff, not me . . . but I suppose that is what I've been feeling and not put into words. Sometimes it *does* feel like the chime is Nana Josie's voice, crying, laughing, calling to me, spurring me on . . .

Pari hands it back to me. 'You're so lucky to have all this,' she says, gesturing around the landing.

She stands on her tiptoes to look at the books on the high shelves.

'I didn't know people had this many books in their houses. This is more like a library!' Pari says, looking closer at some of the leather books in the cabinet.

'My dad loves books, especially old ones with illustrations in . . . and maps,' I explain as she looks at the enormous old atlases.

'You want to take some of those ones?' I ask her, looking at the pile of Mira's old books I've stacked up on the landing. 'I was going to give them to charity.'

Pari's face turns all stony. It's not hard to read what she's thinking now. I would do anything not to have said that. I wish I could grab it out of the air and stuff it back inside my stupid mouth.

Pari jumps up.

'I've got to go now.'

She's already halfway down the stairs when I see Mum's shadow through the glass.

'Hi, girls!' she calls as she opens the door.

'Hi, Mum! Pari's going now,' I say.

'Oh! That's a shame. So early?'

'I've got to take the tube back to Finsbury Park,

Mrs Levenson. But thank you for the food – it was delicious.'

'It's nearly dark! If you can wait a few minutes, I can give you a lift,' Mum offers.

But Pari's already heading down the steps. She doesn't even turn back and wave.

THIRTY-ONE

'She seems like a lovely girl, very polite! Good job I didn't make pizza then!' Mum says, lifting the lid of the cooking pan. 'You two made a good dent in this!' She takes a spoonful. 'Not bad, is it?'

I know Mum's only fishing for a conversation. I don't reply, so she casts again.

'What did she think of your room?'

'How would I know?' I can hardly speak with embarrassment as I replay Pari's visit over and over. I've got this pain behind my eyes. I wish I'd never invited her. From the minute Pari walked in the door when her stomach started rumbling, it was like I got this hollow feeling in *my* stomach that I don't even know what to do with.

'I just thought . . . she's the first friend you've shown it to . . .'

'We didn't hang out in there! We sat here mostly and on my perch. I'm going up now!' I say, and start to climb the stairs.

'Hang on a minute, Laila, we're talking!' Mum follows after me. 'So what *did* you do together then?'

'Nothing much! Ate, talked a bit, did some homework.'

'On a Friday night? She can come again!' Mum jokes.

'She hasn't got a computer at home. Not everyone has all this!' I snap, pointing at the landing bookshelves.

Mum massages her forehead and sits down next to me. I think she must have a headache too.

'Laila, we had a call from your tutor at school. She was talking about you looking tired and she'd noticed you scratching at your eczema. She also told me you were late one morning. You didn't say. What was that about?'

I shrug like I can't even remember being late. 'Oh yeah! Forgot my keys.'

'You'd feel a lot better, more on top of things, if you could just sleep properly.'

'Probably.'

Mum sighs and gets up. As soon as she's gone downstairs I feel bad. It's not her fault it went badly with Pari. I feel so on my own sitting here. No Mira or Krish arguing, no one blasting the house with music, no one trying to pick me up . . . I want to call out to Mum and ask her if she'll lie next to me till I go to sleep, like she used to when I was little.

My phone pings.

> Thanks for tonight. Sorry I ran out on you.
> Will you keep the books for me, please? I really
> want them. Left my homework on your table.
> Can you bring it in on Monday? PX

I feel this glow of relief spread through me.

I text Pari back.

> Glad you're OK. Will keep books for
> you and bring homework in. Laila X

Mum comes up to bed. I don't even bother to hide that I'm sleeping on the landing. She bends down and kisses me on the forehead.

'When's Dad back?' I ask.

'Late, I think. He's at a work-do. He'll try not to disturb you.' Mum looks towards Mira's room but doesn't start on me about sleeping in there tonight.

'Love you, Laila.'

'Love you, Mum,' I whisper.

'I'll take those off to the book bank tomorrow,' she says.

'No, don't!'

'Don't what?' Mum asks.

'Take them. I've changed my mind. I'm keeping them!'

'Oh, Laila!' Mum lets one of the paperbacks drop

259

on to the pile, making it topple. 'If you're keeping them, can you at least get them back on the shelves in your room, please?' She bends down and picks up the books she's knocked off the stack. 'I thought we could go tomorrow and get that new uniform for you at last.'

'Changed my mind about that too. I don't want one any more. There's no point.'

Mum wrinkles her forehead into three deep furrow lines and carries on up to her room. I wish I could explain it all to her so she doesn't think I'm trying to be difficult. It's just that things keep changing. If I had a brand-new uniform now it would feel so wrong.

Dad isn't that quiet when he comes in. I've still got the light on and he sees that I'm awake.

'I am definitely not going to ask you how it went with your friend!'

'Good! Because I'm definitely not going to tell you!'

Dad kisses me on the forehead. 'We won't talk tomorrow, OK?'

'I look forward to that!'

I don't sleep for one single moment, as I pick over every minute of Pari's visit, wishing I could put the whole thing on rewind. I should never have invited her in the first place. I scratch and scratch at the crook of my elbow. I don't care if I make it bleed.

*

Dad's making eggy-bread in the kitchen while Mum casts her line again.

'I was just thinking how independent Pari is, travelling on the tube like that!'

'Not everyone mollycoddles their children like you do,' I say.

'Mollycoddles?' Mum laughs. 'I haven't heard that phrase in years . . . where did you hear it from?'

'Don't know – think I read it somewhere.'

'Well, I know I wouldn't be happy with you taking the bus and the tube on your own, especially with the nights drawing in.'

'Well, Pari still has to go to school in winter!'

'I wouldn't like it either,' Dad chips in, bringing me through my eggy-bread. 'Here you go – not quite like the old fry-up days, but not bad.' He smiles and places his own plate on the table.

'And how's Pari supposed to get to and from school? Are you going to give her a lift every day and night?'

Mum ignores me. 'It's just a shame I didn't get to talk to her.' She tuts at the mess of paper and pens strewn over the table.

'I couldn't face this lot last night. I don't mind you having friends over as long as you clear up afterwards!'

I jump up but it's too late – Mum's already got hold of Pari's charcoal drawing.

'Did your friend do this?' she asks. She's frowning

at Pari's drawing like she's committed a crime or something.

'Yeah, she forgot it.' I take the page from Mum. 'It's for History. I'm taking it in for her on Monday.'

Mum switches the radio on and there's something on the news about a bomb going off in a city somewhere. She switches it off again fast, like she used to switch TV channels when 'inappropriate' programmes came on when I was little.

'Why did you do that? Don't you want me to know about what's actually going on in the world?'

'Oh, Laila, I'm shattered. I couldn't sleep at all last night. You must be exhausted too. It's a big day tomorrow with Janu arriving. Let's hunker down and have a cosy day.'

'I don't have much choice if I'm grounded,' I mumble.

'Maybe we'll see if we can get hold of Mira and Krish on the phone later.'

'That sounds good,' Dad says through a yawn. 'It was a bit of a late one for me too! Let's have a look at your homework then.'

'Can I have Pari's homework, please, Mum?' I hold my hand out and she passes it back to me.

'It would be good to talk about this,' she says.

'I wish everyone would stop talking about Pari. She's in my tutor group and she's my friend, that's all. Here! Have a good read through this too if you want to know everything!' I slam all our homework down on the table and run into the hallway.

'Come on, Laila, stay down here for a bit!' Dad reaches through the banisters for my hand. 'We only want to chat.' He lifts up my homework. 'This is interesting – family connections to history. I don't remember Krish and Mira doing this. I could tell you a few stories . . .'

I pull my hand away, walk up the stairs and close Mira's door. I lie on her bed playing my sad empty picture-frames game, except this time instead of trying to remember what pictures Mira used to have on the wall, I start to fill up the blanks with my own . . . of Kez, Pari, Bubbe, Simon, Hope and Nana Josie.

About half an hour later there's a knock. Dad pushes open the door and peers around.

'Can I come in?' He does his funny hunched-shouldered, head-bowed walk, the one he always does when he wants to make up. He's carrying the CD player.

I half smile at him and he straightens up as if me not being angry with him any more has made everything in the world right again. He hands me back my homework.

'I thought you might like to hear something. Glad I didn't throw this old player out now!'

I shift over on the bed.

'I've dug around and found a few vintage items,' he

says, plugging it in. 'I had your grandad's recording transferred to a CD after your Nana Josie's funeral. Felt right to put them together . . . but I've never played them since.'

Dad presses PLAY and comes to sit next to me on Mira's bed.

'When I was about your age I had this microphone recorder kit for my birthday. I got it into my head I was going to be a reporter or something. The recording's a bit crackly, but—'

A boy's bright little voice cuts through the interference.

'Dad, can you tell me two things you've done that you think are important?'

'Is that you?' I mouth at Dad as if Grandad Kit is in the room and I'm interrupting them.

Dad nods.

'Mmm, good question!'

That's Grandad Kit's voice. He sounds a bit like Dad now.

Grandad's talking about something called 'The Battle of Cable Street' in the East End of London, when people stood up against someone called 'Mosley'. He's talking about how he and his friends could see the evil that Hitler was doing and how they had felt that they needed to do something to fight the rise of fascism here too. He talks about putting on anti-fascist concerts and plays, and about his political cartoons.

Now Grandad Kit is talking about how he gave up smoking and used the money to start his book business. He sounds like he's really enjoying telling this story. It's just getting going when the tape cuts out.

'That's all there is of Grandad's voice. I know – it's a shame. I think my batteries must have run out!' Dad sighs.

'You sound so sweet and Grandad sounds funny!'

'He was a one-off. Laila, I know you find it hard to believe, but Mum and I were once your age, asking some of the same questions you're asking . . .'

I rest my head on Dad's shoulder. The voice has changed on the tape now, and the recording is clear. Nana Josie's voice sounds all smooth, almost like a professional reporter.

'Your Nana Josie . . . Mum,' Dad whispers.

It seems like she's being interviewed for radio about being in the hospice. I feel Dad's chest heave up and down and he reaches out for my hand as he listens to her talking about her life. The strangest thing is I feel like I already know what her voice sounds like, even though I've never actually heard her speak.

265

'She sounds really happy, even though she was ill . . . like she'd had a good life,' I say.

'She was, Laila – and seeing you born was one of the reasons she was so happy.'

'Have Mira and Krish heard this?' I ask.

'The interview with Nana? Yes, at her funeral. I haven't played anyone the one with me interviewing Dad. I should though. Krish never met Dad either.'

I never thought of that. I suppose I think of Mira and Krish both knowing the same things. But even when you're in the same family, each person knows different stories – and even when they are part of the same story, they probably wouldn't tell it in the same way.

I am just about to take the Protest Book out from under Mira's bed and come clean about going to pick it up from Simon when Dad says something that stops me.

'Thinking about it, I'm not sure I've ever played that to anyone since I recorded it. I think I wanted to keep it for myself. It was just a father-and-son chat . . . until now.' Dad squeezes my shoulder. 'When I was your age I was looking for something too, and that interview with my dad – well, it was just what I needed at the time. I suppose it was me saying, I want to understand what's going on in the world, I'm not a kid any more.'

So he *did* hear what I was saying about Kez's bat mitzvah.

Dad unplugs the CD player and heads for the door. I don't even know why I do it, but I run at him and nearly knock him over I hug him so tight.

'Steady!' He laughs. 'Don't knock the old boy off his feet!'

'You sounded just like Grandad Kit then.'

In the morning, on our doorstep, I find a hand-delivered card addressed to me. It's an invitation to Kez's bat mitzvah. There's a little note with it too, asking us all over for 'Sunday supper' at the end of half-term 'to round off Janu's stay'. He isn't even here yet! If this had arrived yesterday it would have annoyed me, but something about listening to those tapes with Dad feels like it's changed something.

THIRTY-TWO

'He's landed – shouldn't be too long now!' Dad says, checking the arrivals board.

A group of businessmen and women walk out of the Executive Exit, carrying briefcases. They look like they've been at some sort of conference. They're followed by a short bald man accompanied by a woman in an airline uniform who's wheeling his suitcase for him. On either side of them are two enormous bodyguards. The bald man looks around smiling at people, like everyone should know who he is.

'Who's that?' I ask Dad.

'I think he might be a politician. Or maybe a businessman . . . actually, maybe an actor? I think I might have seen him on TV.' Dad shrugs, like it's all the same thing.

After a while, crumpled-looking people start to stream through the main exit. A little boy who's just woken up is crying and snotting into his mum's shoulder. An old man's struggling to manoeuvre his suitcase because one wheel is broken. Then there's a rush of people meeting each other and hugging. But even after waiting for another ten minutes, there's still no sign of Janu. Dad starts to pace.

'Just a moment!' He goes over to a desk to talk to an official, who telephones someone else. Then he comes back over to me, sits down and sighs.

'Where is he?' I ask.

'They say they're going through some final checks in customs.'

Dad's phone rings.

'Yes. I can confirm that he's staying with us. Yes and after that he goes to visit his relative in New York. We're waiting for him in Arrivals now.'

Dad pulls a face at the person on the other end of the phone.

'Yes, I understand. Thank you . . . What a weird thing to say!' Dad shrugs as he ends the call.

'What?'

'She suggested I buy him a pair of shoes!'

I had completely forgotten about the barefoot blog thing Janu's doing. I wonder if Mum's forgotten to tell Dad too. There's a shout and then this tall, shaven-headed man comes running towards us.

'Sam! Lai Lai!' he calls. 'Sorry for delaying you!'

As he runs through the crowd, people turn and stare at him . . . and I suddenly feel really embarrassed.

I can't believe he's actually come on the aeroplane barefoot, but I suppose he did *say* that's what he was going to do, so he has to stick to it. He looks different from the way he looked when we went to India. Definitely older than he seemed even a few weeks ago on Skype. Maybe it's his shaved head. He's wearing skinny jeans and a thick navy blue salwar top with a baggy jumper over it . . . and no shoes. He looks like a model on a photo shoot at the seaside, not like someone who's just got off an international flight.

'Ironic, isn't it? If you wear shoes, they make you take them off to go through the scanner. If you have no shoes, they want you to put some on!' He laughs.

'Did they give you a hard time?' Dad asks.

'No, not so hard!' Janu smiles. 'After I explained –' he points to his feet – 'and showed them my website. While I was waiting I was planning my first blog post: "Barefoot in Heathrow Airport"! The security woman who pulled me over says she's going to pledge my first ten pounds on British soil!'

Dad looks down at Janu's feet and shakes his head, like he can't quite put this thing together.

'Didn't Anjali say? I'm going barefoot from Kolkata to London then on to New York and back again!'

'I didn't think you would actually go through with it!' I say.

'I think she did mention it a while back,' Dad says. 'It would have been easier in the summer.'

Dad looks at me and away to a few people staring at Janu's feet, then grins and shakes his head as if to say, *This is going to be fun!*

It's weird how you can go the whole day without noticing what kind of shoes anyone's wearing, but the moment someone doesn't have any on, especially in an official place like an airport, people really notice. I suppose barefoot people don't usually travel by plane.

Dad pays for the parking. 'Come on then, let's get you home! It's good to see you, Janu – shoes or no shoes!'

Dad drives out of the airport. Once someone lets him into the right lane of traffic he starts chatting again.

'What happened to the hair? You haven't turned into a holy man or something, have you?' Dad asks.

'When I had *long* hair you thought I looked like a holy man. Now I have no hair I am accused of the same!'

'True!' Dad admits.

'It's the same as Krish's,' I say.

'Yours too, Sam!' says Janu, pointing to the back of Dad's head.

'Nothing to do with fashion in my case, I'm afraid!' Dad shakes his head, but I can tell he's amused. 'I don't know – you and Krish could have a full mop. Hair is so wasted on the young!' He laughs and pulls on to the motorway.

'So, what's new, Lai Lai?' Janu asks.

'For a start I'm not Lai Lai any more . . .'

'Sorry, yes, Anjali told me of your reincarnation!'

'Where's this wild weather come from?' Dad asks as he attempts to heave Janu's rucksack out of the boot. Janu takes it off him and lifts it out as if it's not that heavy. The wind's whipping under the boot now making it difficult for Dad to close.

I look up at the tree outside our house with the snake sign still pasted on it. The few leaves that were still clinging on have been blown off, leaving the branches bare. Mum opens the front door. The wind blasts so strongly that the door bashes back against the wall. A cascade of leaves races into the hallway ahead of us.

There are lamps and candles lit everywhere – I didn't even know we *had* this many candles. To be honest it's a bit over the top. Mum's even lit the sandalwood joysticks that Dad always says remind him of Nana Josie, the same ones that Aunt Anjali burns in her flat in Kolkata. I suppose she's only trying to make Janu feel at home. There's a feast laid out on the table, with a cloth and proper napkins Mum only gets out for visitors. Can houses have feelings? Before Janu walked in, this house felt a bit sad and empty and decrepit to me, and now it's like everything's suddenly got brighter . . . It's not just the candles either . . .

After Janu's washed and changed, we all tuck into Mum's spread of food.

'Delicious paneer, Uma,' Janu tells her as he scoops some into his mouth. 'At least as good as Anjali's!'

'Well, she taught me how to make it!' Mum shrugs off the compliment, but I can tell she's pleased.

'Cheers, Janu, welcome!' Dad says, and everyone raises their glasses. Mum's poured a bit of red wine and water into mine. I clink glasses and go to take a sip, but it smells gross so I don't bother.

'So this barefoot thing is a kind of fundraising experiment . . . ?' Dad says.

'Not so much an experiment – it's already started working. How to explain?' Janu takes a sip of water. 'I've been on a few barefoot protests, mostly about treatment of the poor in the villages. It got me thinking maybe I could do it as a final fundraising push for the new refuge. I have a target of one hundred thousand rupees by the time I get home.'

'How much is that in pounds?' I ask.

'Around ten thousand pounds.'

Dad whistles. 'And how much have you raised so far?'

'The equivalent of about three thousand pounds. Thanks to Anjali I've already had support from some businesses in India and sponsorship for my blog from one of Priya's music-producer friends. She's putting on a concert when I'm in New York. The blog side was actually her idea. I can't believe how many followers I'm getting, from all over the world too! They seem to like the idea . . .'

'Well, I know I wouldn't fancy walking round London barefoot,' Dad says. 'No one would blame you if you changed your mind!'

'It will be OK; I think I have survived worse!' Janu laughs. 'You know Chameli, my ma, was worried about me travelling here. She has never moved outside the village, so she went to consult her sadhu to see if it was an auspicious time for me to make the trip. You know how important it is to consult the stars! I think she was hoping the holy man would tell me to forget about my barefoot travels. But no!' Janu closes his eyes, nods wisely, points up to the ceiling and speaks really slowly in a solemn whisper. '*No, Chameli – your boy must travel barefoot so he takes his orphan brothers and sisters with him. He has been fortunate, so he must always remember to keep his purpose on track. After all, Gandhiji showed us: it is hard for a barefoot man to become arrogant.*' Janu opens his eyes and beams at us. '*I tell you the stars are with him, Chameli. Let him go!*' He shakes his head and laughs.

'So thanks to the alignment of the constellations, I come with her blessing.'

'Well, you can tell the sadhu when you get back that immigration weren't too impressed!' Dad jokes. 'And I wouldn't try it on the next leg of your journey! If you'll forgive the pun.'

I think maybe Dad's getting a bit merry!

After we've eaten, Mum and Dad clear the table and Janu unpacks the presents he's brought. As he takes out the gifts in the top of his rucksack, a jasmine smell that reminds me of Anjali's balcony spreads around the room. I don't remember us taking this many presents with us when we went to India.

There's a cotton salwar and kurta for Mum and Dad from Aunt Anjali, and a beautiful notebook with handmade paper covered in green-and-turquoise sari silk for me.

There's a weird-looking musical instrument for Krish, and a tiny square-shaped leather box . . . Janu sees me looking and quickly tucks it in his pocket.

'Just a small gift for Mira. I'll give it to her when I see her.' He smiles. 'Do you think she's going to be able to come back from college?'

'Hasn't she been in touch?'

Janu shakes his head.

'She's going to try,' Mum says.

'Good, good. I would like to see her after so long.'

I'm not sure if I'm imagining it, but I think Janu looks a bit emotional. He digs further into his rucksack, hiding his face.

'I could hardly carry any clothes because of all this weight, but my ma insisted I bring this . . . I showed her your snake in the kitchen on Facebook, and afterwards when I asked her what I should bring as a gift for you, nothing would do except this statue. She kept telling me, "Can't you see it's obvious they've entered the cycle of change?" I told her, "Ma, that may be, but if I take this statue I will not have room for my clothes and I'll have to pay excess!" "You can get clothes anywhere!" she told me.'

Janu lifts out the statue with both hands and inspects it.

'So *that's* why your bag weighs a ton!'

Janu smiles. 'You know about Shiva? Too much the priest or too much the party guy until he finds his Parvathi to keep him in balance.'

'So, have *you* found your Parvathi?' Dad asks.

Why do parents have to be so embarrassing?

Janu laughs, but doesn't answer.

After dinner Mum takes Janu off to Krish's bedroom to settle in, and I go into Mira's room, close the door and phone her. It rings and rings. Krish and Mira promised they would call me all the time, but they hardly ever do. So I text them both the same message.

Janu's here. He says he really wants to see you both.
He's got presents for you.
I really want to see you too.
Come home soon.
There's only Mum and Dad left to argue with!
Love, Laila X

THIRTY-THREE

'Laila has told me of this grounding, Uma,' says Janu the next morning. 'I don't know what naughtiness she has done, but make one exception for me! I'm going to have a lot of planning work and travelling around to do with Hannah over the next two weeks. There may not be another whole day to spend together, if not today.'

'I suppose . . .' Mum laughs. 'Has Laila put you up to this?'

I shrug. It *was* actually my idea to take Janu up Parliament Hill and show him the view of London.

I'm in my trainers on the concrete path and Janu's walking on the grass barefoot.

'Aren't your feet freezing?' I ask.

'A little, but I'll get accustomed. My soles are hardened from walking barefoot at home.'

'Careful!' I push Janu's arm as I spot the splinters of a broken bottle on the path, but he's already seen it and takes a wide circle around it.

'Apparently Ma's sadhu told her I have to find green parks on my path. He has this theory that when you walk barefoot it sends a charge from the earth through you.'

'Well, I'd watch out for the dog poo if I were you!' I point to a sausage-shaped turd on the grass.

Janu throws his head back and laughs.

'Come on, little cynic . . . I'll race you!'

Before I can argue, Janu's sprinting up Parliament Hill. There's no contest. His legs are twice as long as mine.

'Unfair advantage!' I manage to splutter out between puffs as he reaches the top of the hill, way ahead of me, and sits on the bench.

'That's life!' Janu laughs. 'Fantastic views from here!' He takes out his iPhone and scans from left to right and then down to his feet.

'It's for a competition thing on my blog. I'm trying out different ideas to get some traction. For this one, people must guess the location of where I'm standing barefoot!'

We look over the city and Janu points out the landmarks. He names some of them: St Paul's Cathedral, the London Eye, the Houses of Parliament – and I fill him in on the ones he doesn't know: Canary Wharf, the Gherkin . . .

'The Gherkin! Like a pickle? In Kolkata maybe they

will build a shiny glass chilli!'

I start laughing, and I don't know if it's the relief of having someone more Mira's age to talk to, but I can't stop giggling.

'What's so funny, Laila?'

'I don't know . . . You being here.'

Janu nods. 'Do I seem so out of place?'

I look down at his feet and pull a 'what-do-you-think?' face.

'I suppose I do . . . But I hear you like to do things your own way too.'

I don't know how to answer him.

'You know we sat up talking a bit after you went to bed last night. Your ma and pa are worried. They told me that you've been quite unsettled these last few weeks.'

Janu doesn't look at me, but I feel my face and neck heat up. How dare they talk to him about me! If Mira and Krish were here too, they probably would have called another full-blown what's-happening-with-Laila conference.

'And what's that one?' he asks, pointing at a glistening peak.

'The Shard,' I say.

'All that glistens is not gold!'

'It's more silver, I think!'

Janu laughs and turns to me, waiting for an answer. It's hard to escape those dark eyes that look right into you.

'You know, my sister Priya used to get grounded all the time for sneaking out to her music gigs. Perhaps you are a little rebellious like Priya? But look at her now, building her musical kingdom in New York! Tell me, how is Mira? I haven't managed to speak to her yet.'

'Fine, I think.' I tap the bench. 'This is her favourite place.'

'In that case, thanks for bringing me here,' Janu says.

An old lady with a rainbow-striped cardigan walks up the hill slightly out of breath.

Janu stands up to give her his place, but she pats the air for him to sit again. Instead she places her hand on the back of the bench and admires the view. She looks down at Janu's bare feet and smiles.

'I used to walk around barefoot all the time when I was young. Still do sometimes – not at this time of year though! Feels good, doesn't it?' she says.

Janu gets into a conversation with her about the refuge he's raising money for in his village. It turns out that when the old lady was young she travelled all over India and she worked with some disabled children from a place called Bhopal that Janu seems to know all about.

'Ah!' the old lady says. 'And still no proper compensation for those families.'

Janu says he'll include her story on his blog post if

she signs in. Fifteen minutes later he's given her a tiny card that has a picture of bare feet on it and says:

Barefoot Blogger
Donating with 'heart 'n' sole!'
www.barefootblogger.com

On the way down the hill we watch the old woman pause at a bench, take her shoes off and carry them in her hand, swinging her arms as she goes.

'Makes me think of Nana Josie,' I say. 'She used to live just down there!'

'Yes? Mira talked of her many times when she came to India. So, Laila, what have you done to stop your parents allowing you freedom?'

Mum and Dad must have been up half the night talking to him about me. No wonder they went into the front room and closed the door. There doesn't seem much point in holding things back from Janu now, so I decide to tell him *some* things, like how much I miss Mira and Krish and how I feel like I'm losing Kez and I just want things to be like they were before.

'Relationships can change over time, and that can be painful indeed.' Janu looks into the distance.

I tell him about the day of the Unfriendship Bench and Kez's face when Dad carried her down the steps.

'That must be humiliating for a young woman! She is strong-minded. That's good. But maybe things will change. I'm thinking of my ma – she has her own unique way of looking at things. When I offer to buy her a wheelchair, she refuses – she thinks it is sometimes a privilege to be carried by someone you love . . .'

'No, Kez *really* doesn't ever want to be carried again!' I say.

'I wasn't being literal, Laila! I'm speaking of a love that is not reduced because you accept help. That is not always weakness.'

I really like Janu, but some of the things he says I don't get.

'Well, you should at least have a choice, shouldn't you? There's loads of places Kez can't get to without asking for help . . . and why should she?'

'True,' Janu says, and turns to me as if he's seeing me for the first time.

I keep thinking how hard it would have been for Kez to just decide to go on the Women's March like I did the other day. She would have had to go by bus. The underground's a nightmare for her. Maybe one day we'll go on a march together.

'*Chalo!* Let's go,' Janu says, standing up from the bench. 'Have you made new friends at school?'

I tell him about the other day with Pari. How I wished I hadn't invited her over, because it was awkward.

'She is proud, Laila. Who wants to be pitied?'

'It wasn't pity!'

'But you don't know how Pari lives, do you? You have to discover more about her before you can understand.'

'I'm trying,' I say. We walk on in silence for a while.

'Why don't you join me barefoot walking? What does it matter what people think?'

I take my trainers and socks off and we walk across the grass together. It actually does feel soft and fresh on my skin. My mind fills with the banner painting of Nana Josie, Hope and Simon walking barefoot together, and then Fliss's little hands clinging on to the bamboo sticks with such determination that her knuckles turned white.

Janu takes a photo of my feet.

'What are you doing?'

'I'm making a barefoot photo page! Everyone I walk with, everyone who donates, must post a photo of their bare feet on the blog. Shame I didn't get that lady's!'

Once we're on the pavement I have to pick my way around the rubbish and cigarette butts. Janu seems to see things before I do. He takes my arm and guides me along the pavement. On the bus on the way home he gets into conversation with a few other people on the top deck. He's good at picking out the ones who'll listen, but one or two don't hang around when he mentions the charity. It doesn't seem to bother him though. He talks Bengali to an Indian man on the seat behind us for ages. I can't believe he actually gets him to take his shoes off. He takes a photo of the man's bare feet before they part. The way he's smiling and waving to Janu as he gets off the bus, you'd think they were best friends.

'Original bus journey indeed!' the man's saying.

Someone's texted me.

Sorry Laila, I won't make it back, I don't think. I've got to get a painting ready for the first-term exhibition. Your painting actually. Say hi to Janu. Hope he has a good time. Mira X

I show Janu my phone. I don't understand why Mira doesn't speak to him herself. It feels really rude after how good his whole family were to us when we went to India.

'A text only. Thanks for showing me.'

He doesn't say anything else about the message, but after I've shown it to him he sits quietly and looks out of the window.

I've forgotten my keys so I clank the letter box.

Dad answers the door and looks straight down at our filthy feet.

'Is this barefoot thing catching?!'

THIRTY-FOUR

'Don't forget those books today, Laila, or I'll take them to the book bank. I can't have them cluttering up the place any more. I wanted them out of here before Janu came,' Mum says.

She reminds me every day, and every day I forget. Maybe it's because each time I look at the pile that I've dragged back into Mira's room, I can't help replaying the scene where Pari ran out on me – and even though she said she wanted them, just the thought of it takes me back to what I said.

'Laila, I have to go into work now! If you don't hurry you'll get another late!' Mum calls up the stairs.

I grab a bagful of the newest-looking books from the pile. I don't care if they're heavy.

When school's over, Pari, Stella and me get on with our music homework. It's easier when there's just the three of us. We can take our pick of the keyboards and percussion instruments and the best thing is that we can actually hear what we're doing.

'It turns out I actually do like school,' Stella jokes, '. . . when no one else is in it!'

'Hello! *We're* here!' I wave at her.

'Yes, but just the three of us. You know what I mean.'

'You really do get stressed with the noise, don't you?' Pari says.

Stella nods.

'Me too!'

'Can you imagine what it would be like if once in a while everyone took off their headphones and listened to the same happy, peaceful music . . . just for one journey,' I say.

'Actually, yes, let's do that . . . it feels a bit grim if the whole composition stays with everyone all in their own heads. Anyway, I like fantasy!' Pari laughs.

I wish Pari and Stella could have been on the underground the day of the Women's March, even though it was so noisy. It was a peaceful noise. That carriage was one of the friendliest places I've ever been with total strangers.

We work on what Pari calls 'our happy ending'. It only feels like we've been here for about half an hour when Mr Rivera comes in.

'A-star for dedication! What's this composition of yours called?' he asks.

'I thought you were supposed to guess, sir,' Stella

says. 'Anyway, we're still working on the end. We've got to sample all different kinds of music for the beginning too; we want to get the feeling like you're moving from what's playing on one person's headphones to the next. Like everyone's trapped in their own head.'

'Intriguing! Let's see what you've got so far.' Sir listens like he's actually really interested and not just doing his job.

'You three should definitely work in a group again. This is great. I'll be giving a commendation to each of you, and one for your tutor group too. But I'm afraid I'm shutting up shop now – it's not officially a practice night.'

Usually after we've rehearsed the piece, Stella and Pari head off for the tube together because they live quite close to each other, but today Stella has to go early 'to help out at home' and Pari needs to print something out in the library, so we go there together.

'She's like me,' Pari says as we wave to Stella at the gate. 'It's not easy for her at home.'

I want to ask Pari why it's not easy for her or Stella, but I don't know if she tells me these things because she wants me to ask her or not. So I don't ask anything and we just walk side by side into the library.

The Malala book's on the Human Rights display shelf. I point it out to Pari as we head to the computers.

'They're good books, I know, but I can't read that stuff. I need fiction.'

Sometimes Pari says things like that and I always expect her to follow up with something else, but she doesn't. Maybe she's hinting for me to give her some of Mira's books.

I'm just plucking up the courage to take them out of my bag, but then I change my mind. Giving them to her in the library feels like making too much of a big thing out of it. How can it be so difficult to give away some old books to a friend without making them feel bad?

'Sorry, girls. We've got a meeting in the library tonight,' Mr Coulson, the librarian, explains. 'I'm afraid you can't work in here.'

'But I need to use the printer! It won't take me long,' Pari says.

'Sorry, Pari. You'll have to come in early tomorrow,' Mr Coulson tells her.

Pari looks at me. I know she won't ask.

'We could print it off at mine,' I suggest.

She hesitates. 'Is Janu going to be there?'

Maybe she's a bit nervous about meeting him after everything I've told her about how different he is to anyone else I know.

'I doubt it. I've hardly seen him. He goes off to work with Kez's mum all day and he mostly doesn't get back till late. We'll have the place to ourselves!'

Pari calls her mum and has a long conversation in Arabic with just a few scattered words in English: 'Homework' and 'Library' . . . Listening to Pari talk makes me feel as if I know her even less than before. I think she's arguing with her mum. Then I know for sure because Pari hangs up while her mum's still talking. At least it's not just me!

'Sorry, I can't come. Mum needs my help tonight. She hasn't been feeling very well so she couldn't get out to the market. I need to go home. I'll have to come in early, that's all.'

I wish I could picture Pari where she lives and I wish I could ask her more questions about her life. The way she talks sometimes makes me think that Pari has to help her mum as much as her mum helps Pari. I would so love to know what Pari's room is like. I'd like to be able to picture her there. I walk her towards the tube, wondering if we'll ever get to know each other any better. My shoulder aches so I keep transferring my bag from one side to the other.

'Laila, I really want to invite you to where I live, but it's nothing like your house! I don't ask people back . . . usually,' she says, as if that's a good reason not to invite me.

'I don't care what it's like.'

'Actually . . . ever.'

'What . . . ? You've never had anyone back after school . . . not even in primary?'

Pari shakes her head.

'I've never really wanted anyone to . . . before now . . . but I do want to invite you . . . I already asked my mum. She wants your home number, so she can speak to your mum and arrange for you to come over in half-term.'

I feel so stupidly happy I could jump up and down and punch the air. I want to hug Pari, but I just smile and say, 'Yeah, no problem.'

'You don't have to walk me all the way to the tube,' she says 'Your bag looks heavy! I'll catch this bus.' She sticks out her hand.

This is the perfect time.

'Oh – I forgot I brought these . . . if you still want them!'

I take out the books right at the last minute and hand them to Pari as she steps through the closing doors. She sits down at a window seat and mimes, 'Thank you!'

As I walk home a text pings into my phone.

You are my first ever best friend. P x

THIRTY-FIVE

I lie on the landing sofa staring up at the ceiling, wondering about Pari's journey home and trying to imagine where she lives from the bits and pieces that she's told me. I don't know why I feel so happy that she's asked me over to hers, but I do. I slip Nana's chime out of the drawstring bag, rattle it and let the sound fill the air . . . and these thoughts come to me really clearly.

I won't really get to know Pari until I've seen where she lives. It matters that it's not just me inviting her to mine. But she seems so worried about me going there, it's making me a bit nervous now. It can't be that bad where she lives, can it? Anyway, how can we be true friends unless we know more about each other?

Maybe that's the same with Kez . . . why it counts so much that I can only go around to hers now and she doesn't feel comfortable any more to come back to mine.

I hear the key turn in the front-door lock.

'Mum?' I call down.

'It's Janu!'

He's standing at the bottom of the stairs, cleaning his feet with wipes he keeps in his backpack. I can't believe he's actually going through with this barefoot thing.

'Hi, Landing Laila! That's what I'll call you.' Janu laughs as he comes up the stairs and heads through to the bathroom to wash his feet properly. I suppose the wipes and the washing are his way of taking his shoes off at the front door.

'That's better,' he says, coming out again and sitting next to me on my perch. He unpacks his iPad and opens his Barefoot Blogger site. 'Let's see if there are any more donations . . .'

He reads out loud:

'£10 from Heathrow Airport!'

He laughs. 'Well, she was as good as her word, I have to say!'

I read the next one over his shoulder.

> I met you on Parliament Hill. I have been despondent about the world recently and meeting you and your little cousin gave me hope! £500 donated.
> With heart 'n' sole!
> Lizzy Melrose

'Ah! The Bhopal lady. She hasn't forgotten. Thank you, Lizzy Melrose!' Janu says 'The kindness of strangers.'

> On behalf of the Tagorian Society. We have
> discussed at our board meeting and
> researched your project . . . we think it is
> fittingly poetic! Tagore himself would
> approve. £1,000 donated.
> Dilip Sen-Gupta

'The man on the bus! I can't believe it! So generous. I wonder who he is . . . I'll look him up.'

Janu flips over his iPad screen and leans back on Nana Josie's sofa with his arms behind his head.

'What's happening in *your* world, Laila?'

I've noticed from the teachers at school that people have questions they get into the habit of asking. A lot of the time they don't really want your reply or to know what you really think . . . That's why 'fine' does fine for most questions. But some people, like Mrs Latif and Janu, have a way of asking that actually gets you thinking. Janu seems to know how much I hate it when Mum and Dad always ask me about school.

'You first,' I say.

'OK!' He rubs his forehead for a moment while he thinks. 'I would say . . . my perception of this city being so different to back home is wrong. Today I visited a place called Centrepoint with Hannah. Do you know it?'

I shake my head.

'Well, it's for homeless young people. Not unlike my refuges. Many of them seemed to be struggling in their minds. I can't believe there is so much of this here too. I didn't expect it!'

I nod. 'I had this thought that I won't get to know Pari until I go to her home. And . . . I think Mum might be a bit nervous about me going . . . she's so overprotective.'

'She's your ma!'

'But she might not let . . . well, I was wondering . . . if Pari does invite me at the weekend could *you* take me over there?'

'No problem.' Janu nods and smoothes his hand over his head. 'That is partly the reason why I came here, to see where you and Krish and Mira live.'

The front door clicks open.

'Hi, Laila! How was school?' Mum calls up.

'Fine!' I call back.

Janu's grinning as he flips the cover of his iPad over and heads off to Krish's room, leaving me alone to chat to Mum. He winks encouragingly at me as he goes.

THIRTY-SIX

On Tuesday evening Pari's mum telephones. I sit so close to Mum as she talks to her that I don't even have to guess the other side of the conversation.

'No problem at all. Pari's always very welcome. They seem to be becoming such good friends. Doing their homework too.'

Mum's talking strangely again, like she thinks that Pari's mum will understand her better if she speaks that way. It sounds weird. I roll my eyes at Mum and she pokes me in the side to make me laugh. I lean into the phone to hear Pari's mum better.

'Return this welcome, yes? Saturday afternoon. Stay evening. Bring sleeping bag. I make a special meal for them. No problem.'

Mum agrees, says her goodbyes and hangs up.

'She sounds lovely! Isn't it funny that her name's Leyla?' Mum says. 'I'd like to meet her too. I'll drive you over.'

'No! Pari's coming to pick me up. We've already

sorted it. We're going on the tube . . . we need to because we've got this music composition for homework. Anyway, it's only a few stops.'

'What's the underground got to do with music?'

'We're composing something about a tube journey,' I say.

Mum looks at me a bit suspiciously.

'What? It's the truth!'

'OK then, I can always take you on the underground,' Mum continues.

'Don't you trust me?'

'It's not that!'

'Then what? Pari takes the tube home alone every morning and night and she's all right.'

'We've discussed this before, Laila. She's used to it and you're not!'

I shrug. 'So as she's coming to pick me up we'll be fine then, won't we?'

'Laila, I'm your mum. I need to know that you're safe.'

'I know what this is about. Pari's mum didn't come over to ours and check us out before she came here.'

I can feel myself start to boil over again. After all the time it's taken Pari to trust me enough to invite me to her's, the last thing I need is Mum deciding I can't stay. I don't know why so many conversations with Mum turn into arguments; they never used to when Mira and Krish were around.

During our 'discussion', Janu comes in.

'If anyone has to take me, Janu can!'

'Laila! Don't be so rude.' Mum looks really shocked. 'Sorry about this, Janu.'

He quietly sits down at the table drinking tea and writing what looks like a letter, but I can't exactly see because his arm shields the paper. Whatever it is he's writing, he has to start it over a lot of times. He keeps crumpling up the pages.

'No! Don't worry at all, Uma; I'm happy to take her. She did ask me earlier.' Janu folds the piece of paper over and puts it in his pocket, then collects up the rubbish, scrunches it up and puts that in his pocket too. 'What day is your sleepover?'

'Saturday,' Mum and me both say together.

'Perfect! I'm going that way anyway with some student friends I met. I've been invited to my own sleepover party!' Janu jokes. Don't worry, Uma, I'll drop Laila there and pick her up on Sunday morning.'

Mum looks like she wants to put up an argument but can't think of a reason to object.

I call Pari and tell her the plan. She asks what I like to eat. I don't want her mum to go to too much trouble, so I say pizza – I think that's pretty safe. As we're talking my feet kick against something on the floor. I peer under the table. There's a ball of paper. I can't drag it closer towards me with my foot so I crawl under the table and pick it up.

The front door's open and Mum and Janu are standing by the wall chatting on the street. I turn my back to them and un-scrunch the paper . . .

Dear Mira,

Sorry we haven't spoken. I have tried calling you and emailing without any luck, so now I am writing this letter. It feels unnatural to write when I am finally in the same country as you and we're only a few hours away from each other! ~~I think you know how much I want to see you~~ . . . Over every other reason, I am here to see you . . .
You will never guess . . .

I feel terrible for him. It looks like I'm not the only one to keep secrets. Does he love her? I think I can guess what's in that little square box that Janu's brought over for Mira. Poor Janu . . . I wish I hadn't see that kiss in the hallway between Jidé and Mira.

I go into Mira's room, close the door and call her. It rings for a while before she picks up.

Me: Hi, Mira.
Mira: Why are you whispering, Laila?

299

Me: Mira, you've got to come home and see
Janu. I think he loves—
Mira: Listen, Laila, I *can't* come. One day I'll try to
explain. Don't ask me again. I'm really busy with
this exhibition.
Me: Have you heard from Jidé again?
Mira: Yes, he's . . . Look, Laila, there are things
you don't understand, and one day . . . Well,
anyway, I can't talk about it now, but I can't
come back. I've got to go . . . I'll call you soon . . .
Me: What if he's going to ask you to—
Mira: I have to go, Laila. Speak soon.

I know when Mira's crying. I can hear it in her voice.
I'm sorry I've called and upset her, but I feel like I'm
in the middle of something and no one's thought to
tell me what it is – as usual. What would little Lai Lai
understand anyway?

THIRTY-SEVEN

Outside the tube station a man about Janu's age sits on the pavement next to a sleeping bag that's all curled up like a shiny grey slug. Tucked inside it are bin liners and beer cans. The homeless man looks down at Janu's feet.

'What happened to your shoes, mate?'

'I'm not wearing them.'

'I can see that!'

'Want a cup of tea?' Janu asks.

'Wouldn't say no!'

'How do you take it – milk and sugar?'

'Milk, four sugars,' the man says, grinning. Half of his teeth are gone and the rest are black.

Janu walks off to buy tea from the little kiosk in the station, leaving me wondering whether to follow him or not. The homeless man smells of stale beer and cigarettes and his clothes are all stained. Maybe he's older than Janu.

'Is he a Hari Krishna or something?' the man asks

me, pointing over to Janu.

I suppose he is wearing an orange jumper today. I stand a bit away from the homeless man. I don't really want to talk to him, but as Janu's left me standing here I don't feel like I've got much choice.

I try to explain a bit about Janu's Barefoot Blog and the refuge. I didn't think he would be interested but it seems like he is.

'I'd like to see him get through the whole winter living on the streets like that!'

I'm relieved to see Janu come out of the station.

'Your tea!' Janu says as he hands it to the man.

The homeless man struggles a bit to take the lid off the tea because his hands are trembling so much. Finally he manages it and takes a sip. He looks Janu straight in the eye and says:

'This is the worst brew I've had in a long time!'

'Thanks!' Janu laughs and holds out his hand for the homeless man to shake.

The man hesitates for a moment and then takes Janu's hand and holds on to it while they carry on talking.

'Not your fault, mate. You didn't make it!'

'Can I do anything to help? Have you got numbers for any shelters around here?'

The man nods. 'You're not one of them that's gonna give me a cup of tea then want my life story?'

Janu shakes his head.

'Thanks for this though,' the homeless man says, breaking his handshake with Janu. 'No one's offered me a hand in a while!'

Janu nods and goes to walk away but the man calls after him.

'Want my advice?'

Janu raises his chin in the air and waits for it.

'Put some shoes on! Take it from me, there's too much filth on these streets.'

The homeless man was right. Janu's feet are disgustingly grimy just from walking from our house to the tube. His soles are already black with dirt. People can't help glancing at them and then quickly away, like they're embarrassed. It feels just like the carriage felt when the tissue family got on . . . only now, because I'm with Janu with his bare feet, I'm part of what's embarrassing. I reach behind me and pick up a free paper. Janu reads it over my shoulder. I'm not that interested, but I don't want to have to sit here and look at people staring at us. Every time the tube doors open I half expect the girl and her family to get on, selling their tissues, but they don't. People notice Janu's feet and look away, like they're disturbed by him. This woman opposite me looks like she's monitoring us . . . Like me and Janu shouldn't know each other. I want to tell everyone that Janu's my sort-of cousin. Why do people have to judge others just because they're different? What is that look on people's faces? It's something like a mixture of pity and disgust, I think. I can see the girl's eyes in my mind right now, as if she's standing in front of me and waiting. 'See how it feels to be judged,' she's saying to me.

'Are you OK?' Janu asks.

I wipe my eyes.

'Yes, I've just got something in my eye.'

Pari's flat is in the opposite direction to the Caring Community. There's not much green where we're walking, and Janu's having to pick his way carefully up the street. There are smears of dirt and liquid all over the concrete. It makes me feel sick.

'That homeless man was right about the pavement. It's disgusting. Are you OK? You're so quiet,' Janu asks me.

I nod.

We pass a derelict house with a few smashed windows and a giant graffiti tag on the outside.

'I really was not expecting to find this here; it's just like back home. Perhaps I was naive.' Janu's talking, mostly to himself I think.

We're walking along a noisy road with two lanes of traffic on either side. Janu says something to me, but I don't hear because his voice is muffled by the roar of traffic and he's holding his hand over his mouth. I do the same . . . I can taste the tinny pollution on my tongue. Janu takes his hand away from his mouth for a moment and shouts over the din of the buses, lorries and cars. As I walk along the road my ears are bombarded with all the sounds that Pari wanted to put into our composition – the clanging, screeching noises that I had thought were a bit over the top. I can see it now. She was doing her whole journey from school to home. No wonder she wanted the music to get louder and more clashing.

'Which block is it?' Janu shouts.

The high walls of three solid tower blocks built side by side cast everything below into shadow, including us.

'Lighthouse Block Two.'

'These super-high-rises are going up all over Kolkata too. They don't look like this when they're new though. Some of them are so smart, but I don't fancy them myself. You know how I like to keep my feet on the ground.' Janu tries to joke but neither of us are smiling.

Maybe these tower blocks did once look light, but not any more with half their windows boarded up. My mind keeps flashing back to the first day Pari came to our house. *'Doesn't anyone try and break in?'*

I understand her question about the stained glass now. It doesn't seem so weird any more.

We make our way along the shadow path, past Lighthouse Block One to an identical Block Two, which is more in shadow than the first tower. We walk up a narrow path to the side of the building. Janu has to pick his way slowly along. There are a few empty parking bays with oversized bins lying on their sides and foul-smelling rubbish spilling out everywhere. In another bay there's the shell of a car parked sideways, as if the driver's screeched to a halt and done a runner. It has one back tyre, one front tyre and no doors. I know that if Mum had driven me here she would never let me stay.

We walk through a rusted yellow metal door into a kind of foyer – although that makes it sound a bit like a hotel, and this is definitely nothing like a hotel. It's not even as nice as that youth hostel we went to in Paris once – at least that was clean-ish. In front of us there are grey concrete stairs and a lift. I can hear Pari's music screaming through my head. Janu slows down, watching where he places his feet. He peers around the staircase, walking up the first few steps, then quickly changes his mind and comes back down.

'Let's try the lift. Twenty floors is a long way to walk on cold concrete,' he says.

I press the button and the overhead light counts down from twenty to one. Pari must live right at the top. The metal doors crank open and we step into the lift. It smells of incense.

'I wasn't expecting a sweet-smelling lift after what I saw on the stairs!' Janu says.

'What did you see?'

'It doesn't matter. Forget I said anything.'

But as we go up through the building the smell underneath the incense is of pee and aerosol. I feel like I'm going to be sick. Janu lifts up one foot and pulls off a piece of chewing gum stuck to his heel. He takes some wipes from his bag, squats down and does his best to clean his feet and hands. As he kneels I see that the walls of the lift are sprayed over . . . to cover up what's written there. It hasn't worked. The messages still show through.

REFUGEE SCROUNGERS GO HOME

Now I can hear the high-pitched drone Pari wanted to have running all the way through our music. I couldn't really understand why she was so keen on it before, but now I think I know what she was trying to put into the music: FEAR and ANGER. If I had to face this lift every single day on my own, I would have that desperate sound in my head too. I can't wait to get away from the reek in here.

'Janu . . . you won't tell Mum what it's like here, will you? If you do, she won't let me come again.'

'No guarantees, Laila. First I need to make sure you are safe; then I will decide.'

I actually feel like asking Janu to take me home, but I can't let Pari down now. What's looking at this every day going to do to her? Janu keeps checking on me as if he's asking if I want to carry on, but he doesn't say anything more.

Flat twenty is a thick metal door like all the others on the floor. Janu rings the bell and someone starts to fiddle with the lock on the other side. It opens slightly. I see wrinkles around worried dark eyes and long grey hair. This must be Pari's mum. She catches sight of Janu and quickly pushes the door closed again.

I hear Pari's voice now. She's speaking to her mum in Arabic and repeating what she's said in English.

'It's all right, Mum, that's Laila's cousin from India . . . I told you about him. Don't you remember?'

Her mum sounds nervous.

'Just hang on a minute!' Pari calls.

The door opens a slit as Pari's mum takes another long look at Janu through the tiny gap, but she keeps the chain across. Pari is talking to her like she's trying to hurry her along. After a while Pari's mum finally unlatches the chain. Her head is covered now.

'Sorry about that!' Pari mumbles.

'*Ahlan wa sahlan*, welcome, welcome.' Leyla claps her hands, says something to Pari and touches my shoulder. 'Pretty friend, looking like sisters!'

I suppose we *do* look quite alike.

Pari's wearing skinny jeans and a thick jumper with some silver sparkle thread through it. Her hair is silky straight and dyed the same colour as Kez's!

'It's not permanent! When I saw Kez's hair I thought I'd have a go too.' She laughs.

'It's . . .'

'You don't need to pretend,' Pari says. 'I don't like it either. It'll be washed out soon.'

I've never seen her hair uncovered. I didn't think it would be so long – it reaches all the way down her back. I wish I'd dressed up a bit more now, instead of wearing my old leggings and sweatshirt.

'Find the flat all right? Did you take the lift? Was it OK? It's better than the stairs.' Pari fires questions at me.

'Yeah, it was fine.'

Pari's chewing on her bottom lip. She looks like she's worried I'm not going to stay.

'I'm sorry, if my husband is here I can invite you in – but I am alone. Sorry,' Pari's mum says to Janu. Then she stares at his feet.

'Oh! *Bismillah*. Why so you walk in dirt with no shoes?'

'It's a long story! Laila will tell you,' Janu says, peering into the hallway. 'Delicious smells!'

'Mum's been cooking for days,' Pari explains, rolling her eyes.

'I'll pick you up in the morning then, Laila. About ten, OK? I'll call Uma to let her know I've dropped you here.'

'OK, thanks!'

'Pari, don't leave your friend to stand in hall. Take your shoes, put there . . .'

I unlace my trainers. There are three pairs of shoes in the hallway: some small, flat, sensible lace-ups, which look like they belong to Pari's mum; Pari's school shoes; and a pair of trainers in Pari's size. She points to some slipper-like pumps on the floor and I put them on.

'How many people live in this house?'

'I know where I'll come if I need shoes.'

'I'm not a charity case.'

Pari's words echo back to me. I can see now exactly what she saw when she came to mine.

'You girls go and wash first,' Pari's mum says, pointing to a door.

I follow Pari into the bathroom. She has to stand behind the door while I edge in, and then we just about have room to close the door if we both stand on tiptoe and squeeze our bodies around towards the sink. The bathroom has a shower, a sink and a toilet, all shiny clean except for where the enamel is chipped away. There's a pile of clean towels by the sink.

Pari and I stand together and wash our hands with soap that smells of medical disinfectant. I would have finished and dried my hands ages ago, but Pari is still washing hers over and over, so I do the same. She must have the most germ-free hands in the world.

Pari's mum is standing in the doorway opposite the

bathroom waiting for us. She's smaller than Pari and plump with a round face nothing like Pari's oval high-cheekboned one. She's taken her scarf off now. She has long grey hair tied in a thick plait and she's wearing an ankle-length blue towelling housecoat like the one Nana Kath sometimes wears at bedtime, but Pari's mum looks like she's got more clothes underneath hers. On her feet she has sandals with socks.

'My name is Leyla and your name is Laila?'

'Mum! You promised – no jokes!'

'Pari told me of you, Laila . . . and I am playing joke with classic song you know it? I say tom-ay-to and you say tom-ah-to . . . ?'

I nod and try to stop myself laughing at the mortified faces Pari's pulling!

'I say I'm Leyla and you say you Laila!' Leyla takes my hand and starts to dance with it. 'You know this song?'

'We get it, Mum!' Pari groans. 'Can we come through now?'

I nod and can't stop myself from bursting out laughing.

'See! She has understanding of good joke!'

Now I get that happy, playful music Pari was so keen to end our composition with. I think it was the music of being with her Mum when she's finally safe in her flat behind the closed, locked door.

'Mum! She's *my* friend!' Pari laughs.

'Yes, yes, I know, but mine also. We are near-to-same-name friends! Now we are all friends, so . . .'

'Mum, you promised me . . .'

Leyla stands aside. There's a cake with thirteen lit candles on the table.

'*Happy birthday to you,*' Leyla sings . . . and after a moment, when it sinks in that this is why she's invited me, I join in. I feel terrible.

'Why didn't you tell me? I only brought chocolates. I didn't know you were thirteen!'

'I missed a lot of school in year three, when my Mum wasn't very well, so they let me repeat,' Pari explains, leaning up close to me so her mum can't hear.

'Kez did too. I feel like the baby!'

Pari smiles at me shyly, and shrugs. 'I didn't want to make a thing of my birthday. I just wanted you to come for a sleepover. That's the best!'

'I phone your mama. Pari makes me promise I don't tell you of birthday tea. But now Laila is here, I am changing promise . . . this is what is friends for. Why not you celebrate together?'

Pari's kitchen is a mini oven with a kind of hob to cook things on the top, a rusted metal sink, a microwave oven and a mini fridge. To the side of it there's a tiny table with a shiny blue top and two plastic garden chairs. The kitchen doubles as a living room – like ours but nothing like ours, because our kitchen living room is pretty much the size of the whole of Pari's flat. There are no curtains and two sides of the room are glass windows smeared with grime and something moss-coloured on the outside. The inside of the flat is sparkly clean but it's hardly got anything in it. The sofa area under the windows is really pretty. It looks like a mattress laid out on the floor, covered with a patterned cloth and a few huge flat cushions in different colours.

'You girls eat cake at table. I will sit on my comfort cushions here.'

Pari spoons some yogurt on to my plate. Leyla keeps looking over at me, checking that I'm enjoying it.

'Laila likes?'

I nod.

'Then Leyla is happy!'

I take another mouthful, trying to identify all the flavours. I think it's cinnamon, honey and nuts I can taste. The combination is delicious.

'So say it! Why is cousin's feet naked?' Leyla asks.

Pari smiles and shakes her head at her mum.

I explain to Leyla about Janu's orphanage and his fundraising and she seems really interested.

I try the yogurt with the cake.

'You don't have to have everything. Sure you like the taste?' Pari asks. She's wearing that on-guard expression, the same one she had when I insulted her pride and she ran out of our house. Even if I hated this cake I wouldn't tell her. I take another bite. I'm glad I don't have to pretend though.

'I love it.'

It's spicy and sweet at the same time and a bit warm, so the yogurt's perfect with it.

'If you'd said it was your birthday I would have brought you a present.'

'You've already given me those books!' Pari says.

Leyla claps her hands, holding up the one she's reading.

'The books! Thank you, thank you. I am becoming a teenager again!'

'Mum's reading them too,' Pari explains.

'I've brought a few more with me, if you want them.'

'Yes, not enough books. I nearly finish this! Leyla is reading Laila's books! My friend says my English improves, especially language for teenage romance . . . Some are quite nice actually.' Leyla laughs.

'They're my sister's books,' I explain.

'Don't try to cover!' Pari's mum shakes her finger at me and laughs. 'I think you have soft romantic heart like me and my Pari!'

'Muuuuuum!' Pari groans.

'And how about your cousin?' Leyla asks. 'Is he married?'

'Mum! This is what I was worried about!'

'No, he's not.'

'Maybe naked feet is making them run away! Instead of businessman they are thinking he can't afford shoes . . . Well, let them think. There are many ways to be rich. My Nuri, my husband, and I have only one child. I want more but . . . Nuri is not so well, even now.'

'Mum! You *promised*.' Pari's smile has disappeared.

'I'm not complain. One child is my riches.'

Then Leyla says something in Arabic and Pari gets up from the table and kisses her on the forehead. Leyla is talking now but looking down towards the cushions like she doesn't want me to see her face.

'She says she wants you to feel comfortable here. She wants you to feel like you are in your own home.'

'Yes, feeling like home,' Leyla repeats, and she raises her hand and flicks her fingers at us, like she wants us to leave the room.

'Come on! I'll show you what my dad made me for my birthday.'

THIRTY-EIGHT

In Pari's room, the double bed that's pushed against the window takes up nearly all the space. At the end of the bed as you walk in the door there are fruit crates stacked on top of each other, all painted in bright clashing colours: red, yellow, green, pink and orange. They're like the crates you get from a fruit market, but they look really pretty stuck together like this. Inside are the books I've given Pari and a few big art books with school library stickers on.

Inside another crate is a small TV.

'My dad's started doing carpentry. He's making something for the kitchen next. Mum fixed these up for my birthday. Before today my things were all on the floor – this is the grand shelf unveiling!' Pari says. I've never seen her chattering on so nervously.

There's a bright green-and-gold bedspread and curtains in the same colour hemmed with a line of tiny, even stitches. The same careful stitches I've seen on Pari's uniform labels. I don't know how they

316

managed to get the bed into this room because there is no space around it at all.

Pari climbs on to the bed and crawls over to look out of the window. I follow and kneel beside her. We are so high up it feels like my head is floating.

All along the window ledge are jam jars with little battery nightlights inside. There's just one photo, in a plain glass frame. It's of Leyla when she was younger, and I suppose that must be Pari's dad holding baby Pari. Her dad looks like the smudgy charcoal drawing she did at our house, as if he's only half in the photo. Pari's definitely more like her dad though, even as a baby. He is tall and slim with the same oval-shaped face as Pari's, the same dark eyes and thick black lashes.

'This is my favourite place right here!' Pari says, looking out of the window. 'It's something like your landing place, where I come to watch the birds and think.'

I reach in my bag. 'And . . . eat chocolate!' I say, opening the box.

We munch our way through half the box.

'Bet you feel on top of the world up here!' As soon as the words come out of my mouth I imagine Kez shaking her head at me.

Pari gives me an *I doubt it* look, then turns around and sits down on her bed.

'Top of Lighthouse Two, I suppose! Want to

watch some TV?' she asks.

She flicks through the channels. The news is on and Pari switches over straight away.

'Hate the news! Don't you? Mum's always watching it and getting me to translate stuff she doesn't understand!' She switches to a programme where someone really needs to have their house done up and can't afford it so this team of people comes in and changes it.

'What if they don't like it when it's finished?'

'It doesn't matter! They're just supposed to feel grateful.' Pari flicks over to a quiz show.

'Dinner!' Leyla calls to us. 'You girls enjoy. I go to shower.'

Dinner is laid out on the little blue table with paper serviettes and a flowery tablecloth. Leyla's even tied balloons to the chairs. It's pizza, orange juice, a different kind of cake and biscuits.

Pari laughs when she sees the table and shouts something to her mum.

She calls back through the bathroom door.

'What did you say?'

'I said I'm not a baby. I didn't need balloons!'

'And what did she say?'

'She said . . . you are still *my* baby!'

We tuck in and I help Pari clear up afterwards. She leaves it looking perfect. Leyla's still in the bathroom when we've finished.

Just before nine o'clock Leyla knocks on our door.

'Sorry, girls – lights out in Lighthouse!'

'Mum! Please don't do it tonight,' Pari pleads.

'Sorry, Pari. Get in sleeping bags, under duvet, heads inside to stay warm.'

'Hang on then.'

Pari lights the battery candles all along the windowsill.

'How will you manage, Mum?'

'I will be OK. I have mattress, cushions and blankets and new-moon curtains,' she jokes, looking at the sliver of a crescent-shaped moon through the window.

'It is not problem for me to stay one night on my comfy cushions! I can dream all happy birthdays from thirteen years.'

'Mum, do you have to?' Pari groans, but she kneels up on the bed and gives her mum a long hug.

In a few minutes the fairy lights and TV cut out and the only light in the room is from the nightlights on the windowsill.

Pari climbs into her sleeping bag and kneels at the window with her nose against the ice-cold glass. I do the same.

'When the lights go out in here I look at the city ones,' Pari says. 'Lots of people in the Lighthouse blocks switch off at nine. Sometimes we can't afford to keep the electricity on all night long. Remember when Mrs Latif asked if anyone knew what "ironic" means? I thought of this! A lighthouse with no light!'

I look to the right and left at the other blocks and it's true, most of the windows have gone dark.

'That's awful.'

'It's how it is.'

'Sorry,' I whisper.

'Why are *you* sorry?' Pari asks.

I don't answer. I can't answer. What can I say? It won't make her feel any better or her flat any warmer if I say what's in my mind: *I can't stand it that you live like this, and I live how I live and Kez too. How can any of this be right?*

'The city never goes dark, so there's always some light,' Pari says, staring into the distance.

'I feel bad taking your mum's bed. Shall we swap with her?' I ask.

'She wouldn't.' Pari shrugs. 'By the way, you need to wear socks.'

It's true; my feet feel like ice blocks already.

I reach down to pick up my socks. One of them's slipped further under the bed. I feel around for it and an aerosol can rolls towards me. There's something else under the bed too – a packet of incense. It smells just like the lift.

'It was you! You lit incense and sprayed over the graffiti in the lift, didn't you?' I ask.

'So now you see why I didn't want to invite you!'

Pari stares out of the window, rubbing the frozen tip of her nose, while I pull on my socks inside the sleeping bag.

'Your mum's made it nice inside,' I whisper.

'She does her best,' Pari says. 'I like the new moon the best! Just when you think it's going to be dark forever this tiny slice of light comes through and you know it's going to get brighter!'

Pari takes my hand. 'You're so cold!' she says. 'It's because you're not used to this.'

I'm trying to hide it but I've already started to shiver. Our breath comes in icy wisps that mist the glass. Pari rummages under her pillow and brings out two woolly bobble hats.

'Hats on!' She laughs, handing me one and pulling on hers.

'Mum knitted these for us, for tonight! My favourite red colour. Look! Birthday pom-poms and everything!'

Pari switches off the battery lights in the jam jars and closes the blackout curtains while I put my hat on and wriggle deep into the sleeping bag. Pari pulls the duvet and a blanket over the top, and we snuggle right down under the weight of the covers.

It's so dark in here with the curtains closed. This is when she tells me. I was never going to ask if she didn't want to talk about it. I think she knew that, but I don't think she ever would have confided in me if I hadn't come here.

'You want to know why Mum and I live here, like this. I've seen all the questions in your eyes. You want to know where my dad is. I'm going to tell you the whole story, now, in the dark, and then I never want to talk about it again. Understand?'

'Yes! But you don't have to,' I whisper.

'I do,' she whispers back and snuggles up closer to me. Curled together in our sleeping bags under the duvet, the two halves of our bodies make a circle.

'I don't remember any of it. I didn't exist! It's just what Mum's told me. It was that time that your nana was marching against bombing our country . . .'

She reaches out for my hand, squeezes it tight, and I squeeze hers back.

'Our whole town was shelled . . . flattened. You've seen those pictures on the news? Grey rubble and dust, houses turned into coffins. My grandmothers and grandfathers were buried there, and my cousins. My mum said we had a beautiful garden with pomegranate trees. Everything was killed. Everything died, even the plants, the fish in the pond, the birds . . . everything. Nothing left to stay for. Mum says that the only precious thing she had she carried with her . . . and that was me!'

I pull my arm out of the sleeping bag and Pari pulls her arm out of hers and we hold each other's freezing hands in the dark.

'My mother was three months pregnant with me

when they left Iraq. She won't talk about how they got away. When I was little she used to make up magic stories like legends and she would put me in them. When I ask her how we travelled here she used to say, "On a magic carpet of hope!" Now I've seen how people really travel, I prefer the fantasy. Every night my mum dreams of drowning. She doesn't tell me, but she talks in her sleep. From what she says, I know we must have come across the sea. When I ask her, all she tells me is, "You travelled in safe, clean waters."'

'You don't have to tell me any more if you don't want to,' I whisper.

Pari ignores me.

'I'm telling you so you know this is why we're here like this. I'm going to get us out of here. I'm going to be the best at things. I'm going to be a teacher like Mrs Latif and find somewhere good to live for my mum and dad, and my dad's going to get better and come back to live with us. Then my mum will be happy, not just acting happy for me, and she'll be able to work again . . .'

I can feel her tears dripping on my cheek, and my tears mix with hers. We don't even try and wipe them away.

Pari's all breathless, as though if she keeps speaking, imagining good things, her words will fill up all the unknown spaces in her future.

I squeeze her hand and she calms down.

'You don't need to tell me . . .'

'It took them six months to get here. The way Mum tells the story, a lorry driver dropped them at the doors of Homerton Hospital and two hours later I was born. She makes it sound easy!'

'So *that's* the photo of you all together. It was taken in the hospital.'

'My mum always ends the story the same way – "And you, Pari Pashaei, were born on British soil." – like I should stand up and cheer at the happy ending! I think I was four years old when we got our refugee status. The papers finally came through, and soon after that my dad became ill . . . in his mind. That's why no one came over on playdates from primary while he lived here. His heart was so sad I used to think he turned the sky grey. Now he stays in the hospital. Sometimes we go and see him. We're going tomorrow with some cake. Mum thinks maybe he might be starting to feel better, because he's building things again – I don't know. She waits for him to get better. We are waiting for new housing. She's seen some flats with little roof gardens up the road. She has this dream of Dad coming home and sitting on a little balcony surrounded by flowers and vegetables . . .'

'Pari . . . I–'

Pari shakes her head. 'I don't really know him. Let me tell you everything. Then it's finished.'

'We have to keep the flat really clean. We need to. I think you've noticed. It's not just me; it's Mum too. She thinks it's because she was worried about getting an infection when she travelled here. She was always trying to wash her hands and be pure to pray too. It was hard for her. The social worker thinks I've caught the clean bug off her.' Pari laughs. 'Funny, isn't it? People think about catching an infection from dirt, but I've caught the clean infection.'

I wait for more . . .

'That's all.' She yawns. 'I've never told anyone all of this before. I can't talk any more now, Laila. Do you mind if I sleep? I feel so tired.'

Pari falls asleep first. I hear her breathing change and I snuggle up closer to her to keep warm. This is the saddest, happiest birthday I have ever shared with anyone.

'Breakfast is ready. Eggs with toast. Come on, wake up . . . it's nearly ten o'clock! Laila's cousin will be coming to collect her and we must be ready to visit Nuri . . . your father.' Leyla opens the door, sits on the end of the bed and looks at us as we peep our bright red bobble-hatted heads out of the sleeping bags. Leyla giggles at the sight of us.

'Looking like seal babies in London Zoo!' She laughs.

'I don't think they wear bobble hats!' Pari smiles.

'Same with four big, beautiful open eyes! Wondering of this world!'

I turn around and peep through the curtains to see what kind of a day it is. There's frost on the ground for the first time. No wonder it was so cold in here last night. The morning sun is dazzling bright. A golden-coloured shaft of light falls across the bed. Leyla switches on the TV and clicks on a news channel. Pari raises her eyes towards me as if to say, 'I told you!'

'Mum, it's so rude! Turn it off!' she says.

They're talking about another march that went on yesterday through the centre of London. It's a Unite Against Racism march. The screen splits to show it happening in lots of different countries. There are people from all over the world, chanting and carrying banners, playing music and looking so peaceful walking together. A family sitting on a statue of Gandhi is watching and clapping. They're holding up a poster:

HERE WE STAND AGAINST HATE.

Pari's mum starts clapping as we sit on the edge of the bed and watch.

'Mum, please can you switch—'

'Wait a minute. Can I see?' I ask, crawling to the edge of the bed.

'If Nuri was well, we would go together.'

'You could go with me, Mum,' Pari says.

'I'll come too!' I say.

Leyla turns to Pari as if she's never thought of it before.

The crowds of people make this incredible noise, like an enormous chanting choir filling up the streets. I imagine Nana Josie, Simon and Hope marching somewhere in that crowd, holding up their banners. I wish I was there too, with Pari and her mum, Bubbe and Kez. Maybe one day we will all march together. I catch a few of the messages on the banners – 'Support the Human Family', 'Unity not Hate' – and then I see a little boy on his dad's shoulders carrying a banner with words painted in gold:

SILENCE ABOUT RACISM IS NEVER GOLDEN.

I look at Pari, and her huge eyes are filled with tears. That's what she remembered, being carried on her dad's shoulders – but now it sounds like she hardly knows him.

'Mum! You promised me we wouldn't have to watch the news . . .' Pari reaches over in front of her mum and switches off the TV.

'You are right, my Pari,' Leyla says, rubbing her daughter's spine where the sun hits her back. 'Sun kiss here!' she says.

Leyla talks to Pari in Arabic and then Pari grabs

hold of her mum and the two of them sit on the end of the bed hugging each other tight and rocking back and forth.

'What did your mum just tell you?' I ask. 'She looked so happy.' I get out of the sleeping bag and stand by the crate-shelves, shivering.

'She thinks you and the new moon coming for my birthday is a new beginning. We're going to the mosque this morning before we visit my dad. She feels peaceful. Last night she slept all through the night for the first time since I was born!'

'Throw open curtains, girls!' Pari's mum calls out to us. 'Our home will be sunshine today, no need for heating – *Bismillah*.'

THIRTY-NINE

Leyla hangs back by the kitchen door when Janu comes to pick me up. She hands me an envelope. 'Give this with your cousin.'

'What's this?' Janu asks, as I hand it to him.

'Please take,' Leyla calls to him. 'If you refuse, you insult me. You sign it in your website. You say Leyla Pashaei from Iraq, refugee in London, she gives to your children refuge school in India.'

'But—'

'No but . . . it is not much, but every pound is helping. There is poor and there is poor. I have seen all in my life, I have lived all . . . So, what about me? No foot photo? I painted!' She laughs and points at her shocking-pink varnished toenails.

Janu stands in the doorway and hands me his phone, and I take a picture of Leyla's feet.

'I am proud my feet in your story.'

'Mum!' Pari groans.

'Thank you, Mrs Pashaei,' Janu says, and lowers his

head in a respectful little bow.

'Thank you for bring Laila to here – this is best birthday present for Pari!'

As she closes the door we both hear her say . . . 'Very handsome boy. I am thinking he looks little like Bollywood star!'

Janu laughs and poses as if looking into a camera lens.

'In your dreams!' I joke.

Just as we approach the station, a boy on the other side of the road waves at me.

'Hey, Mira!' he calls, more than once.

I pretend I don't know him, but it's definitely the the same boy who showed me the way to the Caring Community the first time I came to see Simon. The one I pretended I couldn't speak English to. I want to disappear. I just walk faster, but Janu stops.

The boy runs across the road and catches sight of Janu's feet. Now he's smiling at me.

'Hi, Mira!' he says.

'Hi!'

Janu is looking confused.

I am so embarrassed I can hardly breathe.

'Are you going to introduce us, Laila?' Janu asks.

'Oh, yeah, sorry! This is Janu, my cousin . . . from India,' I mumble in a quiet voice.

'Your English has improved a bit.' The boy laughs.

'Good to meet you. I'm Tomek . . . most people call me Tom.'

'My name's actually Laila,' I explain. 'Mira's my sister . . .'

'Oh, OK.' He shrugs. 'Been to see your friend again?'

I nod. Janu gives me a sideways look.

There's another awkward silence.

'Well, see you again, Laila . . . I hope.' Tom heads off to the tube ahead of us.

We walk further up the road and Janu starts chuckling to himself.

'Why did he think you were Mira?' he asks. 'And what was that about your English?'

I shrug. It seems easier not to even start to explain. Janu carries on laughing to himself.

'What's so funny?' I ask.

'You . . . so full of surprises! You forget I grew up with Priya. You didn't tell me you had a boyfriend.'

'I do *not*!'

I bash Janu on the arm and he yelps.

'He looked happy to see you anyway!'

I roll my eyes, but I do see how it looks.

The train's just pulling in as we arrive on the platform, so we step straight on to the carriage. As soon as we do I regret it, because at the far end I spot Tom. I turn my back and lean against the glass so that even if he sees me I can pretend I don't know he's there. We go one stop. People get off and a group of men get on. They're rowdy and drunk. The space around them grows as people move to the edges of the carriage. One of them's eating a burger that's stinking out the place with stale grease. The way he chews and gulps it down makes me feel sick. Another man takes a beer out of his bag, pulls the tag, throws it on the floor and starts swigging from the can, letting beer dribble down his mouth and on to his neck. The train jolts and the beer spills out over the floor and on to Janu's feet. Janu steps backwards. The man looks at him, squashes his can and drops it on the floor, just missing Janu's toes.

Janu bends down, picks up the can and hands it back to the man, who refuses to take it.

'What's your problem?' the man with the burger asks.

Janu gestures for me to move away from him, further up the carriage. The men all shuffle right up close to Janu, so close that they're whispering straight into his ears. He flinches away as drops of spit settle on his face.

'Lost your shoes in the jungle?'

I look down at their feet. They're wearing huge, heavy boots. There are three other men in the group who move in front of Janu now, blocking him in. This strange noise starts up – they're all making it, and it's loud enough for people around us in the carriage to know what's going on. I think it's supposed to be a monkey noise. I feel sick and frozen, like my feet are stuck to the floor.

At the next stop people get off and move into the carriage further up. I want to grab hold of someone and ask them to help us but everyone's moving away. I turn around. Tom hasn't moved. He must read the panic in my eyes. He walks up the carriage to the far end, away from us. I don't know why I thought he would help. Janu's face is set in this stern mask that I haven't seen before. Now that the carriage is empty the men switch up the volume on their monkey noises and they stand either side of Janu and start to march on the spot, every so often stamping hard on both of his feet. Janu winces in pain. The man with the beer is eyeballing Janu, but he looks somewhere past him and doesn't step back or move or react at all.

I look for Tom in panic. Please let him do something to help us.

Tom nods at me and pushes the red 'alarm' button.

I think I'm going to be sick.

I can't believe how quiet Janu's being. One of the men cuffs the back of his head where his tattoo still shows under the stubble of his hair.

'What's with the tat?'

They start up their monkey-chanting again.

'Leave him alone!' I shout.

'What's it to you?'

'He's my cousin!' I say.

'Are you one too then? That's the problem – you can't tell now.' The man with the beer starts up the monkey sounds again and spits on my shoes.

'That's what they do!' The man with a mouth full of burger says, spitting bits out as he speaks: 'Breed.'

'At least this one's got the sense to wear shoes!' One of the other men laughs and shoves me out of the way. I stumble back and my head bashes into the glass.

Tom runs up the carriage towards me and holds my arm. He's been so quiet that I don't think the men knew he was there.

'I would give it a rest if I were you! The police will be on at the next stop,' he says.

'Just having a bit of fun, mate!'

The doors open and the men step out into the arms of security police.

'I'm not your mate,' Tom says.

An announcement blares out across the station.

'Due to an ongoing incident, this train will be delayed. We request that any witnesses please report to the transport police on this platform.'

I look through into the next carriage, and a few people walk towards the police. Janu collapses on to a seat and Tom sits down next to me. The police get on and start interviewing the three of us.

I can't stop crying. I'm so angry and sad for Janu. Tom sits by me. I take out a tissue from the pack the little girl gave me and I try to wipe away my tears, but they just won't stop coming. I use up the whole packet.

'And you're a friend of Laila's?' a policewoman asks Tom.

'Yes, I am,' he says, as if we've known each other for ages. He takes my hand and holds it tight.

'My dad's had abuse,' he says softly. 'I never get it because they don't know I'm Polish – not till I tell them my name. That's why I'm Tom to most people.'

The police tell us that they're taking this kind of racial abuse seriously and they want to take it further, but Janu explains that he's only visiting and he doesn't want a legal case. I'm holding my phone and Tomek gently takes it out of my hands and keys in his number.

'If you ever want to talk, Laila.'

'Thank you, Tomek,' I say.

My head's so foggy I don't even remember him going. The police officers drive me and Janu back home. In the car they try to make conversation with Janu. They want to know why he's going barefoot. He tells them a bit about his blog, but he's so quiet it's worrying. He hands them his card when he gets out of the car.

At home there's a message on the table.

I'll be back by 3 p.m. Mum x

I go through to the kitchen to make some tea for Janu.

He's taken himself upstairs and he's slumped on my perch when I hand him the mug.

'Thank you, Laila. I think I'll take my bath now and sleep a little.'

'Are you OK, Janu?'

'I'll be fine, Laila. But it takes time to wash away that sort of hatred. How's your head? Did you get a knock?'

He puts his hand up to my forehead where I can feel an egg-shaped bruise growing.

'It's nothing. I'm fine,' I say, and I walk back down the stairs. I stand at the bottom, not knowing what to do or say to make Janu feel any better.

'I'll be OK, Laila. You know, reality is I have met so many friendly people here. I won't let this spoil my visit. We're both a little bruised, that's all!'

He leans on the banister as if he needs to hold himself up.

'It would be better not to mention this to Uma and Sam or anyone else –' I think he means Mira – 'no need to upset them . . . not necessary.'

Janu's mobile rings.

'Oh, hi, Krish!' Janu smiles, limps into the bathroom and starts running the tap.

I listen to Janu speaking through the running water.

'So you managed to get away from work? . . . Ah, that's a shame, but you've got to promise me you'll come and see me for the opening of my new refuge . . . OK, OK, that's a deal . . .

'Don't put the blame on me! I only sent you a photo! What will Uma say?'

It's so annoying when I can't work out what the other person's saying.

'. . . Yeah, yeah, all good, man! Love this city!'

I feel so ashamed this has happened to Janu in my city, and it doesn't even look like Krish or Mira are going to come and see him. But now something Krish has said has got him laughing and choking at the same time.

'Yes, I know that song . . .' He's humming and singing something I've heard Krish play before. I think Krish must be singing it. 'And we live in different worlds . . . forsake me . . . brothers in arms.'

'Sorry, I don't understand.' He listens to Krish for a bit longer, then bursts out laughing. 'I hope Uma and Sam won't blame me! I'll show it to Laila.'

I sit on my perch listening to Janu humming along to the song as he bathes. He only seems to know a few words, so he hums along and sings when he gets to the lines he knows: 'I will not forsake you, my brother in aums . . .' And then he starts laughing all over again. I have no idea what the joke is.

Janu comes out of the bathroom with a towel wrapped around his waist and another draped over his shoulders, still laughing. He hands me his phone.

'Your brother!' he says, shaking his head.

There's a photo of the back of Krish's head with an Aum tattoo in exactly the same place as Janu's. Underneath the photo he's written: 'Brothers in Aums.'

'Mum's going to kill him!' I say.

'Hope not!' Janu laughs. 'It's supposed to be the symbol of peace!'

FORTY

'Laila's not that bothered about going either,' Dad argues.

'Well, she's not getting much encouragement from you, is she? It's only a Sunday-night supper. The girls have school tomorrow so it won't be a late one. '

'I suppose.'

'Come on, Sam. Hannah and Maurice have been so helpful to Janu – and Kez is fundraising for his charity at her bat mitzvah.'

'Yeah, I know, Uma. I just think things are settling down a bit with Laila. I don't want her feeling all left out again because of the bat mitzvah. Shouldn't we be doing supper for them?'

'Probably! But they invited us first, and I think this might be Bubbe's way of getting the girls together. Anyway, Janu's raring to go. He's gone out to buy sparklers.'

*

We're sitting around Kez's family's table, eating and chatting under their sparkly chandelier that shoots star shapes all over the ceiling and walls.

Janu's talking to Kez about the Durga Puja festival that's going on in Kolkata now, and they're comparing ceremonies for that and Hanukkah, which has just finished. I should have sent Kez a card. I always used to. I think it's strange that all these festivals come at more or less the same time. Pari says she'll be able to come back to mine after Eid in a few days' time. I have this thought that millions of people must have had before, and it sounds too obvious to even say it, but why don't all the religions get together at this time of year and do one *big* light celebration, no matter what the differences are between them?

Then Janu says exactly what I'm thinking – and it makes me feel like it's not such a stupid idea after all:

'Basically the same principle. Expel the darkness, let the light rise, and after all that have a feast! You should come to my village at this time. Why not plan your trip to come at Durga Puja next year? We will be having a very special celebration then. Why not all come? Go to Kolkata, visit Reena in her school, stay with Anjali, then come to see the new Vimana refuge. It'll give me a deadline to work towards! One year to the day we should try to open. You can come for the opening ceremony! Krish has promised me he'll come too. Chameli and Anjali will welcome you like you've never been welcomed before!'

It actually feels a lot less awkward here than when me and Kez meet on our own. I miss that hum of lots of people talking over each other at mealtimes, scrambling for a place in the conversation.

Mum's chatting away to Kez's parents about how much she's starting to enjoy her new work now she's getting to know the students she's working with. I feel a bit bad that I haven't even thought to ask her much about it.

Bubbe's sitting next to Dad and they're deep in conversation.

'No, Sam! I can't believe this!' Bubbe hardly ever raises her voice. 'How long have we known each other? But I used to go to that bookshop. I didn't know his surname! Isn't that incredible? It can't be we're only just discovering this now . . . Fancy you being Kit's son!'

'Can you fathom this, girls? Laila! Your grandad's shop was one of my Stan's favourite haunts in London. He dealt in those books that got saved by Jewish refugees in the war. He called them his Kinderbooks . . . That's how Stan and I got talking to him.'

'Sounds like my dad!'

'We spent hours in his shop looking through all those precious books. Stan used to say it was like "holding a bit of history in your hand". I was always under the impression your father didn't want to sell

them – I suppose, like he said, they were his Kinder!'
Bubbe laughs. 'Definitely more of a bookkeeper than
a bookseller . . .'

I'm so happy Dad played me that tape now, because
I can hear Grandad's voice in my head while they're
talking about him. I think I understand why Bubbe
tells Kez so many stories about her Grandad Stan,
because it does make you feel like you're part of this
big web that you haven't even started finding out
about yet. I suppose that's what Mrs Latif's getting at.

'This is far too much excitement. I think I'll put my
feet up!' Bubbe gets up from the table and walks over
to the sofa.

Kez is chatting to Janu about her idea to blog about
her journeys to different places in London.

'Even though it's better on the buses and some of
the new stations, it's still really hard. There's loads of
stations on the underground I still can't go to,' she
tells him. Thinking about the day of the march, I
don't know how Kez would have got there if some of
the stations don't even have working lifts. She's
right . . . how can it be that she doesn't even have the
right to protest? Bubbe looks in her handbag and gets
something out. I can see it from here. It's the photo of
her and Stan. She's switched on the TV news with the
sound turned down. I see her eyes fill with tears so I
go over to sit with her. She's watching pictures on the
news of refugee children being carried on to a beach

from a kind of dinghy. Bubbe has subtitles on all the time because of her hearing. I read the words as they scroll across the screen.

Just one more day and the storm would have taken all these Syrian children.

I hand her a tissue. I don't know why but I found myself in a shop buying more after the ones from the girl on the underground ran out. Now I've taken to carrying some around with me wherever I go. Every time I open a packet I think of the little girl on the tube's hands and her eyes full of hurt and I wonder what she's doing at this moment. Where she is now. I think of her so often I wish I knew her name. Where she came from. I hope she's not on a tube somewhere begging.

'Why don't we *all* go and sit on the comfy seats?' Maurice suggests. 'Fish soup, chicken and baked apples. It was all delicious . . . but far too much! Bubbe, why do you have to be such a good cook? I'm getting a proper paunch!'

'I made the veggie risotto,' Kez reminds him. 'I didn't think it would need that much stirring though – it was tougher than physio!'

Janu laughs. As he and Kez come over, Bubbe reaches out her arms to all three of us.

'Sit with me, young ones.' Bubbe holds my hand

on one side and Kez's on the other. 'I think it's up to you now to get the heart of this world beating again.'

'Mum! Let's switch this off. We don't want to spoil the evening.' Hannah takes the remote control, presses the OFF button and the screen goes blank. She sits on the back of the sofa and places a comforting hand on Bubbe's shoulder.

'I'm sorry, Hannah – I *can't* switch off and I don't think you should either. Stan and I wouldn't have been here if people had switched off back then! Nor would you, for that matter!'

'Please, Mum, try not to get too worked up; you know the doctor said you should rest more. Maurice, let's have a bit of music.'

Kez pulls a face at whatever it is that her dad puts on. I like it. It sounds like folk music. 'Sorry! Not to your taste, Kez? You two girls want to go and hang out in your room for a bit then?'

Kez closes the door to her bedroom.

'Is Bubbe all right?' I ask.

'She has to take blood-pressure pills now,' Kez explains. 'She gets really upset with everything that goes on in the news, like it's happening to her all over again. Mum and Dad don't want her watching it, or listening, but she's obsessed. She keeps saying history's repeating itself and she gets really angry with Mum and Dad when they try to calm her down.'

I think of when I sat with Bubbe on Stan's yahrzeit day . . . when we listened to that little boy talking.

'What do you think of the makeover?' Kezia asks, following the wall-grip around her room to her bed. I'm behind her, looking at the walls that used to be covered in photos of her and me from when we were little. I don't even have to look up to the ceiling to know that the parachute silks have gone. It feels like ages since we had the argument, and I do feel a bit childish now for getting so upset.

The wall by Kez's bed is painted bright yellow.

'Do you like the colour?' she asks. 'If it's not sunny, at least I've got my sun wall! I've just finished this collage. What do you think?'

In a huge frame on the sunshine wall is a massive collection of photos. There are some people I've seen before, but lots I don't know.

'We're there, right in the middle!' Kez points to a cluster of photos of the two of us together – photos ranging from when we were in nursery together right up to the one we took on the last day of primary school – but none after that. There's a photo of Reena, the little girl in Janu's House of Garlands Orphanage that Kez's family has kind of sponsored. She's holding the teddy that I helped Kez choose for her. I look at another, more recent photo, of Selina and Kez wearing their sports kit and raising each other's arms in victory. All these other people I don't know I suppose are from her summer camp. I can't believe I was so jealous before. Now I just want to know more about all the people she knows.

Hannah knocks and opens the door. 'Sorry, girls. Janu wanted to check something again about the design of the bathroom . . . Do you mind if he has a quick look at your pod, Kez?'

'Yes, they're all adapted depending on the site,' Kez's mum explains as she and Janu look in the little bathroom in the corner of Kez's room. 'More a matter of proper engineering, imagination and, of course, funds. But you'd be surprised; we've got the costs of a basic one right down now. Half the time there's quite a simple solution. The beauty of this system is that you can keep building sections as you grow the refuge . . . start small.'

'Actually, Kez and I were talking about something concerning this principle and I would like to get your advice . . .' Janu's voice trails away.

'What *were* you two talking about?' I ask Kez.

'Oh! He's going to help me set up a website, that's all.' Kez takes my arm and turns it over. 'Your eczema's getting better,' she says, and keeps holding on to my arm. 'Laila, I was talking to Bubbe and I really want to invite Pari to my bat mitzvah. I know she's not really my friend yet . . . but I like her and we probably all will be friends, won't we? What do you think? Should I ask her or would you like to?'

'I don't mind asking her.'

Kez hands me an envelope already addressed to Pari. She's obviously thought this through.

I don't quite get why Kez wants to invite Pari to her bat mitzvah, but just the fact that she does somehow makes me feel like it's less awkward between the three of us. It doesn't feel like it has to be Kez *or* Pari any more.

'Oh – and I've made you a playlist . . . some new stuff I'm listening to. Thought you'd like it.' Kez smiles at me a bit shyly, like she's not sure if I'm going to accept it. 'I'll share it with you if you want?'

'Thanks, Kez!'

It feels so good to be doing these normal things again.

'Sparkler time, girls!' Kez's dad knocks on the door. Kez raises her eyes to the sky – but when we're all standing in the garden with that smell of flint in the air, swirling our sparklers around to make star-tracks and patterns in the dark like we used to every November, it doesn't feel childish. It just feels like *us* again . . . me and Kez as we've always been.

Before we leave, Janu makes everyone take their shoes off and stand together while he takes a photo of our bare feet all in a line.

'They're not my best asset!' Bubbe laughs, looking down at hers. 'You can probably tell that these old feet have done some walking! I still can't get over it,

Sam. To think that after all these years of our girls being such good friends, that I knew Laila's grandparents.'

'Did you know my Nana Josie too?' I ask.

'A little . . . but to be honest, Laila, I was always a bit in awe of her arty ways!' Bubbe strokes my cheek and gestures for me to bend down so she can whisper in my ear.

It feels like she's shrunk, but I suppose it's just that I must have grown.

'You will let me have a look at that Protest Book one day, won't you, Laila?'

I nod. I really would like to sit at Bubbe's table and read it together. She could probably tell me more about all the things in there than any googling could. I just hope Mira's not so angry with me that she takes it away.

Bubbe kisses me on the cheek as we say goodbye.

'Funny! Now I remember. The first time I saw your little face in nursery I thought there was something familiar about you.'

'*Please* don't sleep on the landing tonight, Laila. You'll get disturbed by Janu leaving,' Dad pleads. 'I have to set off with him so early in the morning.'

So I go and lie on Mira's bed, just to keep him happy.

I can hear Janu on the phone to someone through the wall. It's Mira. I hear him say her name. And the way he says it makes it sound like he loves her. I feel so sad for Janu. I don't want to hear this. I plug my earphones in and listen to the playlist Kez has made for me. It's not the same kind of music that she used to listen to. There's dance music and a bit of rap, and some of the ambient instrumental tracks that Krish likes, but I think my favourites are still the ones we used to sing together. I turn up the volume on 'To Make You Feel My Love' and play it over a few times, trying not to think about Janu and Mira's conversation. The boy hugging Kez in the photo, the one she didn't want me to see before, comes into my mind. There

349

was something about the way she snatched the phone away that made me wonder if he *was* just one of the crowd. As I sing along I keep thinking about how kind Tomek was that day. I suppose there are lots of things Kez doesn't know about me too, like that I've thought about texting Tomek so many times but can't think what I would say. I blush up all over again at the memory of when we first met. What was I thinking, pretending I was someone else?

While I'm listening to the rest of Kez's playlist I think about how Bubbe and Nana Josie met each other, and Grandad Kit; how Simon and Nana knew each other; how they were marching against that war in Iraq; how that's the reason why Pari's here; and how I'm like a link between them all . . . And it was me who found the chime. Maybe without it I would never have opened Simon's letter and gone to collect the Protest Book and the Banner Bag . . . I feel like I should know where all this is supposed to lead me . . .

There's a knock at the door.

Janu peers around it. 'I could hear you ringing that chime of yours! My friend Yannis uses his worry beads like that!' He smiles. 'Mind if I come in?'

I can't tell if he's really sad or happy.

He sits next to me on the floor, leaning against the bed.

'I've just been speaking to Mira.'

'You were on the phone for a long time,' I say.

'Were you listening?' he asks.

I shake my head and unplug my other earpiece.

Janu spreads his arms out, 'Your sister and I had much to talk about after being apart for so long.'

I check Janu's face. I feel so sorry for him. After that racist attack the other day I don't want him to go away feeling sad.

'Don't look so troubled, Laila. She asked me to give these to you, for you to keep safe till she gets home.'

Janu lays a red-and-gold envelope on the carpet and hands me the ring box that I saw him hide away when he first arrived.

'You'll keep these safe till Mira comes home, won't you, Laila? I was hoping to hand them to her myself . . . but seems like there was something of a misunderstanding!' He smiles at me and pats the back of my hand. 'I think *you* might also have misunderstood, Laila? Open it!' he says.

I hesitate for a moment.

'Go on! Mira told me to show it to you, as long as you guard it with your life till she comes home. No pressure!' Janu grins.

I open the lid and inside is not a ring at all.

'And to think your sister doesn't believe in Karma!' Janu laughs.

I take Mira's artichoke charm that she used to wear all the time out of the box. The one Nana Josie gave her, with all the little silver layers and the tiny ruby right in the middle.

'I though she lost this.'

'Yes, that's what she *told* you.'

Janu looks at his watch. 'Mira's made me go over the story five times already so she can fill in the details for you – but no, Laila, she didn't lose it. She gave it away to a girl on the train near my village.'

'But she loved this . . . Why would she do that?' I can't believe what I'm hearing.

'Something like a reflex instinct. She was feeling sorry for this girl we were sitting with in our carriage. She felt guilty because she, Mira, had –' Janu gestures around the room – 'everything . . . and this girl had not even enough to feed her brothers and sisters.'

The eyes of the girl on the tube come into my mind again. I think I know how Mira felt.

'Your sister's like you, Laila. She has a big heart. I told Mira that the girl would sell it and she would never see it again.'

Janu takes out his phone, scans through his album and shows me a photo of this beautiful woman with shiny bobbed hair, wearing skinny jeans and a bright turquoise salwar kameez with the sleeves rolled up. She's standing next to Janu by a river.

'Can I?' I ask, taking the phone from him and homing in on her. 'She's got amazing eyes!'

'Yes, she's very beautiful – but look what she's

wearing on her wrist.'

It's the artichoke-heart charm.

'She came for an interview to work with me, to set up the website for my blog . . . I was wrong – she never sold it.'

'I've got to tell Pari and her mum about this!' I laugh.

Janu shakes his head.

'I know! Now Leyla will really think I'm out of one of her Bollywood films! But seriously, sometimes these things do actually happen.'

Janu hands me the envelope and I open it.

'Her name's *Parvathi*!' I say, laughing.

'I know – it's like a saga! Mira's going to paint us as a wedding present. It's next year, just after Durga Puja. I hope you will come. I'm going to invite Kez and her family too.'

I can't believe how stupid I've been.

'I thought you were going to ask *Mira* to marry you! I thought you loved her.'

Janu laughs.

'I know that now . . . and I think maybe you conveyed it to Mira, and that's why she was too afraid to meet me!'

'Sorry!'

'No, no! It's also my fault. There was a little romantic idea in me that I should return it to her myself. I wanted to see the look on her face.' Janu looks down at his hands. 'Love is complicated, Laila. In a way I will always love your sister – after all, she brought Parv and me together.' Janu picks up the little bracelet. 'Or maybe this charm did!'

I nod and hug Janu tight.

'It's been good to get to know you, Laila. Keep in touch . . . And remember: no need to say anything about –' he points to his bruised feet – 'All healed now.'

I'm lying on the landing when Janu goes. I pretend I'm asleep so Dad doesn't get annoyed with me. 'Bye bye, Landing Laila!' Janu whispers as he passes.

I watch Mum, Dad and Janu getting his things together at the bottom of the stairs.

'Mira called me late last night. She had an idea that I should give you these. She seems to think they would definitely fit you,' Mum says, handing Janu a pair of black shiny shoes. 'They belonged to my dad, Bimal.'

'I can't take these . . .'

Dad hands him a pair of his socks. 'Here, Janu. Look, it's a miracle! I even found a matching pair!'

Janu puts the socks on, bends down and slips his feet into the shoes.

'We can always buy some at the airport if—'

'No need, Sam!' Janu says. 'They're a little tight, but they'll be fine for the journey. It will be an honour for me to walk in these shoes.'

'You promise you'll keep them on till you get

354

through JFK? Anjali's concerned that you don't make things more difficult for yourself. You know how tight security is everywhere now,' Mum says.

'But are you sure, Uma? These are your baba's shoes.'

'Please wear them, Janu – he would have wanted . . .' Mum's voice falters.

'My ma has this saying, Uma . . . "As long as the footprint of the person is remembered by someone living, then we will always walk with them."'

Janu and Mum hug for a long time.

'Right then,' says Dad. 'Looks like your dad's travelling with us too, Uma! Come on, you've got to let Janu go. He'll miss his flight!'

Every now and again it's like I've got this new power to see things from a distance. If I was looking at myself as a character in this scene, sitting here on this landing, I used to only be able to see the close-up picture. But recently, just sometimes, I can pull back and see myself and everything else that's in the frame too, and that makes me feel things I never used to, like Mum's sadness not just being about Janu leaving, and why Mira wanted Janu to wear Grandad Bimal's shoes.

I hold Nana Josie's chime in my hand and ring it. I imagine Janu's plane taking off, flying through the night. I imagine him looking out of his window at the moon and the stars and falling asleep and waking up to a sunrise in a new country wearing Grandad's old shoes.

FORTY-TWO

The synagogue looks a bit like a community hall. Outside there's a sign that says 'Reform Synagogue'. I should have dressed up like Pari. She's really gone to town on her scarf sparkles, sequinned top and green net skirt like a long tutu. Maybe I should have worn a dress too. Too late now.

Hannah comes to the entrance and greets us all, hugging Mum and Dad and shaking hands with Pari. She looks so happy and sparkly-eyed, excited and nervous at the same time. She tells us that we're Kez's special guests so we should go and sit at the front with Kez's other friends.

Dad picks up a white cap and fixes it to the crown of his head.

A woman standing behind a table hands us two heavy prayer books.

'Do you know how to read these?' she asks us.

Mum shakes her head.

'I'll be the guide.' Dad takes the books from her,

and Mum gives him this look as if she didn't expect him to know what to do.

The room is full of people of all different ages. Kez is sitting at the front with her mum and dad, Bubbe, her uncles, aunts and cousins. She looks beautiful. Her hair's gone back to its normal chestnut colour and she's styled it into loose curls that flow down her back. She's not wearing any make-up and she looks like the Kez I've always known. She's wearing a silvery straight dress with long sleeves and little pumps on her feet. She keeps smiling over at us and waving while we wait for the service to begin. Rebecca and Selina are in front of us . . . and Stella. She turns around and smiles at me and Pari. I didn't know she'd been invited. I even didn't know Kez knew her. Rebecca turns around and introduces us to all the other friends. 'And that's Adam!' she whispers, raising her eyebrows and pointing to a tall boy with wavy black hair sitting on the front row. 'She kept him a bit quiet, didn't she?' Becks laughs.

For the first time in secondary school when we're all together I don't feel like we're all in different camps.

'That's our rabbi, Miriam,' Becks whispers, and everyone hushes as she walks up to the platform and does the welcome. She wears a flowery shirt and a shawl around her shoulders and something like the cap that Dad's wearing. I thought the rabbi would be a man. Rabbi Miriam looks about Mum and Hannah's age. She smiles at us before she greets everyone on behalf of the family. She says what a joyous occasion it is to be here to celebrate the bat mitzvah of Kezia Braverman.

Bubbe's eyes are glistening with pride.

The rabbi says a bat mitzvah marks a transition from childhood into the responsibilities of adulthood.

'. . . And to do this we need to bring all our voices together in celebration. We are lucky to have Ruth here today, our cantor – she'll be playing the guitar and helping us to keep vaguely in tune!'

She asks us to turn to the welcoming prayer. Rebecca twists around to show us that the page numbering starts at the back. Me and Pari struggle a bit with the thin paper, holding the heavy book and turning the pages backwards, but we finally find the prayer. I like the sweet sound of the singing along to the guitar. It's a bit folky, like the music Bubbe plays sometimes. You can sort of predict where the tune's heading, and even though I don't understand Hebrew apart from the odd word I've heard from Bubbe, I pick up the repeated words and phrases.

'What does *Adonai* mean?' I whisper to Rebecca.

'Lord!' she whispers back.

Rabbi Miriam starts talking about Kez's family. She says that in a moment we will make the prayer to the Avot . . . the forefathers. Bubbe's glistening eyes overflow and tears roll down her cheeks. She catches my eye and nods in my direction, and just knowing what I do about her story makes me feel so close to her. Kez reaches for Bubbe's hand while they pray and sing 'L'dor Vador' – 'from generation to generation'. Bubbe wipes her eyes so that by the end of the song she's singing along with everyone else.

The singing in Hebrew takes you somewhere else. I thought it might be boring not understanding the language. At first I look in the prayer book to try to keep up and read the translation, but soon I just let the sound of the chant-singing take me over. Pari is swaying a little bit backwards and forwards as she listens.

'I can actually understand some words,' she whispers.

Rabbi Miriam smiles at Kez reassuringly. 'Now, Kezia, let us take a little time to breathe and reconnect to our soul breath – our Neshima – before we begin the prayer of the Covenant. Kezia has requested that her bubbe be by her side for this part of the service as we open the doors of the Ark.'

'This is my favourite bit. That's where the holy book's kept . . . the Torah,' Rebecca explains to Selina.

Rabbi Miriam leads everyone in prayer again, then introduces Kezia. An older girl called Sarah stands by Kez's side. The rabbi thanks her for helping to guide Kez to prepare for her bat mitzvah. I see now why it's taken Kez so long to get ready for this day.

The whole family and some of the men and women in shawls stand together. Hannah's on one side of Kez and Maurice on the other. Kez's Uncle Leonard is there too and her youngest cousin Noah with his cute curly hair. He's so smart in his little navy-blue suit. I didn't even know they made suits for four year olds! Now Kez's Uncle Leonard is holding the enormous scroll. Kez stands with Hannah on one side and Maurice on the other supporting her as she walks slowly around the whole room while a prayer is sung. People reach out to touch the holy scroll as it's carried around.

The scroll is finally unrolled. Kez keeps standing and leans hard on the lectern. Rabbi Miriam squeezes her hand and Kez starts to sing her verses from the Torah.

She sings the whole of her parsha in Hebrew in her soft, smooth voice . . . I could never sing like that, without any music or anything. Mostly the chant-singing is along the same kind of notes, but sometimes she adds a bit of her own sound to an end note, like she does when she's singing along to Adele!

Rebecca turns to me and grins. 'She's rocking it. It's faultless!'

After the song Kez speaks to Rabbi Miriam, who goes over and whispers something to Hannah. She wheels Kez's chair up to the platform, and Kez looks relieved to be finally sitting. That must have taken a huge effort. Now Rabbi Miriam moves the lectern aside so that everyone can see Kez. She takes her notes off the stand and hands them to her. Kez pauses and arranges them on her lap.

She looks over to us and explains. 'The parsha I'm about to interpret is the portion of the Torah that I've studied. It's about the power of community in our world today.'

She looks much more nervous now that she's talking, and her voice wobbles.

'My parsha talks of three different aspects of community. "Edah" – this is the side of community where we are all witness to what's happening around us. My bubbe has helped me prepare for today and we've talked about this a lot. I have asked this community to contribute to the new refuge our friend Janu is building in India for street children.' Kez looks over and smiles at me. 'When I was in primary school my friend Laila and I saw a video of a four-year-old girl with cerebral palsy sitting on the floor waiting for hours for someone to come and help her. It made us see how much we have, and Laila and I decided that we had to do something in our community to raise funds for the refuge in Kolkata. So this helped me to understand that "community" has a wide meaning . . . that little girl is now my sponsored sister Reena. One day soon we will meet each other. Even though she lives so far away from me in the world, she's part of my community here too because I am witness to her difficulties.'

Selina and Stella turn around and smile at us. I've never seen Stella looking so emotional and gentle.

'I'm so happy she invited us all,' Pari whispers.

After a pause, when Kez sits for a moment and takes a few deep breaths, she repeats some more words in Hebrew.

'The second meaning of community is "tzibbur". I interpret this to mean when we come together for the same reason, even though we may not have things like religion in common. It was my bubbe's idea to invite some people today who I know well and some people I want to get to know better. In my school there are many students with different religions who are my friends. I think that, if we needed to, we would stand up as a community for things that we know are right and also stand against things that we see are wrong.'

Pari's shoulder touches mine as she leans in to me. Now I get why we're all here together.

Then Kez again repeats some more words in Hebrew.

'The third and final aspect is "kehilla". This can be used for good or to create conflict. It's how people come together as a powerful force. and take group responsibility for a situation. My bubbe and I have talked about this a lot. When I see what is happening

362

with refugee people, especially children, I think that the kehilla aspect of community is not being followed by the leaders in this world today. When there are so many people in chaos it is easy to say, "I can't do anything to help with this." But I've been thinking that if everybody says, "I will help to make this change" – like when Quaker people helped my family when they came here as refugees – then kehilla could become a powerful movement for good.

'Everything I have said about my parsha comes from thinking about my friends and family and how they have supported me to help me stand here. My friends coming together for my bat mitzvah gives me hope that the three aspects of community I have learned about in my parsha can be a guide for me in my life, for us. I think we are all witnesses and so we are all responsible.'

I feel the tears roll down my cheeks and I don't even try to stop them. I feel so incredibly proud of my friend Kez. I look over to Mum and she's crying too. She smiles at me through her tears.

The rest of the service, the prayers and the standing and sitting, is a bit of a blur to me.

There are more prayers and singing, and the Torah scroll is rolled up. Kez's uncle walks with it around the room again. It's placed back into the Ark and the doors are closed.

As Rabbi Miriam is doing 'notices and news', Kez

turns around and gives us all a huge grin. Bubbe hugs her close. I want to run over and sit with them. I still feel choked up that she made us all so much part of her story. It's like she's used her bat mitzvah as a way to bring us closer together, and all this time I'd thought she didn't think much about me any more.

'Party time!' Rebecca says.

Now someone's throwing sweets, and all the little children scrabble around for them and then it's over. Kez looks so relieved and happy. The rabbi does a prayer to bless the wine and food and invites everyone to go into the next room for the kiddush.

Pari, Stella and I follow Rebecca and the others into the hallway where Dad's coming out of the bathroom with Kez's dad. The two of them have their arms around each other's shoulders and they each take a drink off a tray and cheers each other.

'Yes, much nachas!'

'Well, rightly so, Maurice. You've got every right to be proud.'

'But it all starts here!' Kez's dad nods over in the direction of the door.

I follow their eyes and find Kez by the door chatting to Adam, and it's impossible for anyone not to notice the look that they give each other as he waves goodbye.

Afterwards we all go back to Kez's flat for her party. Every wall is hung with fairy lights and there are huge bouquets of flowers on the table. Pari says the flowers are called 'birds of paradise'.

As we walk through the door, Pari pulls me aside. She has the same look on her face as when she first came to my house.

'You won't tell anyone about the Lighthouse, will you?' she whispers to me.

I shake my head, but now I feel bad again. I don't want to feel like this at Kez's party. I go through the motions of dancing and having fun, and Pari joins in too, but I can't stop thinking about everything Kez said about being part of the same community. What she said then made perfect sense, but now with Pari dancing by my side and knowing how she lives I have this feeling again in my gut that this can't be right. Why *should* Pari feel ashamed of being poor? Why *should* I keep quiet about those racists who attacked Janu? How can we all dance together if we don't tell the truth about how things are?

FORTY-THREE

On Monday Kez texts me just as I'm passing the Unfriendship Bench on my way into school.

> I've done myself in. I'm so tired I'm having a few days off to recover. Teachers have given me leave to work from home this week. Will you come for a sleepover next Sunday to chill? My parents are away. Just me, you and Bubbe!

I sit on the Unfriendship Bench and wait for Pari. I text Kez back.

> Yes please!

After school when I ask Mum she seems really into the idea.

'That works out well. We've got builders in, sorting out the wall, and I think Dad and I might go away for the night to Suffolk. Get a bit of sea air!'

We sprawl out over Kez's comfy sofas in front of a new version of *Peter Pan*. We've watched this film together tons of times since we were tiny, but I like the way they've updated it so the children are teenagers – it's like they could be us . . . Kez, me, Pari, Stella and Rebecca. We know whole sections of the words off by heart, and when they come up we shout them at the top of our voices. Pari would love this.

'So come with me, where dreams are born, and time is never planned. Just think of happy things, and your heart will fly on wings, forever, in Never Never Land!'

Bubbe laughs at us as we reel off the words. 'Glad to see you two aren't too old for this yet!'

'I didn't know you were friends with Stella in our tutor group,' I say to Kez.

'Yeah, she's really nice. She comes with me and Selina sometimes for PE and to physio too. I've seen her in the hydropool a few times. She has a twin brother; he's got a brain injury. She helps him swim. His face lights up when he knows she's there. She's got such a way with him. She told me she gets really stressed being apart from him.'

As we watch the rest of the film I can't help winding back through everything I thought I knew about Stella. It turns out I knew nothing at all.

Bubbe makes us some doughnuts and lets us eat on

the sofa, and the time just slips by like it used to, with neither of us saying or doing anything much – just hanging out.

When the film's over, Kez and I head back to her room.

'Do you want to hear a real-life love story about Janu and Mira and Jidé?' I ask Kez.

'Do I want to breathe?' She laughs.

We lie in bed in the dark, top to tail, and I tell her the whole thing as I twiddle her feet like I always used to when we were little and had sleepovers.

'That story's so . . . romantic!' Kez says when I finish. 'And Mira never told you any of it?'

I shake my head. 'I suppose everyone has secrets. What about Adam? I saw the way he was looking at you all through your bat mitzvah!'

'You think so?'

'Yes! And so do you!'

'If I tell you something, promise you won't tell anyone else? Because I'm not sure yet whether it'll turn into anything.'

'I promise.'

For a moment I think about telling Kez about Tomek. But what can I say? It's not like there's anything between us, and even though I keep thinking I might call him, every time I go to do it I change my mind. He must think I'm so weird, pretending not to speak English when I first met him. There's nothing to tell.

368

'At camp we were doing abseiling. You know me, Laila, I'll try everything, but there was this one moment when I got really scared and Adam talked me through it. We sort of got to know each after that and we sang together at this silly show thing we did.'

'And . . . ?'

'And when we were leaving he kissed me! But I wasn't sure if it was just like an end-of-summer-camp thing.'

'Are you going out together then?'

'I don't know! I can't believe he came all the way from Manchester for my bat mitzvah.'

'I think he really likes you. The way he was leaning forward and hanging on every word you said . . .'

'You think? He only texted me once to say thanks after my bat mitzvah . . . then nothing.'

Kez's phone beeps. She switches on her bedside light and I catch the time on her clock radio. It's gone midnight already but it feels like we've only just come to bed!

A grin spreads across Kez's face as she reads the message.

'His ears must have been burning!'

She hands her phone to me.

> Can't sleep! Got Kez on my mind!
> When can I see you again? We need
> to practise for our duet! Love Adam X

I wake up first. There's a picture poking out from Kez's pillowcase. I pick it up and take a closer look. It's the sweetest painting of Kez with her bright red hair floating behind her all entwined with a little girl's jet-black hair as they're flying through the sky in a sort of spaceship palace. I look at it for ages, until I feel Kez stir beside me. I hand it to her. 'Who did this?'

'That's one of Reena's,' she tells me, yawning. 'It's me and her flying around in our Vimana chariot!' Kez points to her chair. 'Remember in primary I used to ask you to run for me?'

I nod.

'You understand, don't you, Laila, why I had to break away a bit?' Kez hugs me close.

It's taken me a while, but I do understand. I think I needed to break away too; I just didn't know it. The old Laila would never have gone on a march on her own.

On Monday morning we do a bit of homework and go out to the park. I love Inset days; they make the week seem so much shorter. We sit on the Unfriendship Bench that's lost its 'Un'. Pari calls and I talk to her for a while and it feels fine chatting to her with Kez by my side, not awkward at all.

When we get back Adam calls and Kez blushes red. I keep making her giggle so she goes through to the bathroom and chats to him for ages behind the closed door. I lie on Kez's bed and Mum and Dad text me to say that they're having a peaceful time 'walking by the wintery sea'.

After lunch Bubbe pulls on her coat.

'I'm going to the cemetery. Thought I'd go and tidy up Stan's headstone; I've been meaning to do it for a while,' she says. 'I know it's not exactly an outing, but do you girls want to keep me company?'

'I thought you weren't supposed to drive?' Kez says.

'Nonsense. I'm perfectly fine!'

'We'll come with you then. I'll take Vimana.'

I get the feeling Kez is worried about Bubbe driving herself there.

As I watch Bubbe get into the car and lower the ramp for Kez, I wonder how this family would actually manage without Bubbe's help. Maybe Kez is as confident as she is partly *because* of Bubbe. As we drive past the end of our road, I look towards our house and there's a big yellow skip parked outside and some builders working on the wall.

Bubbe's in a chatty mood as she drives along.

'Back in the day, Stan and I started out at the West London Reform Synagogue. I always feel quite lucky that he's buried here, so close . . . I'm happy we've organized it so I'll be by his side too when my time comes.'

'That won't be for ages,' Kez says. The muscles in her cheeks tense up like she can't stand the thought of Bubbe not being here.

'It'll be when it will be.' Bubbe smiles to herself. 'Anyway, nice and convenient for maintenance!' she jokes, waving to a security man on the gate as we enter.

We park and Bubbe walks ahead of us along the path.

The cemetery is so peaceful. You can hardly hear the road from here. Bubbe walks ahead, putting more space between us. It's like she wants to be alone for a bit, so we hang back. Suddenly she stops and sinks to her knees. I think she must have found the grave, but the way Kez speeds up makes me think something's wrong. I have to run to catch up with her.

When she reaches Bubbe, I see Kez put her hand over her mouth and look up at me in panic.

'Lai Lai!' She screams my name.

At first I think maybe Bubbe's fallen and hurt herself. But she's pointing at the graves, sobbing, and then I see what they're both looking at. On Stan's headstone, underneath his name, someone has spray-painted a red swastika. The headstone alongside and all the others as far back as the cemetery wall have all been defaced too. Bubbe stares and stares, tears running down her cheeks, as if she can't believe what she's seeing. She takes a handful of earth and scatters it across the gravestone to try to cover up the ugly red stain, but the soil slides off.

I get out my phone to call Mum. Why do they

have to be so far away right now?

'Don't bother anyone.' Bubbe straightens up and begins to walk very slowly out of the cemetery without saying a word.

Kez looks like she's in shock too; she's shaking, and when I take her hand, she clasps it so tightly that it hurts.

'I'll call Mum and Dad,' Kez says.

'No! Just wait by the van,' Bubbe orders, and walks over to the lodge to ring the bell. The security man comes out and Bubbe points to the graves in the far corner of the cemetery. The guard shakes his head, takes her arm and walks her back to the car.

'Appalling! It must have happened last night. I'll make sure it's dealt with straight away. I think we need to build the wall higher in that corner.'

'I don't think walls are the answer,' Bubbe mumbles.

'They must have got in over the footpath. Are you sure you're all right to drive?' the security guard asks. Bubbe ignores the question and climbs into the front seat. She doesn't say a word as she drives away. We keep checking on her through the mirror, expecting her to say something, but she has her eyes fixed on the road ahead. I've never seen that look on Bubbe's face before. It's like all the softness has gone out of her, as if she's turned to stone.

When we get in she goes straight to her room. We

make her tea and knock on her door but she doesn't answer.

'I don't care what she says. I'm calling Mum.' Kez dials the number.

'It's Bubbe . . . Mum, you've got to come back home now.' Kez tries to say what's happened but her voice slurs and even I can't really understand her because she's getting so upset.

'It's all right, Kez. We're approaching home now anyway,' I hear Hannah say.

Five minutes later Hannah and Maurice are opening the door. They come into the kitchen and sit at the table while we tell them exactly what we saw.

'Why?' Maurice bashes the table hard and makes us jump. Tears spring into my eyes. Kez looks frightened.

'Dad!'

Hannah puts a hand on Maurice's shoulder. 'Don't, Maurice. What good will that do?'

But I think I understand how he feels. Janu was wrong to tell me to keep quiet about what those racists did to him, and I can't get that vile message that Pari has to look at every day out of my head. If people are afraid to say or do anything about it, how are things ever going to change?

'They've got to call this what it is . . . anti-Semitism . . . If they don't call it—'

'Calm down, Maurice – you're upsetting the girls even more.'

Kez's dad walks to the other end of the room and rests his forehead against the wall for a while, till his shoulders start to relax a bit. He turns around.

'Sorry, girls. Let's go in and see Dara.'

It doesn't feel right for me to follow them, so I stay outside her room. I can hear them talking to her, but she doesn't respond. I go through into the kitchen, walk over to the dresser and pick up the photos of the little girl and boy who grew up into Stan and Bubbe. All these conversations start flowing through my mind: Bubbe talking about Stan and why she came here; Grandad Kit's voice on the tape describing marching down Cable Street; Simon handing me the Banner Bag; the girl with her tissues on the tube; Simon and Nana Josie chanting and marching for the things they believed needed changing. Me . . . keeping quiet about what happened to Janu on the tube and so many other things that I can see are plain wrong. I feel sick thinking about Bubbe lying in bed believing that nothing's changed in this world . . . that everything's just getting worse.

When they come out of Bubbe's room, Hannah calls the doctor.

'I would say grief-stricken, traumatized, yes, that too.'

'Why won't she speak to us, Mum – why won't she

talk?' The muscles in Kez's face and neck are spasming. She shouldn't get into this much of a state. Maurice is encouraging her to take some medicine to calm her down.

It's so wrong. This is the same Kez who just one week ago was flying, she could have done anything, and now she's having to take medication to calm her because of hateful racists. I have to think of something I can DO about this . . . like Nana Josie and Simon did when they saw things that were so unfair. After everything Bubbe's done, bringing us all together at the bat mitzvah. All she and her husband went through to survive as children on the Kindertransport. Janu's wrong. This is not a time to stay quiet. Nothing's healed. I'm not going to let Bubbe think that it's all happening again and we're just going to sit by and watch.

'Laila, I think your parents are home now; we bumped into them on the way back,' Maurice says. He's turned an ash-grey colour.

'Oh yes . . .' I say, placing the photos gently back on the shelf. 'Of course, sorry, I'll go and pack my things.'

When I'm ready to leave, Kez, Maurice and Hannah are all still in with Bubbe, sitting around her bed. I don't want to disturb them, so I let myself out, quietly closing the door behind me.

'You're family too, Laila!' Bubbe's words run through my mind as I walk home.

*

Dad meets me halfway up the street. He wraps his arm around my shoulders and walks me home.

Only . . . it doesn't look like home, more like a building site. The whole of the front wall has gone but it's nowhere near finished yet. Instead of steps there's a muddy ramp up to the front door. Everything looks different now, even our house.

I run upstairs to Mira's room, slam the door, crawl under the bed and take out Nana's Protest Book. I turn the pages that I'm starting to know off by heart. When I look closer at the photographs, I see that the same banner is in a few of the different marches that they went on. It just says: 'Not In My Name'. I think I saw that slogan on the march we saw on TV at Pari's flat too.

Mum and Dad let me be for a while and then the knocking starts.

'Leave me alone!'

They do for a bit, but then they come back. First Mum, then Dad . . . I ignore them and call Pari and tell her about Bubbe. She hardly says anything. I keep asking her if she's still there.

'Pari . . . ?'

'I'm still here!' she says. 'Sorry, my mum's talking at the same time. Hang on, Mum.' I can hear Leyla speaking in Arabic. She sounds upset. 'Mum's saying she saw it on the news . . . it's happened in other areas too. She's worried there will be a backlash against us.'

'I don't get that!' I say. 'Why? They don't know who's done it.'

'But still . . . she thinks it will cause more tension.'

'OK, Mum, OK. I'll tell them. I will make sure they understand . . . Mum says she wants you to tell Kezia's family that she's going to say her prayers for them. There was enough trouble back home. She wants us all to have peace. Anything she can do to help she will do.'

'OK, tell her thank you,' I say.

After I put the phone down, I sit there for a while. What Pari's mum said has made me think. Maybe there *is* something we can all do together?

'Listen to this.' Dad reads from the news on his phone over breakfast. 'A council spokesman said that "our sincere condolences go to the Jewish Community and we will endeavour to remove the hateful graffiti as quickly as possible. Anti-Semitism will not be tolerated in this country or any borough of this city."'

I have never felt like this before. Everything people are saying is feeding my plan . . .

Kez is not at school. I text and call her, but she doesn't answer. I walk past hers on the way home, but the shutter blinds are closed like someone has died. I drop a note through her door asking after Bubbe and telling her to call me when she gets a chance.

When I get back home there's the beginning of a concrete-shaped path, and a man with a mini-digger is pouring soil on to both sides of the pathway. The grinding of the digger drills into my head and I get a sharp pain behind my eyes.

'When's it going to be finished, Dad?' I ask as I walk inside.

'Shouldn't be long now . . .'

I head upstairs and pull the Banner Bag out from under the bed. I press open the catches. They feel a bit looser now. I take the Protest Book out, lay it on the floor and open the bag up as wide as it will go. On the inside, in the faded leather, I spot something I haven't noticed before, someone's handwriting . . . it looks like Simon's. I turn the bag on its side. The words are a bit faded but I can just about make them out:

> 'Days are scrolls - write on them what you want to be remembered'.

I feel this ball of fire in my stomach and I know what I have to do.

I unroll a clean scroll and lay it out across the carpet. I think for a long time about the message. I pick up a paintbrush and choose the same blue paint Nana Josie used for the banner on her last march.

Everything kaleidoscopes through my mind. Those men's faces on the tube, mocking Janu with their chanting, the hateful words in Pari's lift, what her parents had to go through, Bubbe and Stan arriving as children, Grandad Kit marching on Cable Street against the fascism growing in the city, Bubbe's tears at the refugee children on the news, at Stan's grave . . . what if . . . what if no one can tell when they're actually living in a time that's losing its heart? What if that's why evil things happen? No one says and does anything until it's too late; they just change carriage and pretend they haven't seen what's going on.

I want Bubbe to remember us all standing together like we did at Kez's bat mitzvah – and I want Janu to know that I haven't stayed silent, that this is for him too. I think of the sign above Mrs Latif's whiteboard. I want all religions, no religions, don't even know about religion – just people from here, there and everywhere – to come together. I can't stop thinking about the look on Bubbe's face when she drove us back from the cemetery, like she'd given up hope. What if . . . what if Bubbe dies and all this hate is the last thing she remembers?

I paint in bright blue capital letters.

ANTI-SEMITISM
ANY RACISM
NOT IN OUR NAMES

I unroll all the blank banner scrolls and write the same message over and over. Painting in Nana's colours, with the brush she held in her hands, and all these feelings whirring through my head, I feel like she's guiding me through this. Maybe everything from the day I found her chime has been leading to this. Each letter I paint makes me feel closer to her, and I know that this is the right thing to do.

When I'm done I slide the banners under my bed to dry.

I google the address of the Jewish cemetery and write:

Anti-Racism Vigil
Sunday December 10th - 3 p.m.
Crosslands Cemetery
Bring warm clothes, a jam jar and nightlights

Now that I've written it down it starts to feel real.

I don't want to email or text anyone in case Dad checks my account and tries to stop me. I copy the invite over and over and over, then cut them into thin strips and put them in my school bag. By the time Mum peeps her head around the door to say goodnight, I'm all tidied up.

'What's that smell of paint?'

'Working on some art homework,' I lie.

381

'Reminds me of Mira!'

'Have you heard how Bubbe is?' I ask.

'They've cleaned up the graves but she's still devastated. Very depressed. Kez too, I think. Just dreadful, isn't it?'

I'm so tired, but the thought of Bubbe and Kez spurs me on.

I scroll down my phone contacts to:

Tomek

Maybe in the morning I'll pluck up the courage to call him.

I wake up determined to speak to Tomek, but when it comes to it, I text him instead. I write '**Dear Tomek** . . .' then delete it. '**Hi Tomek** . . .' and even that looks strange, so I delete that too and just text him the details. At least it makes sense me inviting him to this, and if he's not interested, it's not embarrassing for me to have got in contact. Remembering what he did for Janu that day on the train makes me even more sure about doing this.

No text from Kez and she isn't in school again.

I tell Pari everything. I talk through my plan and she says she wants to be part of it.

'Don't tell your mum, Pari. This has to be our

thing, to show Bubbe that she's right to have hope in us.'

'I won't say anything. But if anyone would understand, my mum would. I'll tell her I'm coming over to yours,' Pari says.

I pass a wodge of information strips to Rebecca and she promises to spread the word to the people I don't know who came to Kez's bat mitzvah.

'What are you all whispering about?' Stella asks at break-time. I take out a slip from my bag and hand it to her. She looks at it and puts it in her pocket. 'Thanks!'

Mrs Latif is off sick and it's the longest, most boring week in school ever. We don't hear anything from Kez or Maurice or Hannah. It's like they've closed the rest of the world out.

On Friday I text Kez again, but there's no answer.

The weather's turned cold. Really, really cold – so your breath turnes to mist. I decide to wear a vest and one of Mira's old school jumpers like Mum's been nagging me to do for ages. There's a frost on the ground that doesn't thaw all day. Even after school the leaves are crispy white with ice like those sugared leaves you can buy to decorate cakes with. I think of Pari. I hope her mum can keep the electricity on tonight.

*

On Saturday I don't sleep all night, thinking about Kez and Bubbe. I go into Mira's room and sit on the bed. I open the curtains at about 3 a.m. It seems very light. The moon is almost full. As I look out the snow begins to fall. It's just a bit of sleet at first but then it falls heavier, in great soft flakes that fill the sky. I kneel by the window and watch it cover everything with a soft white coat. All the hard edges in the garden are gone . . . I wonder if the snow will stop anyone from coming.

In the morning I run downstairs and look at the road. Nothing's moving. I open the front door. I can't hear anything. It's so quiet, like the whole city's been wrapped in a soft white blanket.

Rebecca phones me. 'Should we cancel?'

'No!' I say. 'It's not that far. It's not till the afternoon. Transport might be working by then. If people come, it'll show that they care even more. Anyway, we've all got time to walk there.'

My phone rings. It's Pari.

'Sorry, Laila. I had to tell my mum or she wouldn't let me come. The tubes are off, you see. She says she's proud of us and she's going to let me walk.'

I give her directions to the cemetery from our street, but she and her mum have already looked it up.

'One hour twenty-three minutes by foot according

to Journey Planner,' I tell her. 'Are you sure you'll be all right?'

'Sure! I know about the cold. I might meet up with Stella on the way.'

'Is she coming?' I ask.

'Yes! She said so.'

I usually hate wearing hats, but the one Pari's mum knitted is so soft. I pull it down over my ears. Mum and Dad are out when I set off. The Banner Bag doesn't seem so heavy without the paints and Nana's big banner in it, but still the further I go the heavier it feels. When it's too much for one arm I switch it to the other. Even though the streets are eerily empty I have the strangest feeling that I'm not on my own. Every time I put a new footprint in the snow I think of all the people this is for: Bubbe, Kez, Stan, Maurice, Hannah, Janu, Pari, Leyla, Nuri, Nana Josie, Grandad Kit, Grandad Bimal, Nana Kath, Mira, Krish, Mum, Dad, Anjali, Priya . . .

Those are the names that come into my head first – then other names drift through my mind . . . Stella, Rebecca, Selina, Adam, Tomek . . .

Most of the way to the cemetery I'm walking in untrodden snow.

I'm the first to arrive. I go over to the lodge where the security guard was when we came last time so I can talk to him about what we're planning, but it's all locked up. Maybe he can't get here because of the snow.

I keep looking at my watch and worrying. What if no one turns up except me, Pari and Stella? *That would still be something*, I tell myself. They should be here soon. I think about phoning Pari again . . . and just as I'm about to, I see someone waving. It's Pari, wearing her red pom-pom hat – and I suppose that must be Stella. They're wearing identical bright blue snowsuits.

'I met Stella on the way!' Pari says. 'She lent me all this warm gear. I'm not cold at all!'

'We're twins!' Stella explains, and smiles at me.

I'm not sure if she's talking about me and Pari and our matching red hats, or about her and Pari in their snowsuits.

'Not *us*!' Stella laughs. 'Me and my brother. That's his kit!' She points to Pari's snowsuit.

We wait, the three of us, for more people to turn up. After about ten minutes a whole colourful crowd of bright coats and hats walk towards us.

I hand Stella and Pari a long taper each – I found them in the Banner Bag.

'Will you light people's candles?' I ask.

Other people arrive with their night lights and their jam jars, and one by one Pari, Stella and me light the candles. All Kez's friends from the bat mitzvah are here, and some people from her tutor group too.

386

There are loads more than I thought would come. I count over fifty of us. There aren't even enough banners to go round.

Even though I'm nervous and I've never done anything like this before, somehow it's not so difficult to tell them my idea, because I'm doing it for Bubbe. I ask everyone to turn their phones off and they do. I thought people would argue or think the barefoot idea is too weird, but when I tell them that our footprints in the snow will show how much we care about this, nobody laughs at me.

'I get that!' Stella says. 'And when people see these footprints they won't know who they belong to.'

I feel like hugging Stella . . . but she's not the sort of person who looks like she would let you hug her.

I hand my iPad to Becks. 'Can you film it all from the start? I'm going to send it to Kez and Bubbe.'

'OK!' she says. 'Ready?' She points the iPad towards us.

We are standing outside the cemetery, and the graves inside look like little even hills of snow. I can just about make out the path still.

When you first take your shoes off, the softness and coldness of the snow takes your breath away. I feel like this is the first time I have really felt what snow is.

I say my name and lay my shoes by the cemetery gates. Then Pari follows:

'Pari Pashaei' – and she places her shoes neatly behind mine.

'Stella Firn.'

'Selina Sen.'

'Carmel Baninga.'

'Nathan Mathews.'

'Louis Falks.'

'Riba Allan.'

'Akil Husseini.'

'Milena Aleksandrov.'

'Kian Edwards.'

'Carlos Mandego.'

The shoes, snow boots and wellies line back and back along the path. There's something so strange about that line of shoes in the snow that I get a bit hypnotized by it and by the people speaking their names, so I don't see him arrive.

'Tomek Romanek.'

I turn and he smiles and nods at me like he doesn't want to make a big deal of being here.

'How's Janu?' he asks.

'He's fine . . . gone to see his sister in New York,' I tell him.

I can feel Pari and Stella staring at us. Pari pulls a face at me as if to say, *Aren't you the secretive one?*

I ignore their grins and hand out the banners to

people who want to carry them. People collect their jam jars and lit candles. We line up in little groups and start to walk barefoot down the path to Stan Braverman's grave.

Tomek doesn't say anything to me. He just walks by my side and occasionally his hand grazes mine. Is he doing it on purpose? Every time our hands touch I feel like an electric shock runs through my body. Even though we've only met twice, and he doesn't know any of my friends, he understands as much as anyone here why we're walking together, so the next time his hand touches mine I reach for his fingers and our hands fold together, palm against palm.

Everything is still except for the song of a robin that hops ahead of us, as if it's leading the way.

'Such a tiny little bird . . . with a strong voice.' Simon's words float into my head.

We reach the end of the cemetery where Bubbe fell and lay down the banners. One by one we place the candles around all the graves that were spoilt. I smooth away the snow to reveal Stan's headstone. The stone is bleached where they have cleaned away the swastika, but you can still see the washed-out shadow of the shape. It makes me think of Pari's picture of her dad, and I think of Janu and what he said after he was attacked . . . about the memory of hatred taking longer to heal. I place my candle on Stan Braverman's grave and Tomek places his beside mine. This corner of the cemetery looks so pretty now, all lit up with candles. Nobody speaks, even the robin has stopped singing. The peace is as soft and deep as the snow. Becks spends a long time filming it, trying to capture the atmosphere.

When all the candles are arranged in the snow, we pick up our banners and walk in our own footprints back to the entrance of the cemetery, leaving the candles burning. Tomek keeps looking sideways at me and smiling as we hold the banner together, and even though this is such a small vigil, nothing like the Women's March or big marches that Nana and Simon went on, or the one Pari, Leyla and me watched on the news, this still feels like something.

Rebecca takes a last shot of the empty shoes and stops filming.

'Will you send it now . . . to Kez?' I ask.

'What do you think I should write about it?' Rebecca asks.

We try out a few ideas and finally agree on: 'Our vigil for Bubbe and your family, love from all your friends.'

After we've done the walk back through the cemetery, people turn their phones back on and there's a chorus of pinging and speaking to parents who want to know where they are.

We stand around talking for a while, but even with

their shoes back on people are starting to shiver. I think it's probably all over now. Quite a few people start to say their goodbyes. There's lots of hugging and arm holding. I understand what Nana Josie was saying now in her Protest Book, about how standing together makes you feel stronger, even if you can't see how it changes things straight away.

We take it in turns to walk back to the graves to make sure the candles are still alight. I have plenty of spare nightlights in my Banner Bag, enough to keep it all lit up to the entrance and by the gravesides.

By the time it's dark, the road has opened up and a few cars drive slowly past, but no buses. I suppose people must be wondering what we're doing here.

The cold is biting through my clothes now and I start to shiver. I suppose it would have been really hard for Kez to come and see this vigil for Bubbe.

'Can I walk with you home?' Tomek asks.

Pari and Stella hear him and don't seem to be able to stop giggling.

We're just about to pack up the banners when I hear the engine. I know the sound of that van.

I can't believe what I'm seeing. Bubbe steps carefully out of the driver's seat, walks around and opens the back of the van for Kez.

'I couldn't stop her coming! Mum and Dad are going to kill me. I'm supposed to be at home looking after Bubbe! But . . . thank you,' Kez calls out from the van as she waits for the ramp to lower.

Kez comes slowly across the snow towards us in Vimana.

'Don't want to go flying!' She smiles at me but she looks sad. Her eyes are full of tears. She reaches out to me and we hold each other for a long time. It's a hug that says so many things. It seems such a long time ago that we used to play those flying games.

Bubbe looks so fragile, like the winter twigs all around, but her face is soft again, and smiling.

'My dear, sweet Laila! I'm wearing them!' she whispers to me, pointing to the little black leather shoes she wore the day she had to leave her home forever.

'Can you help me, Laila?' Kez asks, and I pull her wellies off for her.

'Now, where is that camera you used?' Bubbe asks, and shudders with the cold.

I start filming.

'Dara Braverman,' she says, looking straight at the camera.

'Kezia Braverman.'

I light a candle for Bubbe and one for Kez. Bubbe walks carefully towards Stan's grave with Kez by her side.

I follow the path of Bubbe's little-girl shoe prints treading through the snow.

I can just make out the branches of the trees above.

As they walk further down the path, the snow-light and mist merge into one so you can't tell what's earth, air or sky any more. Bubbe and Kez disappear and all that you can see of them is the faint glow of their candles.

FORTY-FOUR

It's a real laugh in the van on the way back, except for Pari, Stella and Kez giggling and elbowing me whenever Tomek speaks!

Bubbe's obviously going to drop me home first. I wish I could stay in the van and drop Pari and Tomek off too.

'The sign's gone!' Kez says as we draw up by the tree.

'What sign?' Tomek asks.

'Oh! Long story . . . We had a snake turn up in our kitchen,' I say.

'OK!' Tomek laughs. 'It does sound like you're going to have to tell me about that one!'

Dad comes out to meet me and waves Bubbe and Kez off.

'She's got a vanful of girls!' Dad laughs, then he spots Tomek. 'But who's that?'

'Just a friend!' I say.

'I've heard that one before! Is Dara feeling better

now? When she told us where you were, we all wanted to drive her and Kez up there, but she was having none of it. Insisted on it being just her and Kez.'

'She's fine, but she's tired now so she's going home, and Maurice is dropping them all back.'

'Lucky Maurice!' Dad jokes.

'What happened with the snake sign?' I ask.

'Oh yes.' Dad wraps his arm around my shoulders. 'Krish's friend Eddie came over with something for you while you were out! He seemed to think you might want to keep it.'

'What is it?' I ask.

'A snakeskin!'

'Eddie said it shed its skin and about half an hour later there was a knock on the door and someone claimed it. They had a photo of it and everything! The owners had moved house and it got out in the move. They couldn't believe it was still alive! And we were all so afraid of it!' Dad smiles.

'I wasn't!

I feel different walking back into our house. The front garden looks so pretty covered in snow . . . you can't see all the mud from knocking down the high wall. But when I get inside, the place is *still* like a building site.

'What's going *on* in this house?'

'It's chaos. We've had a burst pipe. The hallway

floor's going to have to come up. *Please* sleep in Mira's room! I don't want your eczema to get worse,' Dad explains. 'Come on; let's get you into the warm.' He helps me navigate around the dustsheets and a toolbox. I suddenly feel a bit shaky. 'Cup of tea? Mum's made soup.'

'I think I'll have a bath,' I say.

'Not so fast! We want the whole truth and nothing but the truth! Where did that come from?' Dad asks as I place the Banner Bag on the table.

'It's all there!' I say, tapping the iPad. 'Where is Mum?'

'On her way back from the Bravermans'. You're going to have some questions to answer! But come on, get that coat off. I lit the fire for you.'

I stand in front of the fireplace feeling the heat slowly warm me through.

When Mum comes home she won't let me go. She keeps hanging on to me. She doesn't even want to leave me on my own while I wait for the bath to run. My feet itch and burn – like they were frozen before and now they're thawing out.

'You'll all have chilblains,' Mum says, fluffing up the bubbles of the bath. 'I don't know what this'll do for your eczema.'

I haven't been sratching my arm for a while. In fact I haven't even thought about it. I hold my arms out to check and the cracked skin's gone, with just a faint red shadow to show that the eczema was ever there.

'That latest remedy worked then,' Mum says, and kisses the crooks of my arms.

'Mum!' I laugh. 'What are you doing?'

'Just glad to have you home safe and sound!' Mum sighs and sits on the toilet as if I'm going to get in the bath with her sitting there.

'Can I have some privacy now?'

She laughs and leaves, closing the bathroom door.

The house is so dusty that after my bath I go into Mira's room, close the door and snuggle up on her bed. I take out Nana's chime and ring it just once . . .

Old bare feet are walking in the snow in a long trail of people. Old, old feet, black feet, white feet, brown feet. When they lift their heels out of the snow, they're all cracked and sore and pink from the cold.

'Follow the chime, Laila.' I hear a voice and follow the feet and the sound of an ankle bracelet jingling.

'Is that you, Nana Josie?' I call, but the feet keep walking, the chime keeps ringing.

Someone's running behind me, panting, out of breath. 'Wait for me!'

I know his voice but all I can see is feet in the snow. The chime rings.

'Simon, time to go!' Nana Josie's voice calls.

I follow, but the faster I walk, the further they are away from me, walking into the sun.

The chime rings in my hand, louder and louder . . .

I'm still holding it when I wake up. I feel all warm inside like you do when you fall asleep in the sun and wake up feeling like the heat has seeped into your skin. I hardly ever dream. It's Mira who has those dreams that she thinks really mean something, not me.

I walk down the stairs and there's a builder already working in the hallway.

'Sorry!' I say, squeezing past him and grabbing my blazer. No time for breakfast. I'm going to be in so much trouble if I'm late for school again.

The sun's so bright as I walk out of the door I can hardly see the path.

The snow's packed down from all the footprints. The path is icy, so I step on to the grass of the park instead and run. I love these bright frosty mornings when your shoes scrunch on the ice, but I'm happy I'm not barefoot today like Janu is. It must be so cold in New York.

I slow as I approach the school gates. Mrs Latif is waiting for me with . . . Kez, Pari and . . . what's Bubbe doing there?

Mrs Latif walks towards me.

'Are you better?' I ask her.

'I'm not ill! Though I have had a very sickly few weeks! Haven't you noticed my bump?' I look down at her tummy and I can see that her slim shape has changed. Mrs Latif is beaming with happiness.

'Congratulations . . . Oh, I forgot to give you your Malala book back for your bookshelf!' I say.

Mrs Latif shakes her head. 'No, Laila, I'll get another copy when he or she is old enough. Think of it as a congratulations present . . . Come on, let's go and see Mrs Kaur – I think she's got a few words she wants to say to you.'

'Am I in trouble? Sorry, but—'

'Save it for the Head!' Mrs Latif smiles at me, takes Bubbe's arm and leads the way into school.

Kez holds my hand on one side and Pari's on the other and we walk through the gates together. Rebecca, Stella, Carlos, Selina, Carmel, Milena, Nathan and some of the people from Kez's tutor group who came to the vigil are lined up outside our Head's office. Mrs Latif knocks on the door and Mrs Kaur answers.

'It was my idea!' I blurt out.

'I've heard all about it!' Mrs Kaur smiles at Bubbe and motions for us all to cram into her office. 'Now! Let me shake your hand, Laila Levenson,' Mrs Kaur says when we've all finally managed to fit in.

I've never actually spoken to our Head Teacher before. I thought she would be scary, but she looks really normal and friendly.

'Don't look so worried, Laila! I have never had a group of Year Sevens make a statement I'm more proud of. You are an absolute credit to this school.

I'm so happy Mrs Braverman here has gone out of her way to come in and tell me what you young people have done. With all of your permission I would like to bring this to the attention of the media.'

Bubbe turns around and beams at us all. She looks thin and tired but her eyes are sparkling with happiness, like they did when she listened to Kez speak on her bat mitzvah day.

Most of the rest of the morning we spend in Mrs Kaur's office being interviewed by local papers and even for a TV news report.

'Let's just have a small group shot!' the reporter says.

Mrs Latif, Mrs Kaur, Bubbe, Kez, Pari, Carlos, Selina and Rebecca get in the photo, but Stella hangs back.

Mrs Latif calls her over. 'Come on, Stella! We're all in this together.'

The best thing about this photo is something that no one else would really get, except maybe Pari and me and Mrs Latif. On the first day of school I never would have thought that Stella, Pari and me would be the closest of anyone in our tutor group. I would never have put that on Mrs Latif's map.

The end-of-school bell goes and everyone's getting out of their seats. Mrs Latif and Mr Rivera come over and chat to me a bit more about the vigil. Mrs Latif wants to know if we could get everyone who was involved from school together and do an assembly about it. Bubbe's agreed to come in and talk too.

'I'll help you put something together,' Mrs Latif says.

'We should play the "underground" music you made,' Mr Rivera suggests.

'And your film of the vigil,' Mrs Latif adds.

'Yes, and I can bring in my Nana Josie's banner to show everyone,' I say.

They seem to be actually really excited about all this.

'I'll talk to the others about it,' I tell them, and turn around to see what Stella and Pari think. But they've gone.

I wait at the school gates but I can't see anyone. I don't know why, but I feel a bit flat. What I would really love now is for all my friends to be able to come back to mine and sit on my bed, close the door and for us to just talk on our own about everything that's happened. It doesn't look like anyone's going to show now. Maybe Pari and Stella are already on the underground. I give up waiting by the Unfriendship Bench and go home.

As I cross the road there's a crowd outside our house. Kez and her mum and dad and Pari and her mum are all standing on the pavement. Someone's planted a small tree and some bright red and white flowers either side of the new S-shaped path up to our front door. The garden looks really good. And then the door opens and Mum's standing there and I realize that since I left this morning our house has a got a new door that's been painted turquoise.

Dad's standing off the sloped path near the front door, holding his iPhone up and recording.

'Mind the new planting!' Mum says, steering Dad away from treading on a climber with little yellow star-shaped flowers.

'What is that plant?' Hannah asks.

'Winter-flowering jasmine. Janu's choice!' Mum says.

'What's going on, Laila?' Dad asks.

'I dunno! I haven't got a clue!' I look to Kez and Pari for an answer.

'You first!' Kez says, so I walk up the path to the front door.

Mum and Dad go halfway up the stairs and watch.

'Are you videoing all this? Mira and Krish want to see,' Mum says.

'Got it!' Dad gives a thumbs up.

'Me too!' Maurice calls, holding his phone in the air.

I'm in the doorway now and turning around to look back. Kez is at the bottom of the path.

'You going to invite us in, or what? It's steep but

do-able.' She laughs and steers her way slowly up the slope.

Dad gestures to the side of the house that someone's built a little cover over.

'You can come round anytime now. Whether we're in or not!' Dad says as Kez steers Vimana up the path and parks. I feel myself tense, but Dad doesn't attempt to help her.

She looks up at Dad filming and smiles, but then leans in close to me and takes my arm. 'I've so missed coming here with you.'

I must have been so caught up in the vigil not to see that maybe fixing the wall and the 'flood' isn't all that's been happening here.

'Don't leave our guests standing on the doorstep!' Dad jokes, as Pari and her mum walk through the door together.

'Did you know about this, Pari?' I ask.

'I might have done!'

I look to Bubbe and Maurice and Hannah for an answer.

'It was Janu's idea!' Hannah says. 'When you told him how much you wanted Kez to be able to come here and how it was affecting you both.'

'Anyway, we've wanted some more domestic projects in our portfolio. To show people what's possible . . . so this was perfect timing,' Maurice adds.

I look up the stairs at Mum and Dad. That weekend when they said . . .

'Were you here that weekend I went to stay with Kez . . . ?' I look at Bubbe holding the little bonsai tree and stop myself saying any more.

'To tell the truth, none of us were very far away that weekend!' Hannah says, resting her arm on Bubbe's back. 'But it really is Janu you've got to thank for all this.'

Bubbe takes my arm and gives me the bonsai tree.

'A little thank you from our family!' she whispers, and gives me her don't-argue-with-me look.

'Why don't you girls go through to Laila's new bedroom?' Dad asks, pointing to the living room.

I feel for the step and nearly fall flat on my face trying to stop myself from dropping Bubbe's present.

'Steady! It's supposed to bring you balance!' Bubbe says, laughing.

'Don't make me laugh any more, Bubbe. I need the bathroom! Excuse me, Laila.'

I move aside as Kez follows the strip of grip wall like she has all round her flat. The floor's the same as in her house too, with little circles in it to stop you slipping. This is . . . nothing like our front room.

'Where's the living room gone?' I ask.

'We've moved the furniture upstairs. We're going to make Mira's old room into the living room!' Mum smiles. 'I've always liked that view on to the back garden!'

Kez walks into a pod that's been added like a little cube inside the room, just like the one at hers.

Hannah and Maurice grin at me.

'Right then!' Mum says 'Let's leave them to it. Come on through to the kitchen. I've made some tea. There are a few drinks and snacks on the table in your new room.' Mum points to a little low table in the window in front of my perch.

'You brought it down from the landing!'

Mum grins at me and closes my new bedroom door.

Pari goes over to my perch and sits down. She pats the cushion next to me. Then she holds up the little velvet one where she knows I keep my chime and shakes it in the air.

'You are so lucky!' she says, as I place the plant on the mantelpiece next to Nana Josie's little box, the one with the bonsai tree painted on it. Mum must have been going through my things. The Protest Book isn't a secret any more because it's sitting on the mantelpiece. Mum's put the statue of Shiva that Janu brought us right in the middle. It looks good there, and next to it is the snakeskin. I bet that was Dad's idea. My Banner Bag's tucked neatly on the tiles by the fireplace.

I sit down next to Pari. I'm just trying to get my

head around the fact that this is going to be my room. It's been decorated and I've even got a new bed.

'I like that wall colour!' Pari says. 'Isn't that the colour you used to paint the banners? You could put the one from the vigil in here.'

I *could*, but I already know exactly which banner is going up on that wall. Maybe one day Mira will paint a banner of me, Kez and Pari on a march.

The time goes so fast as we plan out how I'm going to have my room. Kez leaves first, and me and Pari sit and chat about the day of the vigil and what we'll say if we have to do an assembly.

There's a knock at the door.

'Leyla needs to go now!' Mum says, as she peers around the door and opens it wider.

Pari looks at her mum, who is standing in the doorway, busy shaking her head at Dad.

'No, no, Leyla. It's no bother at all,' Dad's insisting. 'Of course I can drop you home.'

Leyla starts speaking to Pari. The only word I can understand is 'sleepover'. It seems like Pari's not sure what to do. She keeps looking at her mum, then back into the room at me. Then she runs at her mum and hugs her tight.

'No, no. You girls stay here, having fun.'

'My first ever sleepover!' Pari laughs like she can't believe this is happening.

'You can't possibly go home on the tube, Leyla,

with this heavy cooking pot!'

'I thought I'd use it all the time, but turns out it's just taking space up in the kitchen,' Mum lies.

'If you are sure you won't need . . . I can show you many dishes, Uma: Iraqi Shourba, lentils Biryani, Chelefry – like a stew – Kibbe Batata.' Leyla pats Dad on the arm. 'And for you, some lamb, Makloba . . . So many dishes! We'll go to Saturday market together get fresh ingredients and I show you how to cook, OK?'

'Stop, Leyla, you're making me hungry!' Dad laughs.

Pari looks towards me and I hardly dare meet her eyes in case she tells the truth. Mum cooks with that pot nearly every day. Pari knows that. She tilts her head slightly to the side and lowers her chin, and without saying a thing, I know we're thinking the same thing.

Is it *always* **wrong to lie?**
Is it *always* **right to tell the truth?**

She won't tell her mum that we use it all the time, and we won't ever talk about it again.

Pari kisses her mum and says something to her in Arabic. She looks really worried about her mum leaving.

'No, no, I am sleeping now. I'll be fine,' Leyla says.

It finally dawns on me that it's Pari who's worrying about her mum being on her own and not the other way round.

'By the way, Laila! Not to place bonsai here,' Leyla says, pointing to the plant on the mantelpiece as she leaves. 'It must go in light place. Keep same temperature, not cold from window, so it will grow well.'

When Leyla's gone Pari helps me hang Nana Josie's banner on the wall above my bed.

'This is beautiful,' Pari says, lying on my bed staring up at the banner. 'Now tell me about this mystery boy . . . Tomek!'

It's not until I'm on my own, sitting on my perch looking around my new bedroom, that any of this starts to sink in. I open my laptop and email Janu.

Dear Janu,

I hope you're having a good time in New York with Priya.

I saw that your fundraising's going well with that concert.

Sorry I haven't been in touch for a few days, but I just want to say thank you for what you did for me and Kez. It's amazing. I'm sitting in my new room now. Kez and Pari have just been here. I can't believe

408

that I didn't guess that all this was
going on.

I did this vigil for Bubbe. I'm attaching
the link so you can see what it was all
about. Maybe Dad was right about the
barefoot thing catching on!

As you can see, Tomek came too and he
asked how you are. I've been thinking that
even though I'll keep my promise to you
and not tell anyone here what happened
that day on the tube, I'll never forget it.
When we were doing the vigil I was
thinking of you and so was Tomek. We
talked about it and we both think you were
wrong to stay quiet about what they did to
you. I think it's a bit why I had to do
something. Anyway, I wanted you to know
that I did the vigil for you too.

Love
Laila X

FORTY-FIVE

The letterbox clanks.

I'm sitting on my perch and from here I can pull the side curtain back and see who's at the door. A flash of gold passes my window. I run to the door and a tall woman with a golden head wrap and a long green coat is crossing the road. She points to the bus that's just pulling into the stop, gets on and waves to me.

'Hope!' I call.

She waves back and then holds her fist in the air as if she's rallying me on. Then she blows me a kiss and is gone.

I look down at my feet, and there on the mat is a letter addressed to Laila Levenson.

I take it into my room, snuggle up on my perch, open the envelope and take out a newspaper clipping of our vigil: I still can't believe that it was actually in the paper.

School Celebrates Student's Anti-Racist Vigil
Young people from Jewish, Muslim, Hindu,
Christian and No-faiths came together to stand up
against racism in a moving vigil dedicated to Stan
and Dara Braverman, Kindertransport refugees.

Stan's grave was one of the many recently
defiled in Jewish cemeteries across the city. The
Mayor of London said, 'We applaud this moving
ceremony led by young people. It gives us hope
for a better future.'

Dara Braverman of north London said she had
been in despair but that her spirits had been
lifted by the young campaigners' clear message
against racism and religious intolerance of any
kind. The vigil was organized by twelve-year-old
Laila Levenson. She said, 'One of my best friends
is from a refugee family from Iraq, and my other
best friend's gran and grandad came to this
country on the Kindertransport, so we wanted to
stand together to protest about these acts of
racism and show everyone that they're not being
done in our names . . .'

I can't believe it was me and my friends who made all
this happen. It feels like a long time ago since the
letter from Protest Simon arrived for Mira. But this
one is definitely addressed to me, and my hands are
shaking as I unfold it and begin to read.

Dear Laila,

I am writing with sad and happy news.

Simon died a few days ago, but his last wish was that I send this letter to you. I wrote down exactly what he said, so here it is.

'Thank you for coming to pick up your Nana Josie's Protest Book. The moment I met you – when I opened my eyes and thought you were a young Josie sitting in the sunlight – I had a feeling about you. So I was over the moon when Hope brought me this newspaper clipping of you and your friends on your vigil, holding the same banners we all used. I knew I was right to hand that Banner Bag over to you. Your Nana Josie would have been right there by your side.'

Simon was always saying how he wanted to choose his moment of parting. He died with the newspaper article of your protest in his hands. He left us sitting by the yucca plant, bathed in sunshine, meditating. His trainers sat empty by his side!

With love,

Hope X

The End

Acknowledgements

I would like to thank my husband Leo and children Maya, Keshin and Esha, and all the members of our family in this and previous times who have taught me so much and without whom this and all my other stories could not have been written.

My immense thanks to Venetia Gosling for our editorial walks and talks and for understanding how important it was for me to take time to develop the layers of *Tender Earth*. I would also like to thank Rachel Vale for her beautiful design of all three books in this collection, Helen Crawford-White for the painterly jackets, and the whole wonderful team at Macmillan Children's Books. Thank you to my agent, Sophie Gorell Barnes of MBA Literary Agents, for her friendship, insight, encouragement and guidance.

There are a number of readers of this manuscript to thank. Maya Cobley and Anna Lawrence. Special thanks go to Nina Mansourian and Avisha Patel and the dedicated staff of the Archer Academy, London. Reading this story back to them was one of the highlights of my work as a writer. The idea for the Vimana chariot (with wings), the experience of sporting events, and Kez's commitment to charity came from discussions with them. Finally thanks to Alexandra Strick and Beth Cox of Inclusive Minds for their invaluable checking of the final manuscript.

Thank you to the members of the Islington Centre for Refugees and Migrants for opening my mind and heart to the struggles and obstacles faced by refugee families integrating into a new society. Thanks to my friend Jo Cobley for her support in writing this story.

Thanks to Susu Lawrence and Anna Lawrence for inviting me to Anna's bat mitzvah and for their interview. To Noga Applebaum for inviting me to the bat mitzvah of Dana Taylor Goldman, and to Dana and her grandmother, fellow author Marilyn Taylor, for their interviews. Thank you to my long-time neighbour and friend Stephanie Rose, with her invaluable knowledge from her work on the Jewish Survivors Programme, for her advice on this manuscript.

Thank you to Astrid Griffiths for helping me to find the title of this book that is so in keeping with our walks together. Thanks once again to my dear friend Maria Levenson and to her family for lending me their name.

Thank you to Susan Gould for generously sharing stories and quotes about Simon that have helped immensely in the writing of this book, and to Paula Hollings, Jane Osborn and Marianne Mattison for their encouragement in keeping the memory of Simon alive.

I would like to thank my late mother-in-law Rosie

Harrison (inspiration for *Artichoke Hearts*), father-in-law Bernard Harrison (who marched on Cable Street) and Simon Gould, our family friend and inspiration for Simon Makepeace in this story.

Thanks to my mum, Freda Brahmachari, and my late father, Dr Amal Krishna Brahmachari, whose caring shoes I imagine Janu walking in. I hope the spirit of all these people, their sense of justice, fairness, fun, adventure, common humanity and encouragement of future generations, chimes through the pages of *Tender Earth*.

References

For the barefoot vigil I was inspired by the Shoes on the Danube Bank memorial in Budapest, Hungary.

The teachings in Kezia's bat mitzvah are drawn from Rabbi Jonathan Sacks's online article 'Three Types of Community: Interpreting the Parsha Vayakhel'.

Laila reads *I am Malala* by Malala Yousafzai with Christina Lamb.

Amnesty International UK endorses *Tender Earth* because it illuminates the importance of equality, friendship and solidarity, and upholds our right to protest against injustice.

Amnesty International is a movement of millions of ordinary people around the world standing up for humanity and human rights. Our purpose is to protect individuals wherever justice, fairness, freedom and truth are denied.

From birth onwards we all have human rights, no matter who we are or where we live. The first declaration to set out fundamental rights that need protection in all countries was the Universal Declaration of Human Rights (UDHR) in 1948, created to say 'never again' to the horrors of the Holocaust. It is a milestone document in the history of human rights and was the first to agree common, global terms for truth, justice and equality.

Human rights help us to live lives that are fair and truthful, free from abuse, fear and want and respectful of other people's rights. But they are often abused, and we need to be alert and to stand up for them, for ourselves and for other people. We can all help to make the world a better place.

You can stand up for human rights too:

- Take action for individuals at risk around the world at www.amnesty.org.uk/actions

- Find out how to start a youth group in your school or community at www.amnesty.org.uk/youth

- Join the Junior Urgent Action network at www.amnesty.org.uk/jua

If you are a teacher or librarian, please use our many free educational resources at www.amnesty.org.uk/education

Amnesty International UK,
The Human Rights Action Centre,
17–25 New Inn Yard, London EC2A 3EA
Tel: 020 7033 1500
Email: sct@amnesty.org.uk
www.amnesty.org.uk

About the Author

Sita Brahmachari's career spans writing novels, short stories and plays, including a celebrated adaptation of Shaun Tan's *The Arrival*. She has an MA in Arts Education and regularly runs creative-writing classes for aspiring writers, including refugee communities, students, and teachers exploring the power of weaving a diverse patchwork of storytelling. In 2011 she won the Waterstones Children's Book Prize for her debut novel *Artichoke Hearts*. She has been Online Writer in Residence at Book Trust. Her subsequent novels, *Jasmine Skies*, *Kite Spirit* and *Red Leaves*, have been variously championed by Book Trust, The Reading Agency and the School Library Association, longlisted for the Carnegie Medal and the UKLA Book Award, and endorsed by Amnesty International UK. *Tender Earth* is her most recent novel for Macmillan Children's Books.

www.sitabrahmachari.com
@sitabrahmachari